S. K. Wright is an award-winning author who has previously published novels for both teenagers and adults under the name Sam Mills. She studied English at Oxford and now works in publishing and lives in London. This is her debut book under the name S. K. Wright.

IT ENDS WITH YOU

S. K. Wright

ATOM

ATOM

First published in Great Britain in 2018 by Atom

3 5 7 9 10 8 6 4 2

A CIP catalogue record for this book
is available from the British Library.

ISBN 978-0-349-00317-7

Printed and bound in Great Britain by
Clays Ltd, Elcograf S.p.A.

Papers used by Atom are from well-managed forests
and other responsible sources.

Atom
An imprint of
Little, Brown Book Group
Carmelite House
50 Victoria Embankment
London EC4Y 0DZ

An Hachette UK Company
www.hachette.co.uk

www.atombooks.co.uk

For L.K., with all my love

'You are what your deep, driving desire is. As your desire is, so is your will. As your will is, so is your deed. As your deed is, so is your destiny.'

– Brihadaranyaka Upanishad IV.4.5

IT
ENDS
WITH
YOU

28th September 2016

This video has been removed by the user

Like   Dislike   Share

Bad Things Going Down in the Woods

8 views

Prologue

I hear the scream and then I turn and run.

It's pitch black in these woods. The moon was shining bright earlier but now clouds have covered the sky. I grab my mobile and use it as a torch, a fluorescent square that shows me the way. The mud is squelchy and I nearly slip; I seize hold of a trunk, panting for breath. Another scream and I freeze, torn – *should I go back?* My mind tells me to reverse but my body ignores the command. I'm running, running, leaves kissing my cheeks, twigs curling against my hair, shrubs brushing my jeans. A refrain from that poem we studied in English zigzags through my mind – *'Whose woods these are I think I know. His house is in the village though ... The woods are lovely, dark and deep, But I have promises to keep ... and miles to go before I sleep ...'*

An opening; light; civilisation. I burst out into the road, doubled over, my lungs raw with pain. My car is still there, where I left it. I stab my car key at the lock and only succeed in scratching off paint. Again I try, and again, and on the third go I hit the jackpot, slide into the driver's seat and bang the door shut. I glance around, worried that someone might have seen me. But this is a quiet suburban street and there are no lights on in the houses.

I turn the engine on, startled as rock music blasts from the radio. I switch it off. I mustn't panic, I mustn't drive too fast. *The woods are lovely, dark and deep* ... I gather myself, put the car in gear and drive away down the road, watching in my rear-view mirror as the woods shrink to silhouettes and disappear.

Chapter 1

Luke

The police come to get me on a regular Monday morning. It's just before 9 a.m. and I should be in assembly singing boring hymns and listening to the deputy head speak about the importance of Living Responsibly and Thinking Of Others. Instead, I'm redecorating the Gents' toilets with the help of Rob, my best mate.

I'm in pain. Rob has just shoved my head into the sink. Laughing, he spins the taps and cold water sluices over my hair, stinging icy in my ears. I'm wriggling but Rob is pressing hard on my shoulders. 'So, Batman,' he says, relishing the game, 'you're going downnn ...' I laugh too and try to tell him he's a bastard but all I manage is a splutter. A surge of fury gives me bonus energy points. I thrash about and throw Rob off and he staggers backwards.

A pause for breath. We both stare into the mirrors. We

remember that we're human, not animals. Sometimes when you're fighting, you forget to think. You forget who you are. We look at our reflections, me with my wet hair pasted over my face and Rob with red smearing from his nose. I'm taller than Rob but he's stockier than me. We've painted cuts and bruises on each other's faces; my blood is on his shirt and his blood is on my skin. Maybe we've got just a little bit out of control ...

Rob comes at me—

I spin around and knock him hard—

He falls to the floor.

Now's my chance. I jump on top of him and grab a fistful of his hair. My anger pumps through me. I love fighting and I hate fighting. The pain lasts for days as your bruises turn all shades of blue, but there's nothing like that moment, that exhilaration when the anger and adrenalin rush so hard and fast you feel like you're on drugs. It's a dangerous moment too, because you can't say how far you'll go, how much damage you'll do, and that fear is part of the buzz.

To be honest, this isn't 100 per cent play fighting. Rob wrote something on my Facebook wall yesterday about how sexy my girlfriend is and I've been feeling pissed off about it ever since.

'So, Green Lantern —' I cry, yanking up Rob's head.

'I'm not the Green Lantern, he's a boring wimp,' Rob protests in laughter. 'I'm Spider-Man!'

'Yeah, right. So, Green Lantern, inferior hero that you

are – how do you like this?' I bang his face down on the floor. I hear him cry out and inside my mum's voice warns me – *Don't go too far, stop, stop—*

Right then the door opens. Rob groans and spits blood onto the floor.

'Luke Jones! Rob Pennington! What the hell are you doing!'

Mr Abdul is standing there.

Shame shrinks me. I stagger to my feet. Mr Abdul teaches Art at St Martin's High. Most of the teachers in our school give me The Sneer, but Abdul's different. He's kind to me; he listens; he seems to really care.

'Sorry.' I wince.

'Luke, what the hell is going on?'

I've not heard Abdul raise his voice like this in a long time. He's normally very chilled.

Rob lies there, groaning as though he's just fought for weeks in one of those ancient battles against Napoleon or something.

'Rob, stop trying to play the sympathy card!' I go to kick him for trying it on, when Mr Abdul cries: *'Luke!'*

'Sorry – but – he's fine! We were just messing around.'

'Luke jumped me,' Rob groans again.

'Hey, that's not true!'

I suddenly become aware that Mr Abdul isn't alone.

Police officers. Two of them, a bloke and a woman. They step forward.

'Rob, for God's sake, get up!' Mr Abdul says irritably.

The police are watching us closely. I'm conscious of the little differences between me and Rob. Rob wears smart black shoes, whilst I'm in non-regulation grey trainers with holes in them; one of my laces has broken so I've replaced it with an elastic band. Rob's dark hair is neat and spruce; my brown fringe is swinging over my forehead cos I meant to cut it last night but I hadn't been able to find the scissors in the chaos of our kitchen. Rob is one of those fake rebels who swagger about and boast that they'll do anything, but the moment an adult shows they're all smiles and thankyous and posh accents. Now he gets to his feet, smoothing down his hair, looking contrite and shooting me a glance as though I'm some thug he met in an alley.

The female police officer looks at Rob as though she wants to mother him. The man is watching me, though. He has spruce hair flecked with grey and dark, dark eyes. I realise that he looks familiar and then it comes to me.

He once arrested me for reckless driving. I can't remember his name. He seemed like one of those guys who enjoy being on a power trip. Still, that was months ago, so why are they here now?

'Luke, this is Detective Inspector Jackson and Detective Sergeant Hutton,' Mr Abdul introduces them.

Jackson. That's him. I step forwards, thinking I ought to shake their hands, but Jackson merely raises an eyebrow, so I shove my hand in my pocket. I'm never good with this sort of thing. I see the female detective staring at my shirt and I glance down, noticing the tear.

'They've been given permission from your mother to take you to the station,' Mr Abdul goes on.

'Do I have to go?' Rob cries in disbelief.

'No, just Luke.'

Rob lets out a little cheer and Mr Abdul gives him a stern glance.

'What's it about?' I ask, even though I already know. Somehow they've found out how much I drank at the party last Friday. I drove home oh-so-slowly, at about ten miles an hour all the way. But they must have seen me on CCTV.

'They're—' Mr Abdul begins.

'We want to speak to you in connection with the disappearance of Eva Pieachowski,' Detective Jackson says.

Shit. My last memory of Friday evening: Eva's face, shadowed by the woods, streaked by moonlight, her mouth an 'O' as she yelled abuse at me. She was so upset that night. I hope she didn't go and do anything crazy.

Rob gives me a shocked glance, then quickly looks away. I almost feel like shouting that Rob was there on Friday night too – it was his party. But no. There's something too familiar about this set-up. Rob politely asks for permission to leave the toilets. While he gets to go back to class scot-free, I'm walking down the corridor in between two police officers, with that sharp, twisting feeling in my stomach that tells me this is just the start of trouble. Of course, with spectacular timing, assembly has just finished. Kids are streaming out and they all get a good look at me; a couple even take pics on their phones, until Mr

Abdul tuts at them. This is bloody typical. I'm the outsider in this posh fee-paying school, here on a scholarship, not courtesy of Mummy and Daddy's millions. I'm always in the wrong place at the wrong time. *Why does this always happen to me?*

Then we're out in the playground. It's cold and I want to ask if I can run back in and get my coat. A panda car is waiting. Its blue lights whirl and flash, incongruous and alien in the daylight.

Mr Abdul leans in and whispers: 'Tuck your shirt in.'

I hastily shove it into my trousers, feeling the safety pin which is holding up my belt. His voice is tender with concern; when I look into his eyes I see fear. For one weird moment I think he's going to hug me. Mr Abdul was once a scholarship boy from a family on a low income. He's told me he sees his younger self in me.

'Be honest,' he says. 'That's all you need to do. Just tell the truth.'

I want to ask him to come with me, but when I open my mouth to say it, I worry that I sound childish and pathetic. He has classes to teach. I've let him down. I don't deserve his help.

So I shove my hands in my pockets and give him a casual smile, as though I don't really care that any of this is going on. The walk to that police car is a long and lonely one. What's happened to Eva? Is this another one of her Dares? What do they want with me?

Chapter 2

Anonymous

The Big Bad Blog ~ Monday 26 September

There's an empty chair in Form 4, Year 13 today.

The news has spread like wildfire: *Eva Pieachowski is missing.*

Our school is in shock.

Eva. The star girl at St Martin's. She's taking five A levels in English, Economics, History, Geography and Art, and she's top in every subject, yet Eva's no square – anyone who has ever partied with her knows that. With her long blonde hair and bewitching brown eyes, it's no wonder that she was scouted by a modelling agency on a trip to Paris. She only did one contract – for Topshop – before dropping it in favour of her studies. She's captain of the netball and tennis teams, tipped to be voted head girl in our elections next week, and at the end of Year 12 she was awarded the trophy for Star Pupil. The prom is still nine months away but it's pretty obvious who will be chosen as queen.

She was last seen on Friday night at a party held at Rob Pennington's house. Rob's parties are notorious. So what happened? Did Eva run away? Is she lost? Is she playing a game? Or has something terrible happened to her? We all know that Eva's recently started to hang out with the wrong crowd . . .

Hopefully all is well and Eva's gone to stay with a friend and forgotten to tell her parents. Let's hope that tomorrow her empty chair is filled.

COMMENTS (2)
Lisa – 'with her blonde hair and bewitching eyes' – what is this, a Mills & Boon? *cringe*.
Tristan – hey, I like this blog. I want to know what's happened to Eva. Thnx for keeping us up to date.

Chapter 3

Luke

'Tell me about you and Eva,' DI Jackson says. 'She's your girlfriend?'

We're sitting in a cramped interview room. A videocam squats in the corner, recording us. Jackson has the most intimidating stare. My hands itch for a pencil. If I was going to draw him, I'd capture his lizard eyes, which laser me for minutes at a time without blinking. Drawing always makes me feel better when I'm tense.

'What's happened to her?' I ask.

'Or maybe Eva was just a friend,' he goes on, ignoring me. 'A friend you have a crush on?'

'Yes, she is my girlfriend,' I assert, my cheeks warming. Why do people always assume a girl like her wouldn't go for a guy like me? 'It's serious between us, we've been dating nearly nine months. We're in love.'

'Really?' He looks surprised and I swear there's a sarcastic flicker in his eyes, as if all teens ever do is play Spin the Bottle and snog and lack the depth to ever feel anything deeper than that. At least my anger smoothes away my stutter.

'We have something really special.'

More surprise. His pen hovers above the page for about a minute, until I'm ready to grab it and fling it across the room. Then he writes something down. He's left-handed and his handwriting is loopy and slanted; impossible to read.

'Are you writing a greetings card?' I ask.

'I'm sorry?'

'You're writing down that we have something really special?' Once I say the words, I know they sound bad. I have such a big mouth. Mum's always warning me: *'You always speak and then think and it's too late once you've said it!'*

'Sorry,' I say quickly.

Detective Jackson folds his arms.

'You think this is funny?'

'No! I don't!' My voice is too loud and I try to turn down the volume. My fists are clenched in my lap. 'I just don't get what's going on. Where's Eva?'

'You tell me,' he says.

'I haven't seen her all weekend,' I say. 'I last saw her on Friday night at a party and then I was helping my mum with family stuff on Saturday and on Sunday I went over to see Rob.'

'Rob?' His pen scratches another note. 'The guy you were beating up in the toilets?'

14

'We were play-fighting,' I correct him. 'We were just mess-ing around! We were pretending to be superheroes. I was Batman and Rob was the Green Lantern – well, he wanted to be Spider-Man, but you know.'

'I'm sorry?'

'You know, the Green Lantern. He's the lame hero nobody likes.' I figure that Jackson isn't the type to ever go to the movies; it would be far too much fun for him.

'I see.' Jackson makes another enigmatic note and I swallow. I wish I could be like Rob. He'd know just what to say. If he was here, he'd already know what Eva's been up to, and would be shaking the policeman's hand and arranging a game of bloody golf or something. I'm no good at dealing with adults, especially ones in positions of authority.

'And you've had no contact with Miss Pieachowski since Friday?'

'Well, I did call her but she didn't pick up, so I figured she was mad at me.'

His eyes flicker. Oh. I shouldn't have said that.

'Can I have a drink of water?' My tongue feels thick in my mouth.

'In a minute. First, tell me why Eva would be angry with you.'

'I ... She ... it was just ... '

'Let's begin with Friday. Did something happen that might make her angry with you?'

'Well, a bit. Kind of. I mean, we were getting on really

15

well to begin with. We went to Rob's house as he was giving a party. He wanted me there cos we're good friends.'

'Except when you're attempting to break his nose,' DI Jackson says drily. Before I can defend myself, he goes on: 'So, did Rob's parents know about this soirée?'

'They were away for the weekend, so ... '

'What time did you get to the party?'

Time? I don't own a watch. I use my mobile sometimes to check the time – and usually find that wherever I'm meant to be, I'm late.

'I think I picked her up around eight-thirty.' I don't add that I had to collect Eva at the bottom of her road, so that her parents didn't see me. That might sound odd. 'So it would've been soon after that.'

'Did you drink at the party?'

'Ah, just a bit. I had a beer, maybe. I know you got me for reckless driving earlier this year, so of course, I was being careful. Eva drank more.'

'I haven't forgotten the reckless driving. So, you and Eva fell out? She got upset?'

'I don't know about that ... anyhow, I left the party at, I don't know, eleven – no, maybe ten thirty. I'm not sure about the time. I left before she did.'

'You didn't drive her home?'

'No – she wanted to stay and I didn't.'

'And you weren't worried about her?'

I stare at the desk, chewing on my lip, when there's a

knock at the door. The female sergeant is standing there. She gives me the strangest of looks – a kind of moon-eyed double take. Then she beckons Jackson over and whispers in his ear. Jackson nods. He turns to the camera, announces the time and says that the interview has been suspended, before switching it off. Then he tells me to wait here and leaves the room, slamming the door behind him so hard that the vibrations shiver and echo through my plastic chair.

'Fuck,' I say out loud.

I'm starting to worry that this is more serious than a silly Dare or one of Eva's wind-ups. I wonder if I need a lawyer. Then I remind myself that me and the detective are basically on the same side, right? We both want to make sure that Eva is okay.

I resist the urge to fold my arms over the desk, bury my head in their nest and nap. I'm scared I'm still being watched through that glass window, even secretly recorded; I try to force an expression of calm neutrality.

It's hard to think straight because I'm so bloody hungry. This morning I opened the bread bin to find a loaf so green with mould that I couldn't face scraping it off. Matt and Freya, who are three and eight, started to cry for their breakfast. Mum was already at work, cleaning down at the church, so it was my turn to sort them out. I said they could have Coco Pops, but when I opened the packet, there was nothing but brown crumbs. They cried all the way to school, until I went into the newsagents and bought a Twix, making them swear to share. That was the last of my paper-round money, so I had nothing left to buy my own breakfast. Fighting Rob took the last of my energy.

Breakfast seems like it happened days ago, not hours. I should be in English right now, discussing Robert Frost's poem about the silent woods. But here I am, in a police station, wondering what my girlfriend is playing at. Maybe it's Eva's idea of revenge. Recently her games have started getting more and more out of control, even cruel.

The door swings open. DI Jackson comes striding back in and sets my Nokia mobile down on the table.

'On Friday night, you have ten missed calls from Eva, between eleven-thirty and one-thirty,' he says sternly.

'Ten? I didn't think it was that many.'

'She also left some messages which you haven't listened to. I think you should listen to them now.'

What? How the hell has he got access to my messages? I know all you have to do on a Nokia is press 121, but surely that's not even legal without a warrant?

I forget everything when I hear Eva's voice, tinny on the loudspeaker, raw with rage: *'I hope you're happy now Luke. Thanks to you, I'm out here in the cold, again – not the first bloody time, is it? I need your help, please, please, help me, please ...'*

I freeze in horror. And then DI Jackson plays the next. Eva's voice is a shrill scream and it goes right through me: *'Luke – you can't do this to me! I have to get out of here! Please, please, stop hurting me, stop ... Help, help me!'*

18

Silence.

'Oh my God! Did someone hurt her?' I cry.

'I don't know, Luke, that's why you're here. Were *you* the one who hurt her? It's not clear who she's referring to. It sounds as though *you're* the one she's mad at.'

'God no, it must've been someone else.'

'Are you sure about that? Why didn't you listen to these messages? Why didn't you call her back?'

'Like I said, I did call her!' I protest. 'You haven't checked properly. I did call her – it was Saturday, or maybe Sunday morning. I – I felt bad and I called at some point. I can't remember when. But it just went to voicemail and I – I didn't want to listen to her messages because I couldn't face them. She wanted to break up, okay? I thought she was just leaving them to tell me to f—, I mean, to go away.'

I stare at the phone again, Eva's voice echoing inside me: *Please, please, please . . .*

'I'm really worried,' I say. 'She sounds terrible – is she okay?'

But DI Jackson just looks at me as though I have all the answers.

Chapter 4

Rob

I stand outside the police station, listening to Mozart's Symphony No. 40 on my iPhone, wondering why the hell Luke is taking so long. In the last period before lunch, I was disturbed to find Luke still hadn't been released from questioning, so I decided to come and find him. He's been in there a good three hours ...

Finally, he emerges, hurrying down the steps. I'm unnerved by the expression on his face: he looks as though he's just sat three exams in a row.

When he spots me, he jumps in surprise. He looks so touched that I feel a flash of guilt: Luke thinks I'm here just for moral support.

He gives me a huge hug. I can feel him trembling and I pull away sharply. Just what the hell went on in there?

'Luke,' I say, 'we need to talk.'

We spot a Starbucks down the road and head towards it. Luke's silent for about a minute and then he spills everything. As I hear him describing Eva's messages, my stomach clenches. I don't have a good feeling about this.

'I'm pretty freaked that she might have been kidnapped or something,' Luke concludes. He's blinking hard, and surreptitiously rubs a tear from his eye.

We sit down with our lattes and Luke makes a flippant remark that it's unlike me to cut class. I can tell he's trying to lighten the atmosphere, but I have to tell him that this is no laughing matter.

This is serious.

Luke's right: I'm a grade-A student. I never skip school. Next month I have an interview at Trinity College, Cambridge to read History. After that, I'm going to work in the banking industry for ten years. I'll stand as a Tory MP at the age of thirty for the Wimbledon constituency. By the age of forty, I'll be prime minister. I've got it all mapped out, and if you think I'm crazy to decide all this at the age of seventeen, then remember: Maggie Thatcher went to Oxford knowing that she was destined to be PM, and look how far she went.

Luke's biting his nails savagely and I gently swat his hand. So then he takes a napkin, spreads it over his knee and starts sketching caricatures of people in the café. For a moment I'm distracted, marvelling at his talent. Most of the time, Luke looks awkward in his body, but when he starts drawing, his whole physique changes, becomes fluid and serene.

'Luke,' I say, swallowing. 'We have to think ahead. If they're seriously worried about Eva, then the questions are going to start. She's been missing three days – if she just wanted to scare her parents or do a Dare, she would have been gone a day, max. So this is serious. They're going to come after us and they're going to want to know what happened at my party.'

Luke's pen pauses. He looks peevish, as though I'm being selfish to worry about us at a time like this. I feel sorry for him. He still hasn't figured out how life works. Once when I was a kid, my dad took me to the park and showed me the ducks on the pond. 'See how those ducks over there are pushing the sick duck away? They don't want to be held back by him, so he has to leave the group. That's nature. Survival of the fittest.'

In some ways, Luke's such an old soul, with his dad in jail and the way he's had to father his siblings, but in many respects he's terribly naïve. He doesn't know how to handle adults; that's why he's in so much trouble at school. And when he's in an intense situation, instead of playing it cool, he tends to blow his top. He once joked to me that he's never quite got the hang of 'how to bullshit like a bourgeois'. To be honest, that's what always drew me to Luke. St Martin's is full of posh toffs; I find his down-to-earth manner refreshing. But now it could screw us both.

'Look,' I say, 'what about what we all did at the party in the – bathroom? And when we ... you know ... '

'You should be a spin doctor, not an MP.'

22

'Luke, I'm serious! Don't you get how bad this looks for us? I still have that video on my phone.'

Luke pales. 'Can't you delete it?'

'Maybe.'

'Maybe?' His pen digs into his napkin, ink spreading, ruining his sketch.

'I'll delete it if you just agree to work with me on this. We have to make up a story about my party, we have to rehearse, and we have to get that story straight.'

Chapter 5

Eva's Diary: 1 June 2016

It's weird – I would never have thought of writing a diary before. It always seemed a bit last-century to me, the sort of thing you expect girls in a Jane Austen novel to do because they've got all those hours to fill scratching out their heartfelt emotions about the latest guy with a big *house*. But a famous writer gave a talk at our school where he said it was good to write every day, even if you just keep a diary. He said that writing is like a muscle and you have to keep exercising it. And since I want to be a famous writer, I figured I should follow his advice.

I'm not sure where to begin. I've started all jokey because laughter is sometimes the only way I get by these days. I'm flippant all the time. I've made such a mess of everything, got myself in such a tangle. I know that sooner or later I'm going to fall off this tightrope I'm walking. In the meantime, I just keep going to school every day and getting my 'A's and keeping my dad happy and smiling at everyone.

I guess all the trouble began at the start of 2016. That's when I first noticed Luke.

I was walking across the playground with my best friend, Siobhan. We were on our way to Economics and there was all this shouting and noise. Well, I love a good drama, so I dragged Siobhan over to the crowd.

Everyone was chanting, 'FIGHT! FIGHT! FIGHT!'

That's when I saw him. Luke Jones. I'd never really noticed before how handsome he is. He's very tall and well built – not in a fake, steroid, too-many-trips-to-the-gym kind of way – he's naturally fit and strong. He was messing around with another guy; they'd both pierced holes in their Evian bottles and were shooting thin sprays of water at each other, howling with laughter. I stood there, hugging my books to my chest, and he looked up with his amazing blue eyes and grinned at me. It was such a wild, dangerous, sexy grin, like a big cat daring me to play with him. He swept his dripping hair from his forehead. Then he blew me a kiss.

'In your dreams, Luke,' jeered Mark, the guy he was play-fighting.

Siobhan put her palm to my cheek and made a sizzling noise.

'Don't tell me you like Luke,' she said. 'He's a bad boy, Eva. Don't go there.'

I'd started to get bored of going on dates with guys. It always followed the same pattern – he'd send me a flirty text, we'd go to see a movie, he'd make me hold his sweaty hand, he'd try to kiss me in the last half, and it would carry on like this for a few more dates before I got restless. None of them had any character. They were all so nice. Maybe a bad boy was just what I needed.

When I started telling my girlfriends that I had a crush on Luke I got a secret thrill from seeing the surprise on their faces. By choosing Luke, I was finally saying to the world, I'm not the angel you think I am, there's more to me than that. Because that's the trouble with being me. Everyone sees me but nobody *sees me*. They only see sparkle and glitter. They can never perceive the shades in me, because I can only be one colour, and it's some kind of sickly, bright pink. Several of my friends were convinced it was some kind of philanthropic gesture. As though I felt sorry for Luke, that he was my project and I'd be the one to change him.

I think I did change Luke, but not in the way everyone thought. I knew he was a bad boy but I underestimated him just the same as everyone underestimated me. When I got to know him, he wasn't what I expected at all. And by then it was too late—

I want to write more but Dad's calling me for dinner. Oh God. I have to go down there and pretend everything's fine. For once my surface glitter is handy. OK. Deep breath. Down I go ...

Chapter 6

Rivka's WhatsApp

Siobhan online

U know Eva gave me her diary to look after cos she caught her dad snooping in her bedroom?

Yeah? Did you read it?

No, I kept my promise.

You should hand it over to the police. Maybe they can find her!

I know, but it's been stolen.

What!

It was in my locker. Today I went in and it was bust open. All my other stuff was in there but someone had nicked the diary.

Shit, that's seriously weird.

I know, I'm freaked. There's all this stuff about MR.W in there.

Shouldn't we tell the cops about that?

No way, Eva made me swear. I'm her best friend!

Who knew the diary was there? Do you think Luke did?

Maybe.

You know, I did see him hanging around by the lockers the other day and u know how jealous he is . . .

Chapter 7

Siobhan

When Eva and I were twelve years old, we used to play this telepathy game. We'd sit at the kitchen table in her house, a rainbow of felt pens and paper in front of us. Closing our eyes, we'd attempt to guess what the other was thinking. Then we'd draw it, covering our pictures with our hands. The results were just amazing. Eva would cry: 'I was thinking of an apple!', and I'd hold up my pic of a green Granny Smith. Or I'd cry: 'Tomato!' and her picture would mimic my mind. Soon we started wearing the same clothes outside school and texting each other every morning to ensure we wore our hair in the same styles. We once even attempted to be blood sisters, though that went horribly wrong – Eva's prick went too deep and blood ended up gushing all over her nice pink rug, and we were too panicked to press our thumbs together. Besides, we didn't need to be Blood

Sisters. The connection between us is beyond the body; it's psychic; it's soul.

And now we're traipsing through the woods on Wimbledon Common with the rest of them, searching for her, without a single clue.

Mr Pieachowski has organised the search with the help of a Community Support Officer. We walk, we search, we seek. Rain fell yesterday and the ground's churned up with mud. I'm touched by how many people have turned up to help. There's a gang of us from school, Rivka and Rob, some teachers, including Mr Abdul, and numerous neighbours. Eva is loved by so many people.

A few droplets spit on my face. Twilight's seeping across the sky like blue smoke and I can feel a chill in the air. *Oh Eva*, I say to myself, to her, to the universe, *let us find you* – something between plea and prayer.

Eva's been missing for five days now, and I'm terrified tonight will be another washout and tomorrow will turn into Day Six.

I fall back from the group, pretending to examine a tree, because I need to create space to focus. Over the last few days, it's almost become an obsession. When I'm making a cup of tea, I'll murmur into the steam: *Eva, I'm here, I'm here, you're safe, you're safe*, or when I wash my hands: *I'm with you*, or when I strap on my heels: *We'll find you, we'll help you, just hold on*. I'm certain my words are weaving together and forming a protective net around her. I'm even scared to sleep, for fear that I'm deserting her, that if I falter the net will unravel and she'll slip through.

Now, standing by the tree, I try to focus. *Please Eva, please let us find you, show us where you—*

'Found anything?'

I jump. It's Mr Pieachowski.

'No – sorry.'

He looks as though he's aged a hundred years overnight. Eva always used to moan about him and I'd tell her she was lucky to have such a caring dad (mine lives in his office – I *never* see him), but she'd just sigh, 'Yeah, a dad who loves me too much.'

The rain is stronger now. Mr Pieachowski looks anxiously at the group.

'It's okay,' I tell him fiercely. 'We'll keep going.' *Oh Eva, we'll never give up.* I'm close to tears, and he gives me a sad smile.

Suddenly I'm aware of a girl by our side. She's one of the volunteers, but I don't recognise her from school. She's small and waifish, with pale blonde hair falling down her back, her grey eyes feline beneath her pale brows.

'Mr Pieachowski?' Her voice is barely a whisper. As she raises her hand to shield her face from the rain, I notice a tattoo on her wrist. It looks like an *S* or a *Z*.

He looks at her, irritated, anxious to keeping looking.

'I saw him, Mr Pieachowski,' she says, 'he was threatening her and I – I tried to film them but he was so – he was so—'

Someone shouts in the distance: 'FOUND SOMETHING!'

We turn, shocked. The girl steps back.

'Wait,' Mr Pieachowski instructs. 'Please – just wait here.'

I hurry after Mr Pieachowski. A small group has formed around the edge of a pit. They seem to gather closer as though to conceal something. Dread fills my gut. I find myself slowing down.

'There's a body,' Rivka says, her voice breaking.

Mr Pieachowski cries out. He pushes everyone aside. I watch in horror as he slips down into the pit, his hands grabbing wildly at the mud, gathering mulch and leaves and dirt, not finding a hold.

He hits the bottom and he hits *her*. She rolls onto her front, eyes staring upwards, glazed and lifeless.

Eva.

Everything becomes very distant. There's a midnight screaming inside me. I feel as though I'm in a bubble, a high-pitched ringing in my ears. Voices blur into cotton-wool fuzz. Rob is by my side. Lacing his arm through mine. Saying, you don't need. To see this. Just step away. Someone call 999. But I can't stop. I can't stop looking. My best friend. My soul sister. My heart.

Her skin is pale, bluish. Mr Pieachowski is rubbing her limp hand, weeping, begging her to just say a word, just move her lips. Rain glistens on her face like tears. And then I see the leaves patterned over her body, the leaves stained brown, and the wounds on her body like red eyes that glare back at me.

33

Chapter 8

Luke

I find out that the love of my life is dead via Facebook.

It's not easy to get online in our house. We have a Dell computer that Mum won in a competition six years ago which sits in the corner of our living room/kitchen. There's four of us wanting to use it at any given time, so just grabbing a turn usually involves a fight. Freya is glued to YouTube, watching cute kitten videos. In the end, I have to tickle her and bribe her with half a Twix to get her off.

I sit down, wondering whether to get a cloth. The keyboard is full of crap – dog hairs, biscuit crumbs, dust – and the screen is sticky with splatters of god-knows-what.

And then I see it. Siobhan's Facebook post:

Siobhan O'Hara I can't believe she's gone. Eva was my best friend and the most amazing person I've ever known. She went missing and we all hoped she was just playing a game, a joke. Now we know that she was murdered. I saw her body myself, in a pit, covered in stab wounds – a sight I will never, ever forget and never forgive. Whatever sick bastard did this to my best friend, don't think you'll ever get away with it. I love you, Eva. I will love you forever. RIP my angel and my friend xxx

I stare as it rapidly fills with comments – *Oh my God, I can't believe it, she was only 17!*, or *Eva was the shining light of our school, this is the worst news I've ever heard*, or, *We will love you always Eva, you will stay in our memories and our hearts xxx*. And I think: *This has to be a joke.* I'm vaguely aware of noise in the background, the sound of the TV, of Freya play-practising for *X Factor* auditions, of Matt messing around with his toy trains and Mum cooking in the kitchen, but it fades until I'm just sitting there, motionless.

Eva's photo is blurred by the dirty monitor – a ketchup smear that looks like blood on her cheek. I lick a finger and try to wipe it away. Tears begin to slide down my face. I feel something by my knee and I jerk away violently. It's Buster. He licks my limp hand gently, as though he senses my devastation. I can't pat him. I can't move.

'Hey, Luke, can you lay the table, the burgers are nearly ready!' Mum calls from the kitchen.

'Burgers! Yummy!' Matt and Freya chorus.

'Sure.' I force myself up.

The tablecloth is still sticky with crumbs and cola splashes from last night's 2-for-1 pizza deal fest. I grab a handful of cutlery. For some reason I find it very important to lay it all out very carefully, positioning knife, fork and spoon in a perfect square. My hands are trembling. I can feel my heart thrashing in my chest. My eyes are burning and my throat is sore from holding back the tears. I think of being with Eva. In the back of my car, making love, our lips pressed together, breaking off in a haze of happiness to gaze at each other, feeling desire so raw it hurt, whispering: *I love you.* I remember that she bit my ear playfully and whispered back that I was amazing. She said I was the only guy she'd ever slept with. She said that I was special—

I go into the kitchen and without thinking, I pick up the pan of potatoes to drain them. The heat sears my hand I yell out—

The pan lands in the sink, hot water spraying across the surface—

Potato pieces flying onto the floor—

'Luke!' Mum yells.

My hand is sore, maybe burnt. I hold it under the cold tap. Buster comes up and tries to snuffle up the potatoes.

'NO!' I shout and then I feel bad. Buster is such a

good-natured and devoted dog that I never get mad at him, no matter what.

I run. Out of the kitchen, tumbling up the stairs and into my bedroom. I pull the bolt across the door. It's the only tidy place in our pigsty of a house. Eva used to tease me about the way I folded everything up and put it away neatly – 'Aren't you guys meant to be slobs? You're such a girl!'

I yank the lid off my wicker washing basket and pull out the dirty washing, a tangle of grubby socks and boxers and crumpled T-shirts, until I find the outfit I wore to Rob's party. I remember pulling on my 501 jeans (Levi's on the label; picked up in Oxfam on a lucky day) and my Ted Baker shirt (a present from Rob for my last birthday). I was hoping the designer gear might impress Eva.

I go cold at the sight of the shirt. There's blood all over one sleeve, blood splashed across the front, now dried into crusty brown flowers—

A voice comes through the door: 'Luke, Luke!'

It's Matt. I jump so violently that I drop the shirt. It ghosts to the floor.

'Piss off,' I hiss quietly. The screws rattle in the lock as he yanks the handle. 'Look, go tell Mum I'm not hungry, okay? I feel sick.'

'Shall I rub your tummy better, Luke?'

He's just a kid. My anger dissolves. 'I'm okay, mate,' I say softly. 'Please, I just need to be by myself.'

I listen to the sound of Matt toddling down the hall and

37

then dragging himself down the stairs one at a time, sitting on a step and then – *thunk!* – thumping down onto the next then – *thunk!* – again and again, down, down, down.

I tiptoe into the bathroom and shove the shirt into the sink, spinning the tap. The hot water catches the blood, brings it to life, sluices its colour down the plughole. *Oh God, oh God.* I should've got rid of this last week, after the police first called me in, but that night I pulled it out of the basket, felt sick at the sight of the red patches and shoved it back in again, burying it deep, wanting to forget. Now I hold it up, but the stains are still there. Panic comes over me. If anyone saw this, what the hell would they think?

I ball it up, race back to my bedroom and lock the door, then hide the bloody shirt in a carrier bag and stuff it in the back of my wardrobe.

I sit on the bed and, on autopilot, I go to text Eva. It hits me again, the reeling shock of it. I'll never be able to send her a sweet text again, or a silly gif to cheer her up. I'll never be able to pin her down and bend over her, teasing her with a kiss that never quite reaches her lips, until she laughs and screams in frustration. I'll never be able to hold her against me, bury my face in her hair, smell her coconut shampoo, feel the soft swell of her breasts against my chest. I'll never be able to pick her up at the end of her road, waiting there in my car and hoping she'd turn up because every time, every time I sat there, I feared that she'd finally cave in to her parents and say she couldn't see me any more, and it was always such a relief to see her walking towards me, wearing some gorgeous skimpy dress, and watch her slip into the seat next to mine. I'll never be able to drive out in the dark with her and play Dares and suffer that electric sense of dread, wondering what she might make me do next.

I don't know what happened to Eva on that Friday night. I'm not to blame for her death, I swear. But I do know this: I was the last person to see my beautiful girl alive before the killer came for her, and I left her out there, in the woods, lost and alone. I sob then, sob and sob until the twilight turns to dark and my eyes run out of tears, crying dry racking sobs until I'm spent. The last time I saw her, she left a sweater behind; I wrap it around a pillow and go to bed, my face buried in her scent.

When I wake up in the morning, it hits me again and I think: *Is this what it's going to be like from now on, waking every day like this?* I feel as though my life is cleaving in two: a Before and an After.

I pull on a pair of old jeans and a jumper. Everything feels surreal and in slow motion, as I'm underwater.

When I check my phone, there are six missed calls, all from Rob. *We have to get our stories straight*, that's what he said last week. I thought he was being OTT at the time. Now I can see he's right. We can't tell the police what really happened at the party – we have to make something up.

Chapter 9

Eva's Diary: 8 June 2016

The night after I saw Luke fighting in the playground,
I texted Siobhan who texted Mark who texted Rob and
that way, I got Luke's number. I spent an hour pacing
around my bedroom, coming up with all sorts of witty
openings. In the end, I decided to just be cheeky:

> if u want to ask me out, this is my no. X

No name.

I paced around my room, waiting and feeling
strangely nervous. I know it sounds arrogant but I've
never, ever had trouble getting a guy I want before.
Now all of a sudden my confidence faltered.

Still no reply. What if my mum was right? She was
always telling me that I'm not that attractive.

We live in Wimbledon village, a fancy suburbia. Our road is the epitome of tedium. Everyone here wears a lobotomised grin, chained by their mortgage, competing for the fanciest car. Everyone was always telling me how lucky I was, but all I ever felt was trapped, bored. Yes, it was *safe* but I'd never travelled anywhere beyond France. I'd never taken drugs, never tried a cigarette. I'd only had sex a few times, with my last boyfriend, and it had disappointed me, lacked the wild passion I'd hoped for. When I went out with my friends, I was always home by midnight, just as I'd promised my Daddy.

To be a writer, I needed to live life to the full. I needed to take risks, break rules. I needed to do things that scared me but would be good for me in the long run.

Luke didn't reply that night, or the next. I noticed he was absent from school, which gave me hope. I wondered if he was sick, though Rob reckoned Luke had been suspended for a few days for losing his temper and telling a teacher to fuck off.

A week later, just when I'd sulkily admitted defeat, the reply came:

Hey there, it's Luke. good to hear from u.

I actually jumped around my room in triumph. How stupid is that?! Of course, I didn't reply for a day. If he

41

was going to keep me waiting, I was going to play that game even harder.

We set up our first date and I woke every morning zinging with anticipation. When I thought of his blue eyes, I wanted to touch myself. When I thought of his fights and temper, I burned with unease. Finally, life was about to get interesting ...

Chapter 10

Eva's Last Instagram Post:
Uploaded the Day Before She Died

♥ 45 likes

Chapter 11

Carolina

I guess I should begin by admitting that I'm not a fan of Luke Jones. The only encounter I've ever had with him involved standing in front of him in a lunch queue and feeling him tug my plait. I think his stupid friend Rob dared him to do it. I crossed my arms, coughed loudly and didn't turn round, but I was more upset than I let on. Plus, he has a terrible reputation. He's been suspended a few times and he's always fighting and swearing and getting into trouble. Apparently he comes from a really bad family.

Even so, I can't believe what I find when I decide to check out his Facebook page.

We're not online friends, of course (to be honest, I actually only have three Facebook friends – Eva had 3089 friends on the day she died), but Luke's page is open to the public so I can take a proper look.

As I scroll down, my jaw drops. I'm sitting in my bedroom with my laptop nestled on my duvet and I reach for my iPhone to take some screenshots.

Date: 5 July 2016.

Luke posts a link to a YouTube clip from *Reservoir Dogs*.

Luke's comment:

 Luke Jones such a cool film – gangstas, guns, blood, wit – what more could u want from a movie?

Date: 12 August 2016

Luke posts a link to a YouTube clip from *Hostel*.

Luke's comment:

Luke Jones such a sick film but I luv it. Eva hates it so now I'll make her watch it over and over.

And then I find another Facebook page for Luke, under a pseudonym, 'The Next Francis Bacon' (how modest!). I know it's his as I once heard Rob chatting about it. I have to admit, he does have talent, but some of the pictures are so disturbing. For example, there's a truly disgusting painting of a huge skull, surrounded by a small circle of trees.

Was there ever clearer evidence of a psycho-in-the-making?

I go back to Eva's page and click through her photos. There are pictures of her at parties, wearing a lot of black eyeliner, looking wild and glamorous and much older than seventeen. There are photos of her in school uniform, hugging her books or holding a trophy. There is one very cute pic of her holding Rivka's kittens. Oh – and there's a picture of her under a weeping willow tree on Wimbledon Common. The shades of the leaves have blended around her blonde hair, making her look like an exotic nymph. I took that photo; I remember it clearly. I had no idea she'd put it up online. I feel touched.

Eva's family have posted the announcement of her death on her wall. There are 658 comments underneath. I think of how kind Eva's been to me. Of the day she met with me in the woods and said we should be 'secret friends'. Of the day I gave her a fat red diary as a present because she said she wanted one; she hugged me so tight and said it was the best present she'd ever had.

I feel choked up. If only I'd gone to the party that night. I did ask but Rob was mean and said squares like me weren't allowed. I didn't dare go running to Eva. That would've made it worse.

I rarely post anything too personal online. I don't understand people who gush about their deepest fears or confess their heartfelt secrets; that would make me feel raw and vulnerable, as though I've undressed my heart. Sometimes I leave comments on websites, under news articles, debating a point – though never using my real name.

Suddenly, overwhelmed with emotion, I find myself adding a comment to Eva's wall:

Carolina Jackson RIP, beautiful Eva. I will never forget you. You were a dear friend and I love you. Carolina xxx

Downstairs in the kitchen, the clock says it's 9 p.m. Dad still isn't home. My reflection is vivid on the window. I look so plain. Eva was always trying to persuade me to undo my hair from its plait and wear it loose, but I pointed out that it just ended up becoming a mad frizz. I guess my glasses don't help either.

Not that it matters. I'm not some ugly duckling who wants to become a swan. I'm not looking for a fairy-tale ending. No matter what the stupid teen mags say, we can't all be beautiful and I'm not wasting my money on a load of products in an effort to pretend I can be. I don't need or want anyone to judge me on my looks. I'm going to work hard, join the police and become a detective. I'm going to be a star.

* * *

I hear a key in the front door.

I quickly dish up Dad's dinner, fill a glass with water, and set them down on the table. It's nothing fancy, just a shepherd's pie from M&S. My dad lives off ready meals.

He comes in and says: 'Hey,' very quietly.

I sit opposite him, reading a book as he eats. I know that for the first five minutes when he comes home he needs to be in peace. He's still in the world of work, soiled by thieves and sickos and the grime of everyday crime. The book is a guide to birdspotting, though I've not had much time to tick off many species recently. I've been too busy thinking about Luke and Eva.

Finally, Dad looks up and smiles at me.

'They've made me SIO on the case.'

'Wow! Dad, that's great!'

Senior Investigating Officer. My Dad, DI Jackson, in charge of the investigation into Eva's death. The tension inside me softens.

'I'm going to be working very long hours.' Dad gave me a concerned glance.

'Dad, I'm seventeen! You don't have to worry about me. I know this is really important. Besides, I can help,' I add. I pleat the edge of the tablecloth in my fingers, worried that he might fob me off. Instead, he looks pleased.

'You can be my insider,' he says. He's asked me to listen to any school gossip and report back to him.

I know a few more details about the case than the rest of my year do, though I've been sworn to secrecy.

I know that the police are still trying to find Eva's mobile. It's missing and the phone is switched off, so they can't tri-angulate the signal, which is basically a fancy police term for tracking where it's located.

Then there's the girl. Mr Pieachowski reported that the night they found Eva's body he'd been approached by a blonde girl who claimed she had seen a guy threatening her. But the girl has never called or been in touch again. She's definitely not from St Martin's, and nobody is sure who she is or what she's hiding.

'Dad, there's something on Facebook that I think you should see,' I say. 'It's Luke's page.'

Immediately, Dad's face darkens. He recently explained to me that when someone is murdered, the most likely suspect is someone close to them. A friend, a family member, a teacher, even. He said that the clever psychos like Hannibal Lecter that you see in movies don't reflect real life. Murder is rarely calculated. Often, someone flies into a rage and in a fit of madness, they flip from Jekyll to Hyde. In that moment, a perfectly ordinary person can do extraordinary things. Worse, Dad's also pointed out that 44 per cent of murdered women are killed by their partners or ex-partners.

'There's all these violent videos on Luke's page,' I say.

'I've seen those, Carolina,' he says. 'We checked him out.'

'Oh.' I feel deflated. 'But did you see his special art Facebook page, for his paintings? It's not posted under his name, so you might have missed it. His paintings are seriously gory.'

'Now that, I would like to see.'

He's actually excited, which is rare – he hardly ever betrays any emotion. He doesn't even bother finishing his food. He goes bounding up the stairs to my room whilst I pant after him. I click through to 'The Next Francis Bacon' and hand my dad the screen. He looks through it very carefully. My heart is beating fast and I'm scared that he'll tell me I'm being silly. Five minutes go by and then he nods, eyes gleaming, and says: 'Thank you, Carolina. Thank you.'

Lost in thought, he leaves my room and locks himself away in his study.

Maybe I *can* get involved in the case.

I take another look at Eva's Facebook page. Someone has commented on my comment! I feel a thrill inside. So this is why people bother with social media. Then my face falls.

> **Lily Young** Hey, I didn't even know u knew Eva. Are u sure u were even friends? Maybe in ur dreams.

Oh my God. What a bitch. Quite a lot of people have *liked* her comment too. And one of those people is *Siobhan*. What right does she have to judge my friendship with Eva? Maybe she's jealous. Ever since Eva had died, she's taken on the official role of Best Friend, and offered everyone a chance to write their memories down in a white notebook.

Then I see that someone has added a new comment, just in the last few seconds:

Luke Jones How can u judge at a time like this? Carolina's comment was sweet. Eva was friendly with everyone.

I peer at my screen in disbelief; I even rub my glasses clean, to be sure.

Luke has left the comment. He's defended me. Wow.

I get up, awhirl with emotion. I hurry down the stairs, down the hallway and knock on my dad's study. It takes several knocks for him to open the door. When I explain the whole thing to him, he frowns and says he doesn't think it's that relevant. Luke might seem nice now, he concludes, but that could just be an act.

Back in my bedroom, I lie down on my bed, feeling foolish. Whenever Dad is dealing with a case, he never lets his emotions overwhelm him. He is calm, cool and decisive. If I'm going to be a good detective, I have to learn from him. Why would Luke pull my plait one day and mock me, and then defend me the next? It's suspicious. Charming me could easily be part of his strategy; he probably knows that DI Jackson is my dad.

From now on, I have to be the detached observer. I have to hover like a falcon, observing my targets from a distance, swooping softly and only when I have my target cornered. I won't get sucked into social media; I'll just watch, listen, and gather evidence. Me and my dad will catch this murderer. We'll do it together.

Chapter 12

Anonymous

The Big Bad Blog

It's been 3 days since Eva Pieachowski's body was found.
Some people have commented on this blog and said that it isn't appropriate, it isn't sensitive, it's unfair. But, unlike the press, this blog isn't trying to sensationalise or sentimentalise Eva's murder. This blog aims to be a day-to-day news report, each entry a fresh episode in the murder case. You will find the latest developments here before you'll hear it anywhere else.

It seems likely that the killer was someone who knew Eva and attended St Martin's. Speaking of which, Year 13 are in a tizz. The police are planning to interview all the major players who were at Rob's party: Siobhan O'Hara, Rob Pennington, Fiona Heckle, Rivka Young and James Carter. As for Luke Jones, he's already been called down to the station 3 times.

Rob's house parties are infamous. We can all imagine the sorts of things that were going on that night. So who knows who might have played a part in her subsequent death? She was murdered in the woods on Wimbledon Common, the very woods that Rob's garden backs onto. Someone knows something.

The Big Bad Blog has been able to glean a rough timeline of events for Friday night. It goes something like this:

9 p.m. – Eva arrives at the party with Luke.

9.30 p.m. – The police stop by briefly when neighbours complain about the noise, but they don't enter the property or do anything more than request that the noise levels come down.

10.25 p.m. – Luke and Eva are heard arguing in the upstairs bedroom of Rob's house. They leave the party via the back garden, heading for the woods. Both are reported to have looked 'like hell'.

This is where things get blurry.

11.15 p.m. – CCTV shows Luke getting into his car and driving home alone.

However – Luke claims that they went into the woods, chatted, and he walked away five minutes later, at **10.30 p.m.**

There's a forty-five-minute window that Luke can't account for.

Just what happened in that time?

Comments (546)

Anonymous – I love this blog! Keep it up, it's good to be in the loop.

Sarah K – how come you have all this inside info? You're either a cop or you're shagging someone in the force.

Mark – RIP Eva, if this blog helps us find the killer then I'm glad it exists.

Chapter 13

Eva's Diary: 2 July 2016

I've not written in this diary for three weeks now. I keep looking back over the time I've spent with Luke over the last 4 months, as though if I search hard enough I might find a way to fix the mess our relationship has become.

I still remember our first date clearly. It's a time I'll always treasure, even if I was naïve.

I lied to my parents about the date. I'd rarely done that before. It was a Thursday and we'd had an early dinner; Dad was still at work. I was about to tell Mum where I was going, but I found myself saying I was off to meet Siobhan for a Starbucks. She shrugged, and carried on reading *Venus in Furs* without looking up.

I was surprised that Luke had asked to meet me by

South Wimbledon station: a stretch of crappy shops
nearby a patch of dirty grass and a line of railings.
Normally guys tried a little bit harder than that to
impress me.

I felt very self-conscious as I walked over to meet him.
It was all Mum's fault. She is so very beautiful and she
spends a lot of time obsessing over clothes and looks in
general. Mine in particular. Before I went out she looked
me up and down in that judgemental way she has ... I
was wearing jeans and a black camisole top. Her verdict?
'I think you're putting on weight.' Honestly, though,
her face said it all. There's always something wrong,
something I could do better. I scowled, and pointed out
that she shouldn't be encouraging me to become bulimic.
She merely raised an eyebrow and said: 'That is not what I
said, Eva, but really who will tell you the truth if not your
mother? I'm just saying that if you just lost a few pounds,
you'd be so much more gorgeous than you already are.'

My dad says I'm beautiful; he jokes about how all
his friends have warned him to keep an eye on me.
Sometimes when I look in the mirror, I feel confused.
I look at myself and think I'm lucky. And then I look
again and hear Mum's voice snaking around my head
and I think I'm just a fat, ugly lump. It's like those
Catholic holographic holy cards that Dad has; tilt them
one way and see the Virgin Mary and the next you see
Jesus. I flit back and forth, trying to see who I am.

I saw Luke waiting for me, leaning against the railings smoking a cigarette. He looked hot – in a James Dean kind of way – wearing ripped jeans and a black T-shirt. I felt so shy that I had a sudden urge to hide, but before I could do anything he looked right at me and smiled. He told me I looked amazing, and I thought, see, Mum, I'm not so bad! We hung out for a bit, chatting awkwardly. I noticed him looking at my legs a few times and then quickly pretending not to when I caught him out. This made me smile inside.

He offered me a Marlboro. Normally I have no problem with telling people where to stick their offers of lung cancer. But I found myself accepting; I needed something to do with my hands. After just one drag I had a coughing fit like I was some kid in Year 8. Luke smiled and gently ran his finger under my chin. It was such a tender gesture that it took me by surprise.

'You don't have to smoke if you don't want to,' he said softly.

I was all shaken up and stripped bare. Just the touch of his finger had made me body react. I thought: I'm the one who's meant to be in control here. Yet I felt anything but.

It was getting cold and I suggested we go to a bar I knew; it was a classy place, with nice romantic lighting, perfect for a first date. Luke's face fell and suddenly it hit me. Of course we couldn't go there – Luke couldn't even afford the price of a coffee in Starbucks. His 'piece-of-rough' reputation wasn't some sort of pose – he really didn't have money. That's why we were hanging out on a kerb. I felt like a spoilt idiot and tried to salvage things by telling him I was just kidding and inviting him back to mine.

I knew Mum would be out at her book group until 9 p.m. and Dad was such a workaholic these days that he definitely wouldn't be home until ten. We'd have the place to ourselves.

It took about twenty minutes to bus it over to Eversham Close. As we headed up my drive, Luke's eyes mooned.

'What, this is your house?' he asked, like it was Buckingham Palace rather than a regular four-bedroomed semi-detached.

Inside, we went into the kitchen and I asked if he wanted a milkshake. Luke nodded and asked in a small voice if he could have chocolate. Finally, the roles had reversed – now I was the one in control and he felt awkward. He stood there, watching me make the shakes, drumming his fingers on the table. I couldn't think of a single thing to say. Normally the guys I dated just went on about themselves and how great they were and how brilliant the last footie goal they scored was.

'So, you live near the tube back there – near South Wimbledon?' I asked.

'Yeah,' said Luke. 'Yeah. But – we could've lived in a place like this. When I was about eleven years old, my dad showed up out of the blue. He used to come and go a lot, cos he was in and out of jail.'

I felt my insides flutter. God, Luke's dad sounded like the type of guy you read about in the tabloids, or those Channel 5 documentaries that my mum interrupts with a dry warning that they'll give me brain rot and then sits down to watch with me.

'This time he had all these presents for us – a new pair of trainers, new jeans, even a Game Boy. He'd come into money – a lot of money. Mum was even able to give up her cleaning work. We were all worried where he'd got it from, though ...

'Then one of his friends phoned up to congratulate us on the lottery win. Turns out he'd won, like, a LOT. The bastard ...'

His voice was tortured. I so wanted to hug him. I felt ashamed for stereotyping Luke's life, turning it into my cheap thrill.

'Then what?'

'Oh, after a month the dick got bored and left us like always. Mum tried to get him to give us maintenance and even took him to court. After all that, he gave us £500 and then disappeared. The last I heard, he'd lost all that lottery money gambling it away in Las Vegas.'

Luke's voice became hollow with despair; he sounded much older than his years.

This had all got pretty heavy pretty quickly. I was very moved but I wasn't sure what to say. I just gave him his milkshake and said: 'Drink up!', all breezy. Luke looked incredulous. Then he took a sip and shrugged.

'It's good.'

He had chocolate milk around his mouth. I smiled and I still think what I did next was pretty impressive, like something out of a film. I walked up to him and with my index finger gently stroked the milk from his lips. Then I put my finger to my mouth and licked it clean. Luke smiled down at me. I thought he might kiss me then: the moment was there. But he held back and I felt momentarily lost, high with nerves. Most guys are transparent but I couldn't tell anymore what Luke was thinking – did he like me or not?

We wandered into the living room and immediately Luke went for the remote control to try out the TV (our massive 72-inch flatscreen). He clicked the 'on' button, but instead the velvet curtains slowly swept closed over the bay windows. He'd used the wrong remote.

I laughed and in that instant he snapped – rounding on me, calling me a cliché, a spoilt little rich girl who has everything on a plate. It was such a strong outburst that I think it had been building up inside him for some time. I was upset but also angry – what did he know? I wanted to put him straight, but he pushed me onto the sofa and ... started to tickle me. I cried out and he pinned me down so that he was on top of me. I blushed and squirmed, conscious of how strong he was; I even playfully squeezed his biceps.

Looking up at him, I said: 'My dad immigrated to this country from Poland twenty years ago without a penny. He built up a business all by himself. So my parents were poor, once upon a time. We moved to this house when I was about five.'

He grunted, but I didn't feel as though he was completely paying attention. I felt indignant. I mean, my life story did sound a bit bland by comparison to his, but still I'd listened to him and now it was my turn – I wanted him to know the real me. If he thought I was just a lucky little rich girl like all the rest, then what was the point?

He was gazing down at me. His eyes were so blue. The blue of a summer's day when you just want to fly free and swim in the sea. There was a scar on one of his eyebrows and another just by his left ear. I wondered if he'd got those from fighting. Our cheeks were pink. He leaned down and kissed me ...

Here is how I was used to being kissed: a guy pokes his tongue in my mouth and groans while I try to act

sexy while feeling either physically revolted or like I
want to burst out laughing.

This was something else. Luke's kiss was soft and
hard all at once. I found myself reaching up and
threading my hands through his hair. He started
unbuttoning my dress. Normally I'd stop it there because
the best way to keep a boy interested is to make them
wait, but we were in the moment and I wanted a little
bit more, just a little bit more ... He started caressing
my thighs with the tips of his fingers and then skirting
the rim of my knickers until I was gasping for him.
He watched me so intently that I was hypnotised. I
didn't hear the click of the front door, the footsteps in
the hallway.

There was Dad.

Standing in the doorway.

Staring at Luke, bare-chested, on top of me, his
hands in my knickers, his teeth in my neck.

Luke leapt off me and his trousers fell to his ankles.
Dad made a swift exit, but not before he'd given me a
very sharp look.

We quickly pulled on our clothes. In the kitchen, we
found Dad sipping Earl Grey, reading the newspaper. He
set it down and glared at Luke, then turned to me. 'Eva,
what's going on?'

Very politely, I introduced Luke to him. I really did
think Dad might like him. Luke stepped forwards – he

looked so boyish and vulnerable. He gets like that around Mr Abdul too. It's kind of cute. He put his hand out and started to say hello. I could tell he was going to apologise.

Dad didn't take his hand. He didn't even acknowledge him. Instead, he looked at me, told me I had homework, and to tell my 'friend' to go home.

Luke's face fell.

I was furious but Dad was having none of it.

Luke gave me a full-on kiss goodbye, but it felt aggressive, like a 'V' sign at Dad. Then there was the slam of the back door and he was gone.

Silence. I turned to Dad and went for a pre-emptive strike: 'I got an A-plus for my Geography essay today. It was the highest in the class.'

No use. He went for a full-on lecture. On and on, it went. Mum treats me as though I'm 30; Dad treats me as though I'm 3. I usually feel much more relaxed and happy around him, but only because he makes me feel like a little girl who'll never need to grow up. Still, it doesn't sit right. I'm 17. I could get married if I wanted.

'... and his mother is our cleaner too, Eva, she's shown me pictures of her family, so I recognised him. I mean, I do find that a little disconcerting ...'

I suddenly tuned in. I thought of the woman who came to clean for us, Pam. She had greying hair in a perm and crimpled lips and stank of Silk Cuts and cheap hairspray.

I made it up to Dad by helping him cook dinner; he did the pasta whilst I heated up his favourite tomato sauce, sprinkling fresh basil on it. He was relieved that the subject of Luke was over; he seemed to assume, as he always does, that I would just go along with whatever he ordered. But as I sat there, watching him eat and listening to him waffle on, laughing and nodding at all the right cues, I was replaying the evening. Luke. I sighed inside. I wondered if I might be falling in love.

I texted him as soon as dinner was over. I said sorry about my Dad but asked if we could meet in secret. Like a modern-day Romeo & Juliet – forbidden, illicit, exciting. Of course, I didn't stop to think that Romeo & Juliet is also a tragedy.

Chapter 14

Rob

There's a thin corridor by the side of the school gym that nobody really uses. I slip down it to get some space before the police interview me. On my phone, I check out the Big Bad Blog. Just who the hell is writing this damn thing? The comments on the latest post have hit 1,034. An alarming number are saying things like this:

It was Rob's party, maybe he plotted her murder for weeks before and lured Eva over.

God. I need a spin doctor.

And there are even more comments about Luke. The poor guy's in a total state. When I picture Eva, I can't see her as a single person. I always see Eva'n'Luke, laughing together, kissing, rubbing noses in an Eskimo kiss, texting, drawing silly moustaches on each other ... and yelling, pinching, pushing, screaming. Both had petrol tempers; the slightest fire and they would ignite. Fatal attraction.

I just hope he can keep it together today and tell the police the right story. It's so unfair; none of the girls are getting any stick. Just because we're in possession of testosterone, it doesn't mean we feel compelled to knife up the opposite sex, for God's sake.

'Okay, Rob?' Mr Abdul strides into the corridor.

I nod. Mr Abdul's going to be my Appropriate Adult for this interview. He'll sit in and make sure everything's kosher. Me and Siobhan were messing around yesterday, wondering if we could request an *Inappropriate* Adult; it helped relieve our nerves. Joking aside, though, I'm glad Abdul is going to be my wing man.

A DC directs us to a room by the gym. They've taped a paper sign on the door: INTERVIEW ROOM 1.

Here we go.

It smells weird inside: a stale tang from decades of sweaty PE lessons. The set-up looks odd too. On one side is a stack of old mats and a clutter of bats and balls and on the other is a small table, where DI Jackson is sitting. I stroll up to him and shake his hand. He looks taken aback. Mr Abdul gives him a respectful nod.

I sit down on a squeaky plastic chair. 'I'd be happy to answer any questions,' I say, feeling the need to break the silence. 'Anything at all. We all loved Eva.'

Jackson presses play on the black audio recorder. He asks

me to state my name and date of birth and all that jazz, then gives the time and place.

I swallow, knowing that whatever I say can't be erased.

'I just have two questions for you, Rob,' he says. 'The first is this – someone has reported that you, Luke and Eva left the party on the Friday night for roughly an hour at around eight o'clock. Can you tell me where you went?'

I look him straight in the eye.

'I have no idea why someone would lie to you, Mr Jackson, but I can assure you that we never left the party.'

'I see.' Jackson shoots me his lie-detector stare for a minute more, then makes a note.

'Another thing. A number of witnesses have reported that you, Eva and Luke were seen entering your parents' bathroom and not coming out for a good half-hour. What were you doing there?'

I clear my throat and finger my collar uneasily.

'We were having a threesome,' I laugh awkwardly. 'I mean, I'm just kidding. Of course, we'd never—'

The moment I say the words, I regret them. Normally I can control my nerves but today they're winning out.

Mr Abdul frowns. DI Jackson folds his arms. And I'm taken aback by the look in his eyes, the storm of emotion he's fighting to conceal.

'Look,' he says, his voice thick with intensity. 'A girl has died. I don't think it's a good time for jokes, do you?'

Chapter 15

Luke

God, I wish I could have a cigarette. I'm standing outside the interview room and craving a Marlboro like mad, that soft swirl of smoke to ease the coils in my stomach. But I gave up six months ago with a promise to Eva. I can't break it now.

Rob's been in there a long time and I'm worried about him. We rehearsed the story over and over yesterday in the woods behind the school. It does mean that we have to contradict the first statement I ever made to the police. A few timings and details have changed. We figured that even if they did pick up on it, we could argue that my memory was blurry, unreliable; we even Googled the phenomenon of suspects remembering contradictory details after they'd made statements, and it's not uncommon.

I'm dressed smartly today. I've actually ironed my trousers and shirt, which is knotted at my throat with a blue tie. And

Mr Abdul gave me new laces for my shoes. He said it was important that I looked more presentable.

I lean against the wall, aware of how tired I feel. It's heavy in my legs, burns behind my eyes. I've hardly slept this week, tossing and turning. My grades are sliding. Yesterday I got my first-ever C in English since I started A levels. Mrs Yates was disappointed in me – but how am I supposed to concentrate in this state?

The door opens and out strides Rob, tailed by Mr Abdul. Rob gives me a nod as he walks past and now I'm paranoid as hell: *was he okay or not?*

Jackson beckons me in. I don't get to have a chaperone for the interview, cos I'm eighteen, a year older (I repeated a year when shit was going on with Dad and it fucked up my schoolwork). I clench my fists, walk in and close the door behind me.

'Luke.' Jackson gives me a once-over, noticing my suit. He raises his eyebrows and frowns. I can't win: even if I do make an effort, it's seen as a show.

'I just had an interesting chat with Rob,' Jackson says.

Silence.

'Uh huh.' I can feel sweat moving across my forehead like moist insects. *God, I hope Rob did delete that video like he promised.*

But Jackson doesn't reveal any more.

We go over it all over again, the story that's starting to fray and curl at the corners.

Eva and I left the party at ten thirty.

We took a short walk in the woods.

I said goodbye to Eva.

'When I interviewed you on 26 September, you stated that you left the party around ten thirty, maybe eleven. There was no mention of the walk in the woods. I find it fascinating, the change in your story.'

'Well, I just forgot about that bit,' I say quickly. 'And I did leave her just after our little walk and the CCTV proves it,' I exclaim. I read on the Big Bad Blog that Eva's time of death was around 1.45 a.m. The CCTV footage showed me driving back at 11.15 p.m. I was home several hours before she died. Jackson admitted that to me in the last interview. He looked a little disgruntled, to be honest.

I find myself biting the skin around my forefinger. It's a habit that I've developed over the past week and it's not a pretty one; now I have little red scars of raw skin around my fingers. Suddenly the skin breaks; there's blood on my lip. I lick it away quickly, but not before DI Jackson winces.

'Are you thirsty, by the way? D'you want some tea?'

I shake my head, but I'm touched by the unexpected gentleness in his voice. There's no good cop/bad cop act with him. His flips of mood don't seem manipulative, but as though he himself can't make up his mind whether to trust me. I recall Mr Abdul telling me: 'DI Jackson's a really good man. I've met him a few times myself – he's got a daughter at the school.' I can't remember her name, though I have a feeling I once tugged her hair when Rob and I were messing around in the lunch queue. I felt bad about it later as she seemed a no-friends, lonely type of girl.

I just need to make a better impression.

'Look.' Suddenly he's harsh again. 'I don't believe you've told us everything, Luke. I know you're holding some things back.'

'I . . .'

Silence. He looks at me. He waits. He waits. I'm silent. He waits. Then he says: 'Interview paused at 3.48 p.m. for a brief break.' He switches off the recorder and says he'll get me some tea.

Jackson gets up. And then he hesitates, turns back.

He throws me a curveball.

'I should just tell you this straight, Luke,' he says. 'One of the other suspects whom we've interviewed has told us you did it. He – they said you got Eva drunk, you persuaded her to go into the woods, and you were seen running away with blood on your hands.'

I feel as though someone's just slapped me. I open my mouth but I can't speak; I hear myself make a noise.

'I'm just going to leave you for five minutes. To give you time to think it over. I'll be outside, so don't think about running. Just think and then give me your answer.'

The sound of his footsteps, echoing around the room like gunshots. Then, the slam of the door.

Shit. I could really do with that cigarette now.

Chapter 16

Siobhan

An empty chair. Each time a lesson kicks off, my eyes will fall on that one empty chair in the classroom. Once or twice Mr Abdul has taken the register and accidentally called out Eva's name; each time, he looks as though he's about to cry. I sit with my mobile on my lap and I write Eva texts, twenty or thirty a day, just as I always did, except now they sit in my Drafts folder, never to be opened. Dead letters. *I'm allowed to skip class today*, I text Eva. *I've got to do an interview with the police.*

I'm just glad I'm not being interviewed by Jackson: everyone in our gang says he's seriously intimidating. In Interview Room 2, I sit down with DC Okeke. Mrs Clements, my Geography teacher, has agreed to sit in as my Appropriate Adult.

DC Okeke looks young, practically our age. He has a handsome face, bright eyes and a wild Afro. He seems the caring type; he's already given me a can of Tango and some bourbon biscuits (I took two, one for me, one for Eva). Maybe it's because he's so kind that I start crying again. I feel pathetic. I want to text Eva: *god, this is embarrassing.*

Okeke is very patient. Mrs Clements offers me a tissue, but even after I've blown my snotty nose and wiped my eyes, I keep my head down. I don't want to do this interview.

We all agreed a story. It really didn't feel right and I objected at first, but Rob assured me it wouldn't interfere with the police finding the killer. After all, Eva's death has nothing to do with us.

'We just want to clarify what happened at the party,' Okeke says. 'We've got eyewitnesses who say that you left for an hour?'

'Well, I left early,' I say quickly. 'I mean, I was hardly there. I felt a bit poorly.'

'I thought that you arrived at' – he checks his notes – 'seven p.m., and left at nine. You were there for a good two hours.'

'Well, yeah, it didn't seem that long. I wished I'd stayed. Maybe if I'd stayed longer Eva would be … She wouldn't be … ' I add miserably.

Okeke gives me a sympathetic glance, but then he resumes his questions. He asks once more if we left the party for an hour as a group – me, Rob, and Luke. And then, because I'm still dazed and cut up with the thought of what might have been, if only I'd stayed, I find myself blurting out:

'Um, yeah, we did.'

I clamp my hand over my mouth. Rob and Luke drilled me

on this a hundred times: *We did not leave the party. We did not leave the party.* 'I mean – sorry – no, we stayed. I'm just finding this interview hard.'

I look at Mrs Clements and she gives me an encouraging nod, but the DC isn't fooled. He asks more questions, but I stick to the story. *We did not leave the party. We did not leave the party.*

Suddenly I hear a loud *SLAM!* from the next room.

Okeke frowns. Mrs Clements blinks. I'm completely freaked. I know Luke just went in for his interrogation. I have a vision of a scene from one of those cop shows, Luke being shoved up against a wall, his collar tight in Jackson's fists.

SLAM!

And,

SLAM!

'We – did leave the party,' I blurt out in a panic. 'But we – we just went for a walk, to get some fresh air, that's all. I swear, I swear.'

Chapter 17

Luke

SLAM!

I'm waiting for Jackson to come back. I can't sit still: rage is pumping through me.

SLAM!

Who, who, who would say this about me?

SLAM!

Who would say that they saw me *with blood on my hands?*

SLAM!

I've grabbed one of the dusty bats from the back of the room and a squidgy old grey ball and I'm batting it against the wall with a *SLAM!*

I should've guessed this would happen. The spotlight has been darting from person to person over the last week. Now it's starting to narrow on me.

I could clam up and say I won't speak without a lawyer. But doesn't that make me look guilty?

When I think of Rob, I feel the deep tug of loyalty. We've been friends since my first day of high school. We've played footie, got drunk, partied, copied each other's homework. Not once has Rob ever given me a hard time about the fact that he lives in Wimbledon Village and I live in some shithole in South Wimbledon. It never seemed to matter – not until Eva went missing.

I pace some more.

Rob was adamant we had to get our stories straight – which basically meant I have to lie for him. I told him I was sick of going in for police interviews and he was sympathetic, to a point.

'But you can handle them, Luke. Your dad's been in prison, you know how this all works. I'm just some pathetic middle-class wimp who's scared at the first sound of a siren.' He laughed at himself in what seemed like shame and I felt like I was tougher than him somehow. But now that I think about it, it's pretty dumb to feign any sort of ego in this situation. Rob's comment was mean. He'd suggested that this is all second nature to me – crime is in my DNA.

Rob says that if I tell the truth, his university career is over. But what about my future? *They said you got Eva drunk, you persuaded her to go into the woods, and you were seen running away with blood on your hands.* Could Rob have told them that? Would he do that to me?

Finally, finally, finally, DI Jackson comes back. He made me wait twenty minutes. The windowless room has turned into a sauna. My shirt is damp and my forehead is beaded with sweat.

He sits down and I tell him, loud and clear: 'Whoever says I did it is bullshitting you.'

It feels good to say it but Jackson doesn't even look up. He just asks me to wait and starts up the recorder again, announcing the time and place. Then he types a user name and an ID into a laptop, spinning it round to face me.

A video comes up on the screen. It strikes me then that CCTV has the mood of *The Blair Witch Project*, all black and white and blurry. I watch a car pull up at a petrol station. *My* car. I watch myself get out. It's strange seeing myself on film. The trivial thought springs into my mind, *I didn't realise that I was that tall.* I go into the shops and emerge five minutes later swigging from a bottle of cola.

'You remember that?' DI Jackson taps the corner of the screen with his pen. 'One twenty-four a.m. Saturday morning.' He adds: 'For the purposes of the recording, Luke is being shown CCTV footage of his car.'

'Uh ...' I'm completely thrown. This is like something out of *The Art of War*, that annoying book Rob once made me read. I've prepared a defence, only to find Jackson is attacking me in a new and completely unexpected place.

Shit. This isn't even about the time I arrived at the party, or the delicacy of timings involving me and Rob and Eva. It's about *after*.

Chapter 18

Rivka's WhatsApp

Siobhan Online

God, I hope those cops never come back again. DS Hutton is such a cow – seems sweet but so grim.

I think they will.

What? U serious?

It's obvious we're all lying about what happened at the party. They know.

Ok, Ok . . . u still on for seeing Mrs Lambert this eve?

Yeah, I guess.

Cmon it'll be good, then we can work out what to do about the diary.

U don't even have the diary anymore.

I know, but about MR.W! and all that. Mrs Lambert will be able to tell us what we should do.

Chapter 19

Luke

I didn't think Jackson would find out about this. I'd kept telling myself it wasn't relevant, because by that point I'd said goodbye to Eva.

How stupid of me. Jackson told me from the start that he never misses a detail. I watch him rifle through my file, which looks thicker every time I see it. I'm freaked to think of all those statements I've made, carved into computer systems like words on a tomb, ready for anyone to bring out in any number of years' time.

'Yes. In an earlier statement you did mention that you popped out for a snack that night,' he says. 'I'm surprised you didn't just stop by on the way home from the party.'

'Yeah, well, I got up and drove to the shops at around one that morning because I couldn't sleep. I'd had a minor argument with Eva and I was upset, sure. I was also really hungry. My mum doesn't keep a lot of food in the house. Also, I'd had a drink or two, so I needed to sober up ... By about one I felt pretty sober and I figured it was safe to drive. I went to the petrol station, I got some cola and some snacks. Then I came home.'

'Really?' You wouldn't believe how loaded one word can sound. 'Let's look at another CCTV video,' he says.

Now he shows my car driving off from the petrol station.

'You don't head back home,' he says. 'And we lose CCTV footage of you around here. I think that's when you went back to the woods.'

His tone chills me. This is getting really serious. Everything I say is a puzzle piece and he's trying to make them fit.

'I was l-lost,' I quickly improvise.

'It's your own neighbourhood. You've lived there all your life.'

Sweat trickles down my spine and pools in the small of my back.

'I needed some air ... I sat in my car on Wimbledon Common listening to music.'

'So you *were* in the woods!' His voice is victorious.

'No. I was nearby – and then I went home. You can see for yourself, on the CCTV! My car headed home by two a.m.'

'Ten past two,' he corrects me.

Sweat is pouring down my face now. I'm shaking all over. I have to fight this, I have to kick back.

'And what about this person who accused me? I have a right to know who they are!'

Jackson lowers his eyes, shuffling his papers. 'Lots of people have said lots of things.'

'But I . . . ' And then I twig. 'There's nobody, is there?'

Jackson shrugs, unrepentant. 'I'm not sure what you're talking about, Luke. If you could just calm down—'

'WHAT!' My temper erupts. I grab his pen and his eyes moon. My only intention is to fling it across the room, but he cringes as though I'm about to stab him with it. I hear my mum's voice chiding me – *Luke, Luke* – and I let it clatter to the table.

Silence—

A knock on the door.

Maybe there is a God. Jackson ignores it at first. Another knock; he sighs and barks: 'Come in!' It's another cop, a young man with an Afro. He gives Jackson a nod, as if he has something important to share with him. I call out that I'm feeling unwell. Anything to get out of here; I'm going to explode if I stay here a minute longer.

Jackson looks cynical, but the other cop seems concerned, and they wrap the interview up, thank God.

A few days later, the police search our house. Freya and Matt are at school. I'm in the library studying when my mobile rings. By the time I get there, I'm shaking with fury, imagining the place overturned like something out of a movie, the air thick with feathers from torn pillows, books on the floor, everything trampled and wrecked. But they are deferential and polite, sickeningly so, apologising for any inconvenience and showing me the warrant when I demand to see it. We just want to find Eva's killer, Jackson tells me. Mum, looking uneasy, makes him a cup of tea.

I go into the garden and light a cigarette with trembling fingers, thanking God I'd dealt with the bloodstained shirt. I burned it in the end, out by Rushmere Green. I wrapped the remains in plastic, weighted it down with stones and threw it in the water. It made me feel like a criminal; but if they'd found it in my room it would have been far worse.

When it's all over and they're gone, the only sign they were ever here is the space on the desk where the computer used to sit. They took it away to analyse my emails with Eva. Nothing in the house is spoilt, but everything is just a little bit out of synch, soiled with their energy, like a nightmare replica of our home.

Chapter 20

Anonymous

The Big Bad Blog

Here's the shock news: Eva took drugs on the night of her death.

Her friends have denied that there were any drugs at Rob's party but the post-mortem has revealed traces of alcohol and cocaine in her system.

The tabloids can't cope. At first they portrayed Eva as a beautiful angel who died a tragic death at the hands of a ruthless killer. Now they've changed their tune. They're running pictures of Eva in skimpy party gear, drinks in hand, boys in tow. And the headlines are getting more and more hysterical. This morning's *Sun* ran with: PARTY GIRL EVA'S DEBAUCHED TEEN LIFESTYLE – DID SHE DIE FROM AN OVERDOSE? The article goes on to imply that she was a spoiled little rich girl who developed a taste for drugs, took a line too many, and that her family are trying to hush it up. Another, slightly gentler piece in the *Daily Mail* still implies that Eva was to blame for her murder: SHE WAS DRUNK AND DRUGGED THE NIGHT SHE DIED – WHAT REALLY HAPPENED TO EVA?

How about just accepting that Eva was a complex girl, as most human beings are?

There is one issue that remains unclear: did Luke pressurise Eva into taking drugs? He has been in trouble with the police for driving under the influence, so it's reasonable to question his role in Eva's drug use. Her behaviour certainly became more erratic when she started dating him.

Apparently Eva's father is angry that the police have not arrested Luke. And we share his anger. As far as the BBB is concerned, Luke Jones is the No. 1 suspect.

COMMENTS (5046)
Anonymous – If Luke did it, then I going to go over to his house and knife him myself.
Mark – From what I hear, Luke is loved and respected by his close friends, all of whom think he's innocent. Let's give him the benefit of the doubt.

Chapter 21

Carolina

Luke has a knife.

I've been trying and trying to remember why I'm so convinced of this. And as I wake up on Saturday morning, it comes to me. I lie in bed in that twilight zone where your mind is floating in dreamland and all the mundane thoughts of the day haven't yet started niggling you. The memory drifts in.

I remember seeing Luke and Eva, with the usual hangers-on – Rob, Rivka, Siobhan. Luke was much more popular since hooking up with Eva, though he never quite looked as though he belonged with the 'cool gang'. They were standing by the trees, smoking and laughing. Then Luke pulled out his knife, casually, as though he was telling some kind of anecdote about it. It was a big blade with an unusual handle, patterned with red and green snakes. Eva took the knife from him and slowly ran her forefinger across the side of the blade, looking up at Luke from under her lashes.

It made me squirm, watching her do that. I wasn't sure what was going on, but one thing was clear to me in that moment: Luke was a bad influence on Eva.

The reason I was able to watch them was because I was halfway up an oak tree. I'd found some unhatched eggs on the ground and a blue tit was cheeping in distress, so I gently returned them to her nest. Normally birdwatching made me happy, but seeing the gang had made me wistful. I'd never had friends like that, and I never would.

I'm sitting with my dad in the kitchen, having breakfast. I've made us boiled eggs with toast. I wait until he's finished the newspaper and then I blurt out the whole story.

'Dad – what if Luke's knife is the weapon?'

I'm disappointed when Dad says: 'We just searched Luke's house and we found nothing. Well, there are plenty of emails on his computer which demonstrate just how unhealthy his obsession with Eva was, but that's not enough to convict him.'

'He's probably hidden the knife somewhere . . . in his locker at school?'

'It was one of the first places we checked.'

'Sorry, Dad, of course.'

'I'm thinking about draining the lake on Rushmere Green. I reckon he – the killer, I mean – might have thrown it in there.' Dad sighs. He hasn't put in his contacts yet and he's wearing his wire-rimmed spectacles; they make him look older, more tired. I feel like giving him a hug but I hold back. We're not tactile in this family. I think the only time Dad has ever hugged me was when Mum died, five years ago, and we watched her slip away together. I remember him holding me tight and the sound of his crying, a hawking noise like some kind of terrible bird of prey; maybe I was the one hugging him, that day.

Dad looks over at me, and I try to smile, but I think he can tell I'm upset. We *have* to close in someone soon.

'Look, why don't you come over to the woods today,' Dad offers. 'We're still trying to find the weapon and Eva's mobile.'

'Really?' I ask in excitement. All I've been planning to do is homework, bird spotting and a little bit more Facebook-stalking. My weekends always feel baggy, as though they're something I try to shape and fill. Now my Saturday has purpose.

The woods on Wimbledon Common. The very place Eva died. The area around the pit is cordoned off from the public, police tape tagged from tree to tree. Police guard the perimeter, making sure nobody gets in.

'This is my daughter, Carolina,' Dad introduces me to a few of the CSI. They're dressed in white suits like plastic Michelin men. They look at my dad with respect, as though they're all a little scared of him. I feel proud to be his daughter.

I'm disappointed that I'm not allowed inside the cordoned area, but Dad says they keep a strict log; I'm unauthorised and therefore a contamination risk. He adds that we can still search outside the perimeter, because the knife could be anywhere.

The woods are a place I normally feel at home. At first I enjoy looking, because it reminds me of bird spotting. I know it sounds such a geeky hobby, but it involves so many skills. You have to be sharp and alive to detail, to discover all that nature conspires to hide from you.

After about an hour of searching, however, my eyes are a blur. Dad warned me about this. He said a lot of police work is banal and exhausting because it involved such slow, meticulous, careful attention to detail.

I get to thinking about the first time that I met Eva. The memory is a sad echo because it was in the woods that we first met.

I'm convinced that she followed me, that day. I was ticking off bird species and all of a sudden, Eva was there by my side. 'Hey, how are you?' she asked. I felt odd, embarrassed; I even wondered if it was all some kind of set-up, if she and Siobhan were secretly filming something to laugh at. Eva linked her arm through mine and said it would be nice if we could go for a walk. She told me about her parents, how her mother was very cold and her dad was a sweetie. She asked me what my dad was like and I told her that I had the best dad in the world. At the end, even though we'd only been walking thirty minutes, she said to me: 'I feel as though I've known you all my life.'

This was the start of our secret friendship. I'm not sure why it had to be furtive, why we couldn't hang out at school together. I fretted that I wasn't cool enough to be seen with; in darker moments, I worried that Eva was being superficial. Eva's excuse was that Siobhan would be jealous – they'd been close since they were kids and Siobhan was very possessive of their friendship.

Personally, I couldn't see why Eva liked Siobhan. She seemed like a pastel version of Eva, a sidekick. Eva's hair was naturally blonde; Siobhan dyed hers the same shade. Eva would wear elegant, tight-fitting black clothes and Siobhan's dress style mimicked hers. I thought that was pretty creepy. I admired Eva and I was grateful for our friendship, but I refused to change, to try to be like her. I think Siobhan is another person that the police need to include on their list of possible suspects.

At my side, Dad sighs – a long sigh. I recall his warning: the more time that passes after a murder has been committed, the less likely you are to find the evidence. It gives Nature a chance to corrode and hide. The rain that fell on the day Eva was found obscured any footprints around the pit. Today the sky is heavy and the forecast has warned of storms ahead. What if the rain washes the woods clean, sweeps the knife away? I begin to feel frantic. *We have to find the weapon now, today.*

When you're seeking out birds, you look high as well as low. I crane my neck. Who's to say that Eva wasn't walking through these woods and Luke surprised her by leaping from a tree? Maybe he pretended he was going home, climbed an oak and then pounced.

I see something – a glint, up in the branches. I start, fully alert now. I look again, squinting.

'Oh my God – Dad. Dad!' I tug at his sleeve. 'Look!' I point upwards.

He screws up his eyes, peering. He gasps when he sees it, wedged into the trunk. A knife, its handle patterned with snakes.

It all goes a bit crazy after that.

The CSI are called over to remove the knife and bag it up. I'm sure I can see dried blood on it. They congratulate Dad and he beams and says: 'Thanks. But it's not me who's due all the praise. My daughter here's the one who found it.'

On the way home, we stop to pick up an Indian takeaway. We only ever get Indian when Dad is in a really good mood; normally he complains that it's too expensive.

'We did it, Carolina, we did it!' he keeps saying, shaking his head in wonder. Wow. My dad is usually so cool and rigorous. Now there's an uncharacteristic brightness in his eyes. It's exciting to see him like this, so passionate and intent. He confided in me last week that this has been the biggest investigation he's ever headed up. I know solving it means everything to him.

My dad and I never say, *I love you*. He's always been a strict dad. He's never given me much allowance, although I try not to complain too much. Once, when I asked for a raise, he told me to write a 2,000-word essay clearly illustrating its pros and cons; then I had to read it out, like a lawyer in court. He's never even been that impressed by my good grades; he wasn't that academic at school and he says that life experience is more important.

Today, though, he doesn't need to say a word. I know he loves me; I can see it in his eyes. I sense he's been waiting for me to surprise him, to show what I can do, and now he's quietly pleased that his faith in me has paid off.

'We have the weapon, we have the murderer,' he says. 'We'll fast-track a DNA test and have the results by Monday.'

'It must be Luke's. It must be.'

'You know, Carolina,' he says. 'My gut feeling is that you're right. I think we've found our killer.'

Chapter 22

Eva's Diary: 18 August 2016

I'm writing this in the early hours of the morning. I've only just got home. My face and hair are caked with mud from falling in the woods. I still feel shocked and shaken.

I met up with Luke around 9 p.m. I sneaked out and hurried down to the bottom of the road. It was exciting when Luke and I first started dating; now it just made me feel uneasy. As always, Luke's battered Fiat was already there. As I got into the car, I turned my head so that his hello kiss landed on my cheek. He frowned and said that he wanted to go for a drive over in Oaks Park.

I tried to persuade him that a drink at All Bar One would be so much better. I had it all planned, all the words scripted; I'd rehearsed them to myself, to the mirror, the cat and Siobhan, but I was scared of saying them to Luke, out in the middle of nowhere on a dark, cold night.

Luke normally indulges me, but when he's on edge he can be so stubborn. He drove us into the park, down those dark winding lanes, then pulled up on a verge overlooking a steep hill. The wind was strong and all the trees shook as though they were whispering and passing secrets. The moon winked in slivers as the clouds flurried past. I turned to Luke and I told myself, I have to say it. Now. Tonight.

I have to admit that I faltered. His good looks always got me. He leaned over and kissed me softly. There was a lick in my stomach. I reached my hands to his hair, all the time thinking *Stop! Stop it now!* And so the moment he pulled back, I did it.

'I think we should break up.'

He looked ... hurt. I have to admit, I was a tiny bit pleased. Then I felt crap for being such a bitch.

'But,' he said, 'we've been together for six months now. Six months and one day and three hours.'

Oh God. Luke was always doing this: obsessively counting the time we'd been together.

'I know, it's the longest I've ever dated a guy. But now it's time to say goodbye. I'm sorry.'

'But – we're going to get married.'

'What?' I cried.

'The other week – I gave you ...'

'You gave me a mini donut ring,' I said. 'I thought you were joking.'

'Well, it was kind of a joke, but it was serious too.' He seized my hands. 'I've never even looked at another girl in these past six months.'

Why don't guys get it? If he had been looking at other girls, I might have felt less smothered. A few months ago, I'd even taken him out with Siobhan in the hope he might try to flirt with her to make me jealous. He'd spent the whole night acting as though she wasn't there.

'Well, we could just have a break,' I said. 'Not for ever – just for a few weeks.' Thinking: God, I'm such a coward.

He stared at me so hard that I was forced to meet his gaze.

'Why?'

I nearly told him the truth: I've met someone else. But I didn't – I was terrified that Luke might grab the car keys and slash his wrists there and then. All I could think to say was the stupidest cliché in the book:

'It's not you, it's me.'

'Well, of course it's me. I'm the one who's being dumped. Look, I know I'm not your usual ... The thing is, I've been predicted three Bs and an A for Art for my A levels, and as soon as I finish uni I'm going to get a really, really good job and a nice house and a proper car – not like this heap of junk.' His voice cracked as he gestured at it.

I always laugh under high pressure and heavy stress. I couldn't help it: Luke's eyes were lasering me and the air in the car was so hot and dry. I dissolved into hysterics.

Luke snapped.

'RIGHT. RIGHT. GET OUT OF THE CAR!'

'What?'

'GET OUT OF MY CAR!'

'I – but Luke – I didn't mean–'

He pushed me. Hard. I nearly went flying, but I caught the door just in time to get out safely. And then he drove off. The door was still open and he leaned over to bang it, swerving and nearly going off the road. I watched the yellow eyes of his tail lights gradually becoming smaller and smaller, as though the dark had closed over them like eyelids.

I stood there, shocked. I willed and willed him to come back. I had thought that Luke would react badly, but normally he was such a nice guy. I reminded myself that there were two sides to Luke; I'd seen his anger a lot at the start of our relationship, but not in recent months. To be honest, it was all so brash that I might've been turned on, if I hadn't been so cold, my teeth like castanets, my skin pricked all over. Then I started thinking about the reports I'd read in the local paper about the recent robbery at Oaks Park, where a girl took a ciggie break, and the next thing she knew, a guy was thrusting a knife in her side and hissing at her to hand over her fake Prada.

I thought about calling my dad. But what would happen then? He'd call 999, right away. It would be round the whole school in a day. Dad would have me under lock and key. And the next time I even thought about dating, he'd probably hire a bodyguard to chaperone me.

I heard a noise, close by. Quickly, I hid behind a fat oak tree and texted Siobhan: **In Oaks Park all alone – told Luke we had to break up & he drove off.** Then, SEND.

I cheered myself up with the thought I'd soon be safe in my bedroom, laughing at the worst break-up ever.

Then I looked at my phone.

The message hadn't sent.

I tried again.

No reception.

Now I was truly freaked out. The woods sprawled far and wide; I could walk for hours through them and only find myself lost in an oak labyrinth of dead ends. I was stuck out here for the night.

Luke, you bastard.

I heard the sound of a car in the distance. Should I risk it and hitch a lift? Or hide and suffer hypothermia?

It wasn't exactly the best of choices. Then, as the car
drew up, I saw that it was his.

When he saw me, he leant over and opened
the car door.

Until then, I'd felt far more angry than sad. I'd been
trying to be all cool and detached because I knew one
of us had to be. And then the tears came. They poured
out of me, all the guilt and regret, all the sadness that
my love for Luke had died. I think I was also crying
because I'm still uncertain whether or not I've made
the right choice. Luke held me to him and he said sorry,
over and over. I sobbed the whole way home and he
kept reaching out to hold my hand or stroke my cheek
and wipe my tears away. At the bottom of my road he
stopped the car, hugged me again and asked if I wanted
to go to the Rihanna concert on Saturday; he'd bought
two tickets just in case. It was as though nothing had
happened between us, as though we'd been out on a
regular evening to McDonald's and a movie.

How am I ever going to resolve this stupid mess?
How can I ever break up with Luke if he won't let me?

Chapter 23

Rivka's WhatsApp

Siobhan Online

Did Mr P get in touch with u about the service?

Yeah, what are u going to wear?

Black lace. It's starting to look bad for Luke, shouldn't we tell the police about MR.W?

Maybe it's looking bad for Luke cos he did it!

U really think so?

Anyway, u heard what Mrs Lambert said.

I don't care what she says, we should decide.

God, I don't know what to think anymore. I need a smoke.

Pot head.

:)

Chapter 24

Luke

I stare at myself in the mirror. I thought I was hiding my grief from the outside world, but now I see sadness has fossilised in my pupils. I remember how Eva used to kiss and stroke my eyelids when I was tired.

This is the suit I'd been saving up for. Rob always used to tease me that Eva and I were like the Princess and the Frog, and I have to admit I felt both proud and paranoid at the thought of taking her to the Prom, dressing right, looking sharp, proving to the world that we were a serious couple. It would be a V sign at everyone who thought I wasn't good enough.

Now I've ended up buying the same suit for her memorial service. I could never have afforded it, even with my paper round and extra shifts at the local burger bar, but Mum pressed some notes into my hand.

'Don't tell the others,' she whispered. 'I was saving this for Christmas – but this is more important.'

'But Mum—' I protested.

'Ssh,' she said, and gave me a tight hug. Then she pushed me away and went back to sorting her cleaning stuff for work.

In that moment, I loved my mum so fiercely. I loved her because in that hug I could feel all her faith in me. There was not one iota of tension, not one trace of doubt in her smile. Unlike the rest of them.

It's times like this that make life black and white. Until you suffer a crisis, you don't know who your real friends are.

I make the mistake of checking my Facebook account just before I leave. There are fresh comments on my wall, some from people I hardly know:

We know you did it, Luke, just fucking own up!

And:

You are one sick bastard.

And:

I hope you rot in hell, murderer!

At first when the comments started, I tried to stay calm, grit my teeth and give a reasoned reply. I told them all about how much I loved Eva and that I would never do anything to hurt her. But I've given up now – now I just block the bastards.

I know it will be the same tonight at the service. A part of me wants to tear off this suit, crawl away and hide in my bedroom. But then what? They'll all take it as a sign of guilt. Mr Abdul has been a good friend. He's advised that I just have to hold my head high, be calm, be dignified, be honest, and wait it out.

I give Mum another hug before I leave. Freya and Matt wail for one too. It's not been easy for them; Freya's come home from school crying, saying that she's been bullied by friends who've asked her if her brother is a murderer. I hug them both extra-tight, blinking hard.

As I leave the house, I feel as though I'm carrying a very heavy weight, like a huge rucksack, and I just want to put it down.

I realise that I am no longer living life, I am surviving it. Every day, every minute, I am waiting for life to go back to normal. A part of me still believes that one day I'm going to wake up, and everything will be sunny and fresh again, and Eva will still be alive, and back in love with me. That part of me can't accept that it's never going to happen.

I walk into the church between Rob and Siobhan. We're all carrying candles and they form a choir of flickering light. Siobhan keeps giving me weird looks but I ignore her; Rob shoots me anxious stares. He's still convinced that the police are going to spot the holes in our stories and come after him.

We set the candles on a big white table, muttering a prayer, then sit down on a pew together. It isn't going to be a proper funeral – just a service for friends and family while we wait for the police to release her body.

Mr Pieachowski stands up to make a speech.

He speaks about Eva with such tenderness, I can't help but blink back tears. I guess I've demonised him in my head cos he hates me so much. I wonder if I should approach him at the end of the service and try to explain.

To my surprise, Rob gets up and makes a speech.

He's written notes; he's prepared. I feel a bit put out. Rob never told me he was planning this.

Rob's speech is crisp and polite. I can tell that he's practised it. He concludes by saying: 'Eva was an inspiration to us all. She shone so brightly. In mourning her loss and remembering her life, we must strive to follow the example she set.'

In my pocket, I feel my mobile vibrating. Siobhan gives me a look when I yank it out. It's Mum. I quickly turn it to vibrate/silent mode. I feel worried; Mum never calls unless it's an emergency. I text: **r u OK?**

When Siobhan gets up and walks to the front I feel a lump rise in my throat again. The other speeches, even Mr Pieachowski's, sounded like they were describing Saint Eva; Siobhan talks about the real Eva. She keeps breaking off to wipe her eyes and at one point nearly sets her hair alight on a candle, which makes her laugh – 'Oh God, imagine what Eva would have said if I set myself alight at her service.' Everyone laughs in tearful relief.

A realisation hits me. Mr Pieachowski has organised this. He's contacted various people in my class and asked them to speak. Siobhan stumbles back down the aisle and sits beside me, sobbing; I pat her arm gently. Inside I'm falling apart.

Carolina stands up to speak next. I can't believe it. Carolina barely knew Eva. Eva often mocked her behind her back. How come she gets to speak and I don't?

I knew Eva better than any of these people.

When I first got a scholarship to St Martin's, I was scared I wouldn't fit in. It meant so much to me when Rob became a friend, but people only *really* started to accept me when Eva and I started going out. Now it all seems to have unravelled overnight. Are any of these people actually my friends?

I want to grab a hymn book and hurl it at Mr Pieachowski for freezing me out of the ceremony. Then I right myself. I close my eyes. I tell myself to stay calm and focus on my dear Eva.

I think of her beauty, the dimples in her cheeks when she smiled, that wicked look she got in her eyes when she was making trouble. I think of how she refused to ever be bored and insisted on making every moment dramatic and interesting. I think of her love of reading and how she would talk about her favourite books, *Wuthering Heights* and *Dracula*, as though they were her best friends. I think about how it was to watch her sleeping; sometimes she put her thumb in her mouth, a girlish gesture that always moved me. I think of how she had a terrible habit of laughing in the most inappropriate situations. Eva, Eva, Eva – the list could go on for ever.

When I open my eyes, tears are pouring down my cheeks, defying my every effort to hold them back. I can feel Siobhan looking at me, slightly surprised.

I watch Mr Pieachowski go up to the front to thank every-one for coming. I can't bear it.

I stand up. 'Please – please let me say a few words about Eva.'

Everyone turns and stares. Mr Pieachowski's mouth is a thin, cold line. He wants to tell me to shut up, but he doesn't dare.

This is like the moment in a movie where the hero has one opportunity to change people's opinion and he makes a speech so heartfelt and fluid that it's met with spontaneous applause. But this is no movie, I've never been good at public speaking, and I find my words fraying in my mouth.

'Eva was a – a – truly – special person . . .' *Special person*. Four people before me have already said the same. 'It was Eva who first texted *me* to ask me on a date.' But that isn't right. I've started at the wrong point, I need to tell them about how she saw me having a water fight in the playground and I looked up and our eyes met. 'I was having a fight with this guy in the playground and Eva thought it was funny . . .' Shit, shit, that sounds too violent. 'But I wasn't – I mean – Eva was just so—'

'Enough.' Mr Pieachowski's voice is icy. I sit down, burning hot and cold with shame and confusion and rage.

Siobhan, to my surprise, rubs my shoulder. My mobile is vibrating again. What's up with Mum? I have to get out of here.

I exit the pew, muttering *Sorry*s as I step on feet and bags, ignoring indignant looks. Mr Pieachowski is speaking again. I'm aware of my footsteps layering echoes over his words. I open the big oak door and it makes a terrible grating noise as it scrapes against the stone.

Sod them, I think dully, *sod them all.*

Outside in the chill, I listen to Mum's voicemail: 'Luke, they're here. At the house. They're here to arrest you!'

I call back in a state of shock. She answers right away.

'Luke,' she says urgently. 'I told them where you were. I had to – they said they'd arrest me for obstructing – obstructing the course of – I'm sorry' – her voice breaks with tears of desperation – 'I can't even remember the term, but they said I had to tell them. They're coming for you. They think you might run and they're coming for you.'

I can't speak.

'Luke, are you still there? Oh God, this isn't your fault, our bloody family is cursed.'

'Mum, I'm so sorry,' I break down. 'Seriously, it's just that bastard Jackson, he's got it in for me—'

My voice is interrupted by the swell of sirens. Blue lights spin, highlighting the stained-glass windows of the church. Then there are footsteps crunching on the gravel and DI Jackson's face in mine, telling me that he's arresting me for the murder of Eva Pieachowski.

Chapter 25

Anonymous

The Big Bad Blog

Luke did it!

Wimbledon has been in turmoil for the last twelve days. On 26th September Eva Pieachowski was declared missing; on the 28th we heard the tragic news that her body had been found and she had been brutally murdered. Then the murder weapon was found in the woods: a knife, patterned with snakes, which had Eva's dried blood on it and some incriminating DNA. As the BBB predicted from the start, Luke Jones, Eva's boyfriend, turned out to be the murderer. He killed her on 24th September, on Wimbledon Common, after they left a party at Rob Pennington's house to take a walk in the woods.

It transpires that Eva had been trying to dump Luke for some time, but he couldn't accept that a no meant no. Her murder was a crime of passion. In the heat of the moment, he took out his knife and stabbed her 13 times in the early hours of Saturday morning. Then he shoved her into a natural pit where, in the mud and the cold, she bled to death.

There is some speculation about a possible accomplice – someone who helped him to get away or cover things up afterwards. The BBB understands that that there are some significant discrepancies in the various statements taken from others who were at the party. Siobhan O'Hara and Rob Pennington are still under suspicion.

So what happens now?

Today's *Daily Mail* suggests that Luke might be tried in a juvenile court. They are wrong. Luke Jones is no longer a minor – he might be in Year 13 but he is already 18 years old. That's because he repeated Year 9 twice, due to 'family issues'. He will be tried as an adult. It is unlikely he'll be granted bail, so from now and until his trial, he'll be held in jail.

It is the opinion of the BBB that this is the right – and the safest – place for him and for all of us.

Come back to the BBB for the most up to date information on the forthcoming trial . . .

COMMENTS (7,910)

Rob Pennington – Hey, how about someone being innocent until proven guilty?

Mark – But it was obvious that Luke did it!

Chapter 26

Rivka's WhatsApp

Siobhan online

Have u seen the BBB? It's saying we're accomplices

Bullshit!

I hate that blog! Rob is totally freaked and he just came over. He's going to the cops, he's going to tell them the truth about the party.

Whhaaaaat!

He promised not to name names.

I guess he's being loyal to Luke.

We should go back to Mrs Lambert, find out more about Luke.

We did ask and nothing came up. Look, if u don't tell Jackson about MR.W I will.

What! Betray Eva!

It was before, but now Luke's in jail and he doesn't even know about MR.W.

You were never a big fan of Luke when Eva was alive.

yeah, he was a stalker. But the police don't have a full picture.

OK, OK, I'll go.

When?

Tomorrow. I swear.

Chapter 27

Rob

I'm locked in a stall in the boys' toilets at St Martin's, watching a video on my mobile. I made this video the night of the party. A short video that involves, me, Eva and Luke, in the bathroom of my own house ... I must've watched it over fifty times now. When DI Jackson interviewed me, I was even half-hoping that he'd confiscate my iPhone and see it for himself. That way, it would have been *his* decision, *his* fault, and I wouldn't have actively betrayed my best friend.

But he didn't. The buck stops with me. If DI Jackson *did* ever see this evidence, God knows what he'd do.

I hear the bell ring and the muffled din of 800 pupils surging through the corridors, chatting and yelling and looking forward to home. There's a sharp pain pulsing in my temple. When I leave the cubicle, I dig into my bag for a paracetamol – the last in the packet I bought last week.

Damn. I approach the Art Studio, hoping to speak to Mr Abdul alone, only to find that there are still some students hanging about, chatting. They're asking him about Picasso, for crying out loud. *Was Picasso married? Did he watch TV?* I hang by the door, twitchy, impatient. I need to do this now, before I lose my nerve.

As I stare out of the corridor window, into the quad, the statue of Venus in the fountain reminds me of Cambridge. I feel wistful. Last week I went for my interview at Trinity College. It was so good to get away from all of this; ironically, the other applicants were fraught with nerves and insomnia, but for me it was a welcome break. I walked through the streets, explored the sprawling colleges, took photographs and felt like my old self again, ready to study at the best university in the country, ready for a career in politics. My dad went to Cambridge, and his dad too. The interview went swimmingly; I actually felt as though my destiny was unfolding. But when I think of Luke and the video and the party and the – well, my stomach clenches and my head burns with the unfairness of it all.

Then I picture Luke in prison, locked up for the next twenty years. He has no future any more.

I know I have to do this.

Finally, finally, the students leave the studio and I go in.

Mr Abdul is as warm and friendly as ever. We sit in the classroom, surrounded by drying A-level artwork, pictures

114

of a black swan painted in varying degrees of talent. I notice that Eva's last paintings are showcased on the wall. Luke's are nowhere to be seen.

I explain to Abdul that I feel terrible because I haven't told the police everything. I held that house party cos my parents were away and it was my last chance to go wild before getting stuck in for my Cambridge entrance exam. And the girls, Eva, Siobhan and Rivka, wanted to do it *properly*. Jackson was right about us leaving the party for an hour, though we had denied it.

Luke, Eva and I went to the offie to get booze. We used fake IDs. They weren't hard to knock up, with a photo, a fake stamp and a bit of cellophane on the top.

The next bit is hard to admit.

We met up with Ritchie. He sold me a bag of coke. I paid, I took possession and I took it back to the party, divided it into ten parts and sold it on to those who wanted it. I was trying to be a good host and keep my guests happy. I hardly took any myself; someone gave me a joint at one point and I smoked it but I didn't inhale.

I should add that I very rarely take drugs, or indeed deal them. I've only ever done it once before. So this was only the second time ever, ever ...

Mr Abdul's always telling students that we can talk to him about anything, but even he can't help but look appalled.

'And the thing is' – my voice cracks – 'Luke was such a good friend to me. He even changed his statement, shifted the timings just to cover me, so they wouldn't know about the offie and the drugs. But he still left the party at ten thirty, which is the crucial bit, right?'

'Right,' says Mr Abdul slowly. 'But let's consider that by changing his statement, Luke might have looked as though he was lying about all the other details. Luke told me that DI Jackson accused him of drugging Eva before the attack took place. So, Rob, I think we both need to take a trip to the station.'

'I can't! I'm up for Cambridge! I'll never get in!'

'And Luke's life is ruined for good.'

'But – but – there's something else.' I felt hot with defence, ready to show him the video.

Mr Abdul holds up his hand and says: 'Save that for the police.'

'I can't go.' I shake my head.

'If you don't go, I'll have to call them myself. I hope you understand why I have to do that, Rob.'

I don't protest. This is why I'm here, after all. I wanted him to make me.

When I leave the police station a few hours later, I feel euphoric. Mr Abdul turns to me and grins, shaking my hand.

'See?' he says. 'It wasn't that bad, as it? Doing the right thing always pays.'

Yeah, right, I think, as I nod politely, because my dad says life is no fairy tale, and he's a CEO, whereas Abdul plays about with pot paints for a living.

'You'll still be down in Westminster one day, Tory front bench, I have no doubt,' he adds, with a wink. I wink back, frowning, wondering if I imagine the sardonic edge to his voice.

But who cares? I'm free. My future is stretching ahead of me like a red carpet. I decide to go and celebrate with a game of tennis and I win 4 games to 3.

Later, I lie on my bed and listen to Mozart. That cop, DI Jackson, is one moody bastard. I'm not easily intimidated by adults, but it's impossible not to be shit-scared of him. I couldn't believe it when he said he wasn't that interested in the drugs, that it was Luke's fault for deciding to lie and change his story. He also said that the drugs had been and gone, so he couldn't prosecute me, though he warned that he'd be keeping his eye on me from now on.

I kept saying that I thought Luke was innocent. I kept saying sorry. But he only shrugged. 'Luke's DNA was on that knife. It's what happened in those woods, what Luke chose to do and what he chose to tell us, that makes this case.'

And that was that.

I watch the video again.

One last time.

I kept meaning to show it to Jackson, but it was all going so well that I just wanted to get the hell out while I could.

I always make mini-films when I have parties. It's fun putting up them up on Facebook afterwards and embarrassing everyone (*never, ever* let your parents friend you). Needless to say, this one will never make it online.

The first part of the video was shot in the kitchen. We're making a cocktail with Baileys, Tropicana, Jack Daniel's, lime and grenadine. When I watch it this time, feeling more relaxed than I have done in weeks, I notice a new detail. There's a boy right in the edge of the frame. He's standing apart from everyone else, on the patio by the open doors, looking into the kitchen. He's got fair hair and I don't recognise him. He's definitely not from St Martin's, so he must have gatecrashed. He's watching Eva as she squeezes a lime into the mixer. But let's face it, who in that kitchen *wasn't* watching Eva?

God, she looks so beautiful. I never understood what she saw in Luke. I was glad that she made him happy but I admit I felt jealous too. In the video, she does a twirl and blows a kiss directly to camera. I get a hard-on, watching. Then I feel bad. Lusting after a dead girl is just sick, right?

The second part takes place in my bathroom. I've laid lines of coke on the toilet seat. Luke uses his knife to separate them. The camera lingers on the red and green snake pattern on the handle. He turns round with a cheeky grin. I snort my line, then Luke, then Eva.

Then Eva jumps up, all buzzy, and cries: 'Let's pretend to film *Psycho*!'

It's this game we all play. We recreate famous scenes from movies. It's a laugh. Luke's reluctant at first but Eva's persistent. She had a weird hold over him. She jumps up, pulls the plastic curtain across the bath and gets me to film as Luke sidles up. He play-stabs the curtain and Eva lets out a shrill scream. Suddenly, she yanks back the curtain and Luke's knife dives past her; a swirl of her hair shimmers and whirls to the floor. Eva yells with laughter and Luke laughs along too, but he looks strained and the sound is hollow.

The video cuts dead.

I can't work out if this is serious evidence or not. Luke thought it looked bad, so I told him I'd deleted it. But something inside me told me to keep it, just in case.

I watch it again. I watch the way Luke wields the knife as he lunges at the curtain. Who can blame him for being mad with her that night? Eva was constantly playing games, winding him up, goading him. She brought out the worst in him and revelled in doing so. Who knows if they went into the woods and she started some bizarre role-play that all went too far?

I feel tired and cross, suddenly, the victory of the day seeping away from me. I'd thought I'd wrapped everything up – so why this new, nagging worry? Luke has been charged, so what difference would this video make?

Then I remember the Big Bad Blog: *charged, but not convicted* . . .

Luke is my buddy. I love his jokes, his talents, his insights, his loyalty. He's been a great friend to me.

My finger hovers on the delete button and I just don't know what to do.

10 October 2016

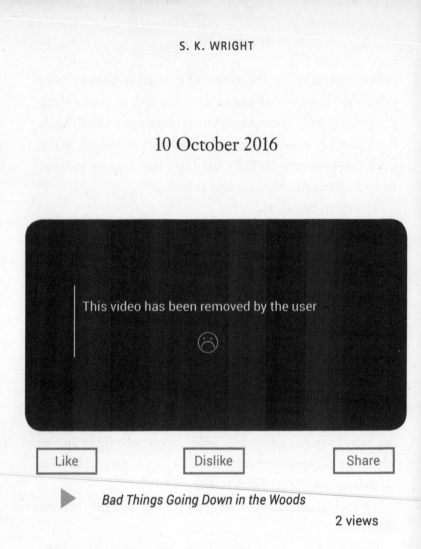

This video has been removed by the user

| Like | Dislike | Share |

Bad Things Going Down in the Woods

2 views

I just want someone to watch it.
I just want someone to *see*.

Chapter 28

Luke

I feel as though I'm watching myself from above. I can't believe this is happening to me. My mind is a fug and everything is hazy, strange and slowed down.

I'm at Prison Reception and I've been photographed and identified and interrogated. They've asked me a lot about my mental state; I think they're trying to figure out if I'm in the suicidal category. I've had trouble saying much more than monosyllables.

They tell me to remove my clothes. It's then it happens. I'm half-naked, and my heart starts to pump ferociously. My trousers are caught around my ankles and I reel, my head swimming. The guard doesn't look too worried. She just sits me down and says: *'Breathe.'* I lean over, gasping in out in out. I hear her telling me that I'm having a panic attack.

Gradually, my breathing slows and she pats my shoulder and says:

'Come on now. Let's get this over with.'

I have to bend over and suffer a bloke's finger up my arse to make sure I'm not hiding any drugs there. I think: *This is what it feels like to be an animal.* There's a roaring in my ears and my heart starts to hammer again, my breathing to quiver.

Then it's over. They tell me to get dressed but the clothes they make me put on are horrible. I brought my gear in a duffel bag Mum packed for me. I was told that if I was on remand I could wear my own stuff. But they store them away and instead I'm given 'greys' – standard prison uniform. They're grubby, old, stained. Even the boxers and socks I have on aren't mine. My skin is crawling with the itchy thought of how many guys have worn these and what they might have done with them.

Then it's time. We go through gate after gate. Each one is unlocked, each locked behind us. I know it sounds a cheesy cliché but it really does feel as though we're heading deeper into Hell. With every *clang* that echoes behind me, the outside world of blue skies, freedom and hope seems to leap away by a continent. Inside me, I feel as though there's a wild animal, screaming and thrashing and sobbing.

I'm shown into my cell.

At least it's not as terrible as I've imagined. In my worst nightmares, I'd pictured somewhere with rats and a wet floor and a thin mattress and a bucket to shit in. There are two bunk beds, an odd-looking toilet, a noticeboard on the wall, a sink and a window. It's so tiny that I can only just move around the bunk.

'Just you in here for now,' says the guard, which is also a relief. 'You'll have an induction this evening with a few other prisoners.'

The door clangs shut behind me. They've put the few possessions I'm allowed into a plastic bag with HMPS stamped on the side. The first thing I do is take the photos out, one of Eva, one of my family, and pin them up onto the noticeboard. I lie down on the bed. The mattress stinks of stale ciggie smoke. The sobbing animal inside me rears up. It warns me that I might be stuck in here for twenty years. It tells me that this is life-in-death. I want my dog. I want to hold Buster tight and bury my face in his fur. I find myself crying, howling. I hear myself making senseless noises. I punch the mattress. I beg Fate, God, whoever, whatever is out there, to help me, to save me, to get me out of here.

All around me, prisoners yell and bang and the walls sing with their sounds of fury.

Nobody comes; nobody cares.

Chapter 29

Siobhan

I open my eyes and my first waking thought is: *Hi Eva.*

While I'm in the bathroom I tell Eva about the crazy dream I had. There was a black cat running across the road and someone was reciting the opening lines of Robert Frost's poem 'Stopping by Woods on a Snowy Evening'. He was her favourite poet and Eva knew it off by heart. I always used to humour her, but personally I couldn't really work out what the poem was all about – it's just some guy stopping to watch snow falling, which is pretty boring, as activities go. Now I read him to feel closer to her.

I open my wardrobe and we have a little chat about what I should wear today. For weeks after Eva died, I kept wearing the black lace top I borrowed from her, but it's too cold now that autumn's set in. I opt for jeans and a charcoal-grey polo neck; something conservative. I need to be taken seriously.

I go downstairs to find my mum in a lilac trouser suit, all powered up for her big business meeting.

'You're up early, darling,' she says. 'I thought your first lesson wasn't until eleven.'

'Uh, yeah – I was just going to the library to study,' I lie.

My parents are pretty worried about my grades; I've been predicted 3 Cs and they're oh-so-keen on me getting into a Russell Group uni. Mum looks relieved, and even gives me a hug.

When I get to the police station, however, I find that I chicken out and dive into the nearest newsagents, buying a Snickers and a Mars bar. I locate a bench and sit down. I place the Mars bar next to me. They were her favourite. *Oh Eva, please can this be OK. I just want to help Luke. I don't mean to betray you.*

About twenty minutes later, I stand up, take a deep breath and walk in.

I show the receptionist the card that DC Okeke gave me. Okeke's not in, but she says that DI Jackson is available, which makes me even more nervous. Everyone says he's really scary.

Here's a surprise: Jackson turns out to be super nice. He makes me a cup of tea and smiles encouragingly as I stumble with my confession.

'I'm really sorry I didn't tell you this before,' I say. I'm weaving a little plait into my hair, which I always do when I'm nervous; his eyes zigzag from my face back to the weave of the plait. 'I promised Eva that I won't tell anyone, but well,

Rob and I are worried about Luke and how we should have been more honest, and I know Rob came to see you, so I felt I should too. Basically, Eva had two boyfriends.'

'Oh, really?' His mouth is still smiling but his eyes have a new alertness. 'Look, forget I'm a policeman, Siobhan. Eva would want you to tell me everything you know.'

Rob has really read this guy wrong. I trust my instincts; I feel myself open up.

'She told me she was seeing an older guy. I think he was married, cos they were seeing each other about three times a month and she was secretive ...'

'And she was still definitely seeing Luke at the same time?'

'Yeah, kind of, but Eva wasn't a slut,' I say quickly. 'She was just all mixed up. Luke was very possessive.'

'And did she ever mention this older guy's name?'

'She called him Mr White, but it was a code name. She didn't want me to know his real name.'

'You should have told me this weeks ago, Siobhan,' he chides me gently. 'We came into St Martin's and I interviewed you and you never said a thing.'

I feel like crying. 'I didn't want to betray her. She made me promise and it was the last thing I had ... Rob thinks that you've got the wrong guy ... And you see, Rivka and me, we went to see a medium. Like, a spiritual healer? I know it sounds kooky but this medium, Mrs Lambert, contacted Eva's spirit and the spirit said I should keep her secret. So I did ...'

126

'Her *spirit*?' Jackson's tone sharpens.

'I know it sounds ridiculous, but Mrs Lambert really connected with her.' My plait is finished and I begin another one.

Jackson shakes his head and touches my arm. 'Siobhan, you need to be careful, these people prey on the vulnerable. It's understandable – you're grieving for your friend. I just hope she didn't take too much money off you.'

'It was a hundred,' I say meekly. 'But the thing is – I think the older guy Eva was seeing might have been the murderer. I think he was a contract killer.'

Jackson raises his eyebrows. I'm starting to regret mentioning the medium thing. When I say it all at once like this, I know it sounds bonkers.

'Why? Was this man assassinating the good people of Wimbledon?'

'Look, I know I sound crazy. I know have no evidence. But I do know Eva told me Mr White had a gun.'

'Eva was killed by a knife.'

'Yes, but surely if he had a gun he could have had knives too? This is why I didn't tell you – because I thought it would sound stupid.'

'Siobhan, this sounds rather ... far-fetched. Did you ever think Eva was making this up? Playing with you a bit? She did want to be a novelist.'

I consider for a few minutes. It seems so disloyal to say that Eva was exaggerating, though the thought has crossed my mind. Then I say: 'Well, this might also sound silly, but ...'

'Please,' he says, very gently. 'I didn't mean to laugh at you. Please feel free to open up to me.'

'She was different after she'd been with her older guy. The day after a date with him and she was all flushed and sparkly and somehow older, as though he'd rubbed off on her. I don't think you can fake that. So whether or not he was a killer, I'm certain he did exist.'

'I see.' Jackson spins his pen. 'Her parents didn't know about this, either, did they . . . ?'

We go over it all a few times, in case I've forgotten any details. I feel bad because I remember so little. I know Eva went to hotels with her lover but I don't know where. I give him a list of dates that I think they met, but even that is uncertain. I have to admit, I've been so stressed since she died that I've been smoking way too much pot and my memory's a little cloudy these days. Not that that's something DI Jackson needs to know.

'Hey,' I say, 'did you ever find out who that blonde girl was?' Jackson looks blank, so I remind him, even though it cuts me to remember. 'She was the girl who approached me and Mr Pieachowski, the night we found . . . Eva.'

'No.' Jackson shakes his head. 'We put a call out, but she never came forward. But I'm confident we have the right guy and enough evidence in place for a conviction.'

I tell him that Mrs Lambert also assured me the blonde girl wasn't significant to the case and Jackson gives me a solemn nod.

*

I leave the station feeling hollow. For the last month, her secret has been a warm weight inside me, something I wanted to carry. Now it's no longer mine; now it belongs to other people.

Now I've confessed I'm terrified Eva will desert me. Rivka asked me how it feels to be in constant communication with her spirit. I tried to explain. It's not that I hear her speak, more that I feel her essence.

It all began a few weeks ago, after the first session with Mrs Lambert. I was writing a draft text to Eva. I was feeling so weepy, so full of longing for her reply, wishing I didn't have to rely on Mrs Lambert for a connection. Then I felt it: a breath, like a whisper on the back of my neck. A sense of peace descended over me. I found out that the word aura was originally a Greek word meaning breath; it was about the first time in my life that I've ever bothered to look up a meaning in the dictionary. And that's what I can feel: Eva's aura, shimmering with mine.

But now the space around me is vast and blank. *Oh Eva, come back. I need you.* Back home, I check on the Big Bad Blog yet again. I check it about twenty times a day but it's not been updated for over a week.

There are no texts from Sebastian either, even though I've texted him three times. Sebastian is my on–off boyfriend and he's sexy as hell, but totally unreliable. When Eva died, he came over and gave me a big hug and a bunch of flowers. But then he went AWOL again.

In my bedroom, inspiration hits. Earlier this year, Eva

and I decided to start a vlog together, where we'd discuss favourite films and books and make-up tips. We did two and it was going pretty well, although the comments underneath were always, always, about Eva and how hot she looked. Then Eva got bored. The filming was much more hassle than we'd imagined, with all the retakes and editing; she said she wanted to focus on writing and I should carry on with them, but I didn't have the confidence to film them by myself.

I watch our videos again with a mixture of pride and sorrow. Maybe I *should* continue what we started. If I think about it too long I know I won't do it, so I take my iPhone, open the camera and press record. I chatter away without censoring myself; I just let the words come gushing out. I say that I've lost my best friend and I don't know how to be without her. I film all the little things in my bedroom that remind me of her: the silver hoop earrings she left behind, the *Pretty Little Liars* book she lent me, a jumper she left hanging on the back of my chair. When I upload it to YouTube, Eva's back again, the peace of her, and I know this is what she wants.

I watch comments start to come, the hits start to roll, and I feel a little less lonely. Maybe I can survive this. *Eva, who was Mr White ... who was he?*

Chapter 30

Carolina

I'm sitting at home in front of my computer. The sky outside is a bright blue, autumn leaves floating from the trees in beautiful swirls of colour. The flat, restless feeling I'm suffering reminds me of when Mum died. In the weeks after she had gone, there was so much to organise. Dad, being Dad, threw himself into the paperwork, locking himself away in his study, filling out forms, copying her death certificate, closing bank accounts. I helped to organise the funeral. I wrote out addresses on envelopes, fingers pinched around my pen; the focus helped to calm the wild thrashing in my heart. Dad read the eulogy. For the first half of his speech, he spoke in a cold monotone that shocked some of our relatives; and then halfway through, tears started to leak from his eyes and I wanted to run up and hug him. He only just made it to the end of his speech.

After the funeral, there was a sense of anticlimax. Sympathy cards sat on the mantelpiece. Flowers began to dry and curl. People stopped saying 'I'm sorry' when they saw us in the street, because, I guess, life had moved on and we were expected to move on too. I went back to school. I used to linger in the library and do my homework there, because I hated coming home to the cold, silent house where every room held a memory of Mum, the baking tins in the kitchen that she used to bake me buns, or her hairbrush, still lying in the bathroom. Dad worked longer hours and got his promotion to DI. That was five years ago.

Going to Eva's memorial service was hard. The church full of candles, the smoke that drifted from them like clouds of grief. It brought back all the pain of losing Mum. I felt so bad for Eva's parents. They looked broken, aged by grief, hollow-eyed, gripping hands tightly. I couldn't believe it when Luke turned up. Dad had warned me that they were going to arrest him – what the hell was he doing here? I felt such a sense of savage triumph when I heard the sirens. *Now you damn well get what you deserve.*

The memorial we made for Eva at school has been packed up and moved to her parents' house now. They've promised to keep it on display in her bedroom. Luke's in jail. Nobody's discussing the Big Bad Blog much anymore. There's a sense of anticlimax that I recognise so well.

I've arranged to meet DC Okeke in Starbucks – I know he works with Dad now, but we've actually known each other since we were kids. Back then we made tree houses together and hid out in them, eating home-made ice lollies that Mum used to bring out for us. He was the first boy to ever kiss me, though we never became girlfriend and boyfriend; he fell for a girl in his own year and dated her instead. Okeke went to St Martin's too. After finishing school two years ago, he signed up to the police force. Back then, I knew him by his first name, Krishna; but over the past few years, I've got into the habit of calling him DC Okeke. It started as a tease and then became a habit.

He's half-African, half-Indian, with cheeky eyes and an ebullient afro. I kind of wish he was still at school with me, especially now Eva's gone. I miss having someone to confide in.

I'm surprised that he seems to be in such a sober mood. We drink our lattes. I thought he'd be happy to have the case wrapped up, but every time I mention the success of it all, he smiles weakly. He keeps tearing away at the plastic lip on his cup. What I love about Okeke is that he has a quirky sense of humour and loves to joke, but he can also be very thoughtful and takes my opinions seriously. He makes me feel clever; he makes me feel valued.

'What is it?' I ask, finally.

He looks at me as though he's not sure whether or not to trust me. For one horrified moment, I'm plagued by paranoia. 'What is it, Krish? Has Luke been let out?'

'God, no,' Okeke says. 'But maybe he … the thing is, we

were all under so much pressure to find the killer. Eva's parents, understandably, wanted it to happen as fast as possible, so did the media, so did our boss. I just worry that we've all been in too much of a hurry.' He puts down his cup. 'Promise you won't mention any of this to your dad?'

I hesitate. Dad would be disappointed in me, but I'm shocked; I have to know what Okeke is holding back. So I nod, hoping this isn't a promise I have to break.

'It turns out Eva had another boyfriend as well as Luke.'

'Oh.' I thought we were close friends, but she never mentioned this once. 'How d'you know?'

'Eva's friend, Siobhan, came in and confessed that she knew.'

'Siobhan is pretty silly and scatty. And Dad hasn't mentioned anything to me ... so he can't have thought it was *that* important. Besides, what does it matter? It's not like there were two sets of DNA on the knife.'

'There's another thing.' Okeke looks nervous.

'I promise, I swear I'll keep it secret,' I reassure him.

'Well, the same night that Eva died, there was *another* guy in the woods. He showed up on CCTV, on the path next to Wimbledon Common. He was wearing a hoodie too, as though he didn't want to be seen.'

I swallow, surprised again that Dad didn't mention this.

'The thing is, all the other passers-by that night were interviewed or came forward. And two confirmed seeing Luke and Eva together. So this guy probably doesn't matter at all.'

'You couldn't run the CCTV of his face through the system, to check for a match?' I ask.

'No – the image was too blurry. Normally with that situation, we'd hire an expert to enhance the resolution quality, but your dad wouldn't authorise it, said there was no need. He was convinced Luke was the perpetrator and that was that.'

'What did the rest of the team think? Like DS Hutton?'

'She agreed with me to begin with, but when the knife was found she was convinced of Luke's guilt too.'

'Exactly!' I glow with pride once again when I think of how important my contribution to the investigation was. 'There's *so* much evidence against Luke – the knife and him being in the woods and the way he's been obsessed with Eva. It would be crazy to think he didn't do it.'

Okeke smiles with relief. 'You're right. I feel better, talking to you. It was all churning round and round in my head but now it's out in the open, it does feel like I'm making something out of nothing.' He smoothes his palm over his forehead and his nod seems like a full-stop. 'Anyhow, your dad's instincts are good. He always knows what to chase and what to ignore. I hope one day I can be as good at my job as him.'

Back at home, I sit at my computer, click open a tab for YouTube and search: *Luke Jones, arrest.*

There it is. Eva's memorial service had been interrupted by the noise of the sirens. We'd all scattered outside and evidently someone had filmed Luke's arrest. I watch the camera footage

135

closely. My dad grabs Luke and cuffs him; Luke struggles back. It's the look in his eyes that gets me. If you were guilty and someone arrested you, you'd be furious that the game was up, right? That you'd been had? But Luke's eyes are huge with bewilderment. His mouth is an O of shock. He can't believe what's happening to him.

Unless Luke is a very good actor. Perhaps he's a psychopath. They're the most dangerous ones of all, because they seem so charming and everyone falls for it. In that space inside where most of us have a conscience, they just have an empty hollow. The thing is, though – Luke isn't especially charming. If anything, I've heard people use that cliché about him, that his bark is worse than his bite, that he means well but doesn't know how to show it, that he's got some issue with authority figures.

I replay the video. This time I try to follow my dad's detective mantra: *Always be objective. Be rational. Never let your emotions sway your conclusions.* And I consider that Luke's look of shock is probably down to that moment of recognition: his life has been changed for ever. I have to look at my own bias too. I mean, maybe I don't want the investigation to be over. Maybe I just need to get out there and find another mystery to solve.

Chapter 31

Eva's Diary: 31 August 2016

Why did it all go wrong between me and Luke? I
haven't even had time to put it all down in my diary
so far. The first few months that we were dating were
great. He bought me flowers. He bought me chocolates.
He told me l was the most beautiful girl in St Martin's,
in Wimbledon, in the world. He made me feel as though
I was wrapped in a big fur coat, warm and safe. When
he first said 'I love you,' my heart pounded just like
something out of a book. We were in a McDonald's
drive-in at the time, picking up our fries, and it was
so funny and sweet, the way he just blurted it out.
But once he'd said it, it all became a bit well, what
next? I noticed I no longer got butterflies before we
went on a date. I begin to find it a hassle, lying to my
parents all the time. And the big joke was this: Luke

wasn't the bad boy I'd pegged him as. He was the gentleman they'd always wanted for me, but they just couldn't see it.

I began to worry that there was something wrong with me. I asked Siobhan and she was supposed to reassure me, but instead she agreed. Great. We're studying *Pride and Prejudice* at school. It's the same old story – the heroine has to choose between a hero or a bastard and she learns to opt for the nice guy hero with his huge house and it all ends happily ever after, tied up neatly with a pretty bow. You wonder if Elizabeth and Darcy really had a good time of it, though. I've seen pics of my parents' wedding day. Mum looked radiant, clutching a bouquet, her long hair laced with a wind-furl of confetti. Now, I often overhear her on the phone saying things like: 'Well, things haven't gone quite the way I thought they would, but that's life, right?' Sometimes she'll stare at me or Dad accusingly, as though we've wrecked things for her. In some ways, I think Dad's rags-to-riches success has taken more from her than it's given; she had ambitions to set up a fashion label but lost the impetus once his business took off.

Anyhow, I remember the night that I began to have Serious Doubts about Luke. We were sitting in his car together and out of the blue he said he wanted to discuss The Future.

'Oh, well, you're going to be a famous artist,' I said, because it was a joke we had. I had this little fantasy of us dropping out, eloping, hanging out in Paris, me writing my books, Luke painting his masterpieces. I'd never do it, of course, but the thought brightened up a dull day.

'I'm not going to apply to art college,' Luke said. 'I've changed my mind.'

'But you're so talented!' I cried, in shock.

But no. Luke said he didn't want to be poor and in an insecure profession. I told him my dad's advice – you should do a job you love. I reminded him that money can't buy you happiness.

'Only people who've never been poor say that,' he replied. And then he started saying that he would need a good job to support me, if we were going to get married after A levels. Like we were in the 1950s! Me, married, at 17! I'm not planning on getting a ring on my finger until I am much older, at least 35.

'I'm bored of talking,' I interjected. 'Let's play a game of Dare.'

My tone was light and Luke looked taken aback. Then he grinned and said sure, we could play.

And that was how the Dares began.

I dared him to take off his trousers and run around the car park in his boxers, which he did. Hilarious! I even filmed him and then teased him by saying I'd keep it *just in case* ... it never hurts to have leverage. He dared me to kiss him for four minutes without stopping, which was less fun.

When I told Siobhan that I was thinking about ditching Luke, she looked shocked. I pointed out that she'd been dead against him at the start. She said: 'I misjudged him. Actually I've learnt something from Luke – people aren't always how they seem. I mean, all the supposedly nice guys you've dated treated you badly. Now you get the nice one you've been waiting for and you don't want him either.'

I feel mean and guilty. I did love Luke's caring side, but, I just wanted him to be edgy more often. That's what I'd liked about him. He was a sheep in wolf's clothing, but I wanted a wolf.

Then the Dares got more interesting.

Or, as Luke claimed, 'out of control'.

But he kept playing so I figured that, for all his complaints, he was getting a kick out of them too. He would sit there, waiting for me to dare him with a glint in his eyes and a smile twitching on his lips. He could be cruel too. He dared me to eat three chillies, to photograph myself topless, to go to school without knickers, and I loved him for it.

Then came the night of Siobhan's party.

We didn't have a good time. Luke said he wanted a

break from Dares and immediately I felt though
all my fizz had gone flat – I'd become
addicted to them.

Luke insisted on being by my side every second
of the party. I felt as though I was on a leash. I
remembered what parties used to be like before we
were dating, how I'd flirt a lot, dance with loads
of guys, enjoy being sexy and free. Now people
came up and chatted to us as a couple. Luke loved
beginning every sentence with 'We did this,' or
'We did that,' or 'Eva and I are planning to ...' I
felt shrunken, subdued. It was getting so very ...
middle-aged. I felt like my parents. I'm seventeen,
for God's sake.

We left the party and Luke slung his arm around
me, sighing: 'I'm way too drunk to drive. Mind if we
get the bus?'

'No way!' I cried, shoving his arm away. I knew
I was being unreasonable but I'd reached a pitch
of drunkenness when I can sometimes be really
belligerent. I was on a high from the party and now
Luke was bursting the bubble, bringing us down to
earth. There was a bus stop across the road, a few
dodgy types hanging out; one was knocking back cans
of beers and shouting abuse at the sky.

'I'll drive,' I said.

'You've drunk far too much as well,' Luke

objected, but I had already swiped the keys from his jacket pocket.

I ran to his battered Fiat, and unlocked the door. He tried to chase me but I was too quick. When he finally caught me, giggling, he sighed: 'OK, I'll drive. I'm sure I'll be OK and sober up on the way home.'

'Good,' I said. 'It's a Dare.'

Luke rolled his eyes and I felt disappointed. He needed to realise that the Dares became way more exciting when they were transgressive. Breaking the law took the game to a new level.

I pulled down the mirror and applied some lipstick. As I smudged my lips together, I had a fleeting thought of Mr Abdul. He'd found me smoking in the playground the other day and confiscated my packet of Silk Cuts, then said: 'I'm shocked that you of all people, Eva, would be doing this sort of thing.' It had been kind of sexy, being told off like that. I put the radio on and turned the volume up. Luke was driving so slowly it was insane; I joked we'd get home next July. He put his foot down and I wound down the window, feeling the warm summer's night. People looked at us as we drove by – they envied our energy and wanted a piece of it.

Then we heard the siren. The car wasn't a proper cop car, but a plain one. It tailed us; Luke groaned and pulled over.

The cop who came up had a very stern face. He said

that his name was DI Jackson and he was on his way home from the station when he'd spotted us. Luke said 'Sorry,' about 50 times, but just opening his mouth incriminated him. He sounded drunk.

DI Jackson gazed over at me. If I try and describe him, he just sounds really lame. Short greying hair (yes, grey!) and a lined face. But his eyes were dark and sexy. I think he noticed me checking him out and looked taken aback. I wondered if flirting might save the day. I decided to play the damsel-in-distress. It's not a hard one to do because teenage girls are almost always underestimated – all we have to do is giggle and everyone just assumes we're flaky, ditzy, hopeless.

'Oh, we're just on our way home, we only had a tiny teeny bit to drink, we're so sorry, we promise never to do it again, I mean our parents would kill us,' I said.

'Well ...' He was wavering, nearly there. Then he flicked another glance at Luke and something cold set into his expression. 'I'm sorry, but I'm going to have to breathalyse you.'

It was all pretty tragic. Luke had never looked so sexy, especially when DI Jackson ordered him into his car; Luke put up a sulky protest, like a proper bad boy. DI Jackson told me to call a cab. We left the car there on the kerb.

Back home, I thought about how thrilling the evening had turned out. My boyfriend getting nicked?

I have to admit, it was kind of a turn-on. But not long after, I got a text from Luke. Thankfully he'd passed the breathalyser test and been just under the limit. But he had been cautioned for careless driving and would have to pay a £100 fine, which he could ill afford. He added: **no more dares for now, OK!**

Maybe an older guy was the answer, I thought. DI Jackson had triggered an awakening in me; it had been gathering energy for a while and now it had blossomed. Older men were so mysterious. Experience made them wise and powerful. And there were plenty of other opportunities. My dad's golfing partner, Ronnie Wright, was always giving me the eye; Mum complained that he was a serial womaniser and always cheating on his wife. Then there was Mr Abdul. He was seriously handsome; probably the only man in possession of a goatee beard who I found attractive, as it set off his chiselled features. When he'd told me off about the ciggie, I'd made a point of checking his left hand: no ring. He was nice, but very principled and straight. Of course, if we did get it on and anyone found out, he'd be fired and I might be expelled (?) so I'd have to play this one carefully. It would be like a Dare to myself.

Chapter 32

Luke

My first week in jail, I have a meeting with my lawyer and he says he wants me to change my plea to Guilty.

'What the fuck!'

'There's no need for bad language,' he reprimands me. 'But, my dear boy, your case really doesn't look good.'

My dear boy? It's like we're in the 1920s.

'You were with Eva just before she died—'

'Hours before she died,' I correct him.

'You were the last person to see her alive.'

'No! I wasn't! The guy who killed her was the last person to see her alive!'

He holds up his hands. 'I am simply doing my best to advise you. If you were to plead guilty, you could receive a more favourable sentence, reduce your time in jail.'

'I'm innocent! I don't want any time in jail!' My hands are

fists and I resist thumping the desk. 'I loved Eva, I still love her, but that aside I'd never kill anyone, d'you get that?'

He gives me a very searching look, as though he's a priest working out whether I belong in heaven or hell. Then, just as I think he's going to say something meaningful, he pulls out an embroidered hanky and explodes into a snuffly coughing fit.

I'm starting to wonder if I might need a better lawyer.

I had to apply for legal aid to get myself a lawyer, and Mr Princeton isn't quite the hotshot I'd hoped for. He's about ninety, for a start. He's wearing glasses with a very thick lens, so that his eyes seem distant behind them. His white hair is streaked with yellow and is combed over his eggy scalp. If I was going to sketch him, he'd end up a caricature. Then I remind myself not to judge on appearances, after all I've been through. His manner is very polite and there's a kindness in his voice that I respond to. It's something so lacking in my life right now that anyone who's half-decent to me makes me want to grab them and hold them tight.

Maybe I'm the one making a bad impression, sitting here in my horrible, oversized uniform, aware that I smell bad. I'm too scared to go into the washrooms. I'm one of the youngest guys in this place and I'm convinced the older guys will all leap on me.

Yesterday I was in the canteen, buying a cheap alarm clock for two quid, when a meaty thug called Jon came up and asked how I was doing. He seemed to be trying to be a kind of father figure, but I was scared that there might be a price for his kindness; that he might be grooming me for sex, drugs and so on. So I just hurried off. This conversation with Princeton is the first half-intimate chat I've had in days.

'Look, this isn't an easy case,' he goes on.

'And I get that. The thing is – I'm innocent and I'm going to plead my innocence. I just want to get out. When will the trial be? They don't tell me anything here.'

'I should imagine that will be three months at the latest.'

Three months! An eternity. The last three days have felt like years.

I close my eyes and concentrate on my breathing. I need to control my emotions, or he might start thinking I can't get a grip.

'You may of course plead Not Guilty. I apologise if my initial suggestion upset you, but you must understand that I'm not judging you. My concern is making sure you avoid jail, or have the minimum amount of time in jail.'

I exhale shakily.

'The knife,' he says, pulling some notes from a burgundy briefcase. 'Detective Inspector Jackson claimed that your DNA was on the knife – well, of course it was. It's *your* knife. We need to ascertain whether there was any other DNA on it and how you came to lose it.'

'Um, I – I think I dropped it at school a few months back,' I say, shifting in my chair.

'Look. You see this?' He shows me a printout; it's from Eva's Instagram page. He points to the image – it's my knife.

'Eva added this to her Instagram a few days before she died. So I wonder if you really did lose it a few months back.'

This guy is maybe sharper than I've given him credit for.

'I – I – just don't remember.'

'Well, you must try, Luke, you must try,' he insists. 'I suggest that you go and rethink everything – write down dates, orientate yourself, and *think, think, think* back to the moment it went missing.'

A few days later, Mr Abdul comes to visit. The wardens lead me into a big room filled with tables, where inmates sit chatting with their family and friends.

It's a relief to be out of my cell. It's like a cooker where I'm slowly being stewed in nightmares and foul thoughts. When I see Mr Abdul I just want to bolt. Every new experience in here – my first shower, first meal, first lesson – confirms that this is my life now. I can feel routines being established, the days setting in, and I can't accept it. I have to keep fighting.

I can tell he's shocked by my appearance. My hair is lank, my skin dry, and my eyes feel hot and hollowed out with grief.

'Luke? I'm so sorry,' he says.

I pick at the graffiti on the desk. I've been looking forward to seeing him all week, but now he's here, I feel furious with him, even though it makes no sense. Apart from Mum, he's been my biggest ally from the start. Mum came to see me a few days ago. Freya and Matt came too. We all just sat and cried, to be honest. I know she believes I'm innocent, but that's not enough any more. She thinks I'm doomed to end up like my dad, I can tell.

'I have a lawyer but he thinks my chances are pretty bad.'

'You must be positive, Luke. You mustn't give up the fight.'

'And what good will that do?' I mutter. 'I'm cursed.'

That's what my mum used to say whenever Dad left us, or the gas was cut off, or we ran out of money for food – *Our family's cursed, we just have to learn to live with that.*

'Luke, I'm so sorry,' he says it again, clearly at a loss for words.

When I look up, I see tears in his eyes. I frown, my rage deepening. His tears are a luxury.

'It's okay for you,' I say. 'You can go to Starbucks. You can go to school and teach and do what you love. You can see the sky and walk in the park. And I'm stuck here for ever.'

My voice cracks.

Mr Abdul goes pale. He passes me some letters from my friends, from Rob and Siobhan. He also gives me a book called *The Upanishads*. He confides that it helped him through a really rough patch once. He was out of work, and his benefits got cut off due to a computer error; he was nearly made homeless, slept on friends' sofas, and became so depressed he contemplated suicide. This *Upanishads* book helped him when he thought there was no hope. He turned his life around. I nod, knowing this is a special confession, but my heart hardens. Why should I feel sympathy for anyone? The world has put me here and I hate the world in return. I don't care about

149

anyone or anything. I take the damn book and ask the guard to get me out of here.

Later in the night I wake up and find my face is wet. I wrap my arms around my ribs, suddenly gripped by the fear that Mr Abdul might never come back. I sit up and stare at the scattered squares of paper on my cell floor, the remains of the letters I tore up. It just felt too much of a torture, reading about their ordinary lives, being reminded of everything I've lost. I gaze out through my window at the tiny patch of sky, indigo tainted with neon, fractured by the barbed wire surrounding the prison wall. The stars look down at me, so cold and indifferent. Why are some people born like Rob and some like me? If there is a God, why does he have favourites, those he blesses and those he curses? I reach for the book Mr Abdul gave me, *The Upanishads*, and I read from the intro:

Human beings cannot live without challenge. We cannot live without meaning. Everything ever achieved we owe to this inexplicable urge to reach beyond our grasp, do the impossible, know the unknown. The Upanishads would say this urge is part of our evolutionary heritage, given to us for the ultimate adventure: to discover for certain who we are, what the universe is, and what is the significance of the brief drama of life and death we play out against the backdrop of eternity. In haunting words, the Brihadaranyaka declares: You are what your deep, driving desire is. As your desire is, so is your will. As your will is, so is your deed. As your deed is, so is your destiny.

I find some peace in the words, even though I mistrust the emotion. I've always been pretty cynical about how people get religious in extreme times. Mum told me my own dad was Born Again in jail – and lost his faith a few weeks after release. But there's too much time to think here. Atheism is a luxury for those with privileged lives.

My lawyer's instruction to *think, think, think* keeps looping round my head. The trouble is, I know exactly when my knife went missing, but I've been too scared to tell anyone. Not even Mr Abdul knows the truth about that.

There's a shard in my heart; the pain of memory. I know, too, that I didn't tell them everything about what happened that night in the woods. Confession: it's a funny word. It's only just struck me that it's the same term that we use for criminals and sinners, for the courtroom and for a box in a church. Prison is so claustrophobic and yet so empty. Sleepless nights and slow days; too much time to think everything over and over, a hammer in my mind. I want to be cleansed of these dark memories once and for all. Should I tell my lawyer what really happened the night that Eva was killed?

Chapter 33

Anonymous

The Big Bad Blog

Today on the Big Bad Blog, we ask a controversial question and we *exclusively* reveal new evidence that sheds new light on the case of Eva Pieachowski.

First, the question on everyone's mind:

Is Luke innocent?

We all rushed to condemn him – the BBB as much as anyone. Luke was the jealous boyfriend, the last man to see Eva alive: the obvious culprit.

The media were quick to demonise Luke and his family, reporting that Luke got Eva into drugs for instance. But everyone at St Martin's knows that Eva was a strongminded girl who was perfectly capable of making her own decisions. To imply that Eva was so weak and impressionable that Luke would make all her decisions for her is sexist at best.

Furthermore, the media drew a link between Luke's background and his guilt. His father's criminal track record has been raked over, and his mother has been portrayed as 'merely' a cleaner, struggling to keep things together. Since when does having a low-paid job mean that you can't raise a good family? By all accounts she is a generous, hard-working woman. Luke got to St Martin's by passing the entrance exam and enjoying a scholarship. In fact, Luke was the star of his art class and had every chance of a successful career ahead of him. Why would he kill Eva when he had such a promising future?

If we entertain the thought that Luke is not guilty, we must also raise the question: who is?

The BBB can announce an exclusive – you'll read this here before you even read it in the papers. Eva had a secret lover. An older man she referred to only as 'Mr White'. Luke knew nothing about him.

In light of this new evidence, we must surely revisit some loose ends in this case . . .

As the BBB pointed out previously, Eva's mobile phone remains missing and it could not have been moved by Luke. What happened? Who has it?

There is CCTV footage showing another man walking nearby the woods just before her murder. He must have heard something – so why hasn't he come forward if only to clear his name? Was he just a passer-by? Or was he Eva's true killer?

COMMENTS (3980)

Tristan – Are you serious? Luke is SO guilty. Mr White sounds about as real as the tooth fairy.

Henry – who is running this BBB, is it you, Lisa? Reveal yourself!

Lisa – not me! I'm no blogger!

Chapter 34

Carolina

A few weeks after Luke goes to prison, something unexpected happens.

It's really odd, but ever since my dad has been splashed across the papers as the cop who caught Eva's killer, everyone at school has been so *nice* to me. One lunch-break, Rob came up and shook my hand in that very posh way he has, as though he was the headmaster congratulating me on a prize-winning essay. He said that he wanted me to know that he bore no ill will. He was sad that Luke had been arrested but understood that my 'father' was just doing his job and he'd been 'very decent' in many respects. I managed to keep a straight face. I know all about Rob's dirty little drugs secret. He was just toadying to get in my dad's good books; that's obvious. Siobhan and Rivka were watching us, giggling. Then Rivka suddenly came up and gave me a hug. Siobhan looked confused, cautious, and then joined in. Soon the whole group had gathered round me and were asking me questions. They didn't seem fussed that my dad had put their friend away. They were just excited because I was so close to the case – they wanted the nitty-gritty.

Even so, when Rob asked if I wanted to hang out in Starbucks, I was flattered. How could I say no?

And so I joined their group.

The cool group. The group of rich, attractive kids that used to blank me if I said hi and sneer at me at every opportunity.

I'll admit that I felt cynical at first. I felt like saying to them: 'Hey, I'm still the same person I was a few months ago, when Eva was alive and you didn't want to know me. Nothing's changed.'

But I must admit, I do feel a lovely glow as I enter Starbucks and sit down next to them. Friendship is like a comforting fire after being out in the cold for so long. As I laugh and joke with them, though, a fear gnaws my heart. I'm convinced this can't last, that I'm not good enough for them, that one of these days they'll turn on me and say it was all a joke.

Siobhan and Rivka are chatting about the mysterious Mr White. Now it's out in the open, it's all Siobhan ever talks about. She starts gossiping about how Eva told her that Mr White had dark eyes and sexy hands. I want to roll my eyes because I'm certain her imagination is colouring in extra details and blurring the truth.

I turn to Rob. He's showing off, juggling some screwed-up paper napkins. 'Do you think there's such a thing as karma, Rob?' I ask.

Rob drops a napkin and looks surprised. 'I think we create our own luck, our own destiny. We have to follow our path in life, and if that annoys other people, it's their problem. So, no, I don't think karma matters. We make our own fate.'

'Ah, okay,' I say, but I don't feel much better.

That uneasy feeling is coming over me again. I tried talking about it with Dad, but he didn't want to listen. He's been pretty stressed ever since the BBB came out ...

I suddenly have an urge to write down all these theories swirling in my mind. So I politely reject Siobhan's offer to read my palm and say I need to go to the loo.

Inside, I put down the seat, pull out my phone and make a list:

Questions which are still unresolved:

Eva's mobile – where is it?

The guy Okeke mentioned – near the woods at time of murder, shows up on the CCTV. Who is he? Mr White? What if he found Luke's knife and did the deed?

Blonde girl on the search – told Mr Pieachowski and Siobhan she knew something. Still a mystery.

I can't hide away in here any longer or the others will start to notice. I flush, wash my hands and rejoin them, my brain still buzzing. I feel better; I realise I've been wanting to make that list for quite a while.

I'm slightly taken aback to see Mr Abdul is chatting with the group. It's always weird seeing teachers outside school. He's got a takeaway cup in his hand.

'We've just been debating whether "Mr White" is a teacher from school,' Siobhan teases him. He laughs, but I note the blush that sweeps across his cheeks.

He quickly asks if anyone has heard from Luke.

Nobody's received any letters from him in a while. Everyone's wondering how he's surviving. Rivka says sadly that it must be very grim in jail, and there's an uncomfortable silence.

Mr Abdul frowns, then leaves and everyone waves goodbye. Nobody wants to dwell on Luke, so the subject quickly changes to Rihanna's latest drama and the next party they're planning ...

I watch Mr Abdul as he strolls away. I've heard he's married but I did notice just now that he wasn't wearing a wedding ring. And, incidentally, he has *dark eyes*.

'You okay?' Rob asks.

I turn and give him a bright smile, joining in with their chat, but my mind is still buzzing ...

Chapter 35

Luke

The classroom clock says 8.50 a.m. Mr Abdul is calling out our names for register. He's on the *H*s, the *I*s. My name is coming up and I've got a nervy feeling in my throat, like a snake is forcing its way up from my gut and into my mouth. I hear Princeton's voice in my head: *All you have to do is confess. He'll call your name and you just say, yes, I did it, I killed her.*

'Luke Jones,' Mr Abdul calls out. Everyone turns to look at me. Siobhan points and whispers to Rob, something about my hands. I look down and realise that they're covered with blood. Quickly, I hide them in my lap. 'Yes!' I confess. 'I did it! I did it!' Wind fills the classroom, scattering their whispers of shock. Then I see Eva, sitting at the front. She turns to look at me, shaking her head and smiling. *'Well, Luke, you've done it now ...'* I watch as a snake slowly winds across the floor between her high heels, heading towards me ...

I wake in a shock, heart pounding *Oh my God where am I who am I?* I'm all disorientated and I reach for the lamp by my bed, only for my fingers to hit a wall.

I remember: *Prison. I'm. In. Prison. Eva. Dead.* A firework of panic; I listen to my breathing flutter and slowly the sparks of shock fade. I glance at my clock. It's nearly four in the morning. I close my eyes again, but my mind is stained with images from the nightmare. Was it a sign, an omen? I'm seeing Mr Princeton in five hours' time – and I have a decision to make.

'This is all confidential, isn't it?' I press my lawyer as we sit down together.

'Of course,' he says. He looks on edge today, his handkerchief at a squiffy angle in his pocket. He starts going on about the knife again, and also some new information that he needs to share with me, but his words fuzz into the background. *Say it*, I tell myself. *Just say it say it say it.*

I cut across him: 'Eva – I think I might have pushed her into the pit,' I blurt out. 'But I'm not sure.'

'I ...' Mr Princeton looks utterly shocked. He shuffles his papers around, then clicks his pen on and off. 'I have stressed, Luke, that it might be a wise decision to plead guilty.'

'No – no, you have to listen,' I say. 'Please.'

He nods, his lips pinched, and I close my eyes. I need to take myself back there, into the woods, into the dark of that terrible night. I feel as though I've painted over that night with every confession, every interrogation, and now I want to scrape all the layers away and find the pure image, the simple truth.

'I loved her so badly, but for some reason she was mad at me all the time. She talked about breaking up but I know she didn't mean it. Or she wouldn't have even come with me to the party, would she? We went there as a couple; she wanted me to pick her up. We argued about music on the way, and when we got there we took a few drugs. It wasn't my idea. Eva said it was a Dare. She said I was boring if I didn't take them. I actually gave up smoking for her, you know. I was trying to set a good example to inspire her. But it just seemed to push her in the other direction . . .

'She was flirting with Rob, my best friend. I was jealous and I got cross and said we should go. She said, no, we should talk. So it was her idea to go into the woods, not mine.

'I didn't like being in the woods. Eva was shivering with cold but she wouldn't take my jacket – I offered it to her. Anyway, that's when she nearly fell into the pit; she grabbed me and I pulled her back. We hadn't seen it. She didn't even thank me. She just said we had to break up. I know that was just the drugs and drink talking because only the day before, she'd told me she loved me – but in the moment I just lost it.

'I loved her so much and I couldn't understand why she wanted to ruin everything. I – I said I would push her into the pit. She laughed and said, go on then. And I took a step forward – I wasn't really going to push her in, but she started, and then – then she fell.'

I swallow. I can still remember the noise she made, like Buster does when his paw is trapped. It still pollutes my dreams every night.

'I looked in and saw her lying there.'

Mr Princeton interjects. 'She didn't cry out for help?'

'Well – yes. I mean, if she'd been silent, I would have checked that she wasn't . . . But she wasn't asking for my help, just hurling abuse at me. She was fine – she was just angry. And. I mean, I shouldn't have left her, ran off back to my car, and . . . I'm sorry.' I break off, tears raw in my throat, hot behind my eyes. 'I loved her . . . and I guess I was to blame for her death. In a way, I did murder her.'

There. I've said it. My confession. But I don't feel cleansed; I just feel lost, naked.

'Was your knife the weapon you used?' Mr Princeton asks.

'NO!' I bellow. Hasn't he been listening to a word I've been saying? 'But by leaving her in the pit – I left her in a vulnerable state, right? She couldn't run. She couldn't escape whoever it was who found her there. It was like I left her like a piece of prey for a wild animal . . . She was screaming abuse at me, telling me she didn't need my help, but I should have done the responsible thing. You see?'

'Luke,' Mr Princeton sighs. He removes his glasses and polishes them; his eyes look smaller without their distortion, small and tired. 'You've made a signed declaration to the police. It doesn't look good if we try to change that now.'

A quicksand feeling: I tell the truth and I've made things

worse? I should've kept quiet. I'm losing my mind locked away in here, memories gnawing at me like rats slowly nibbling my sanity, reducing it to skeleton. *You try to be honest and then they just twist it . . .*

'Well, can't we leave that out and stick with the story I told the police, that I just argued with Eva and left?' I cry. 'You can pretend I never told you, right?' My voice rises. 'Right?'

Mr Princeton sits up very straight.

'Intimidation will not work with me, young man,' he says icily.

I slump in my chair. 'Sorry, I didn't mean . . . I just . . . ' My head swims and I suddenly feel very tired. I want to go back to my cell, curl up foetal, pull the covers over me. I don't want to speak to anyone any more. I'm out of words.

Then, just when I think it can't get any worse, Mr Princeton drops his bombshell.

'Take cheer. One thing that is working in your favour is the discovery that Eva had another boyfriend – an older man known as Mr White. I'm looking into his identity now – it seems that "Mr White" was just a code name . . . '

'I'm sorry, what?' I whisper.

'Yes,' he says brightly. Then he informs me of all the facts: Eva and Mr White had been seeing each other for the last four months; he was older, most likely married; they might have met in hotel rooms.

And this, he assures me, is good for me. It will really help my case.

*

I lie on the bed, heavy with this new knowledge. My past is becoming sketchy, as though the good parts never happened. Oh, Eva. I guess there were signs things weren't that great between us. Did any of it mean anything? Did she ever care for me at all, or was I just a cover for the older guy?

Food comes. It's like dust in my mouth. I am hollow with hunger but I lack the energy to eat. I put the tray on the floor and shove it away. Maybe I won't eat ever again.

Eva's memory used to be a benign, soft presence, a ghost who kissed me to sleep each night, who told me I was innocent, reassured me I'd be out soon.

That was just a fantasy, my mind's bullshit creation. Now I see her as a medusa, taunting me, snakes hissing and biting into my face. And this sickens me, but the fantasy comes. Yes, I am in that pit that night. Yes, I do have a knife. And I do stab her, over and over, I stab the lying bitch, and it feels so good to hear her sob and say *Sorry, sorry, sorry* ... I slam my pillow, letting it all out. Then shame shakes me awake. What am I doing? I'm becoming the sicko they want me to be. Still, nobody in this place can actually see into my mind, can they? I have nothing of my own here but my thoughts still belong to me.

Chapter 36

Carolina

47 Edge Hill. I got Mr Abdul's home address from Rivka. She said she once went to see him to ask for some advice. I was quite startled, to be honest: I know teachers are meant to care, but aren't there rules about entertaining students at home? I asked if Eva had ever visited Mr Abdul at home, and Rivka replied with a shrug and said sure, several times.

Mr Abdul lives in a fancy Edwardian house with two cars in the driveway. Quite expensive for a teacher; I guess his partner must be earning. I hang back, concealing myself up a little path that winds from the cul-de-sac onto Wimbledon Common, dappled by the shadows of chest-nut leaves.

I wait, feeling prickly, impatient. I'm still in an antsy mood after arguing with Dad. All I said was: 'Mr White might have been in the woods that night, as well as Luke.' He went crazy, barking that the case was closed and that was final. I know he's just stressed out about the BBB, but maybe he feels a bit lost too: the case was everything to him and now he's got nothing to obsess over.

A bird bounces onto a nearby branch. A blue tit. It's been three weeks since I last visited the woods, which is forever. I miss the silence and peace of my green refuge. Just as the boredom and weariness start to feel unbearable, making me wonder again whether I'm cut out to be a detective, the front door of number 47 opens. Mr Abdul comes out.

A girl with blonde hair follows him. She's stuffing something into her bag – a video camera? She looks waifish and her gait is shy. She seems to be thanking him. As she pulls on her coat, something snags my attention. A flash of something on her wrist. I suddenly remember what my dad told me, right at the start of the case – Siobhan had been approached *by a girl with fair hair and a tattoo on her wrist.*

Of course, loads of people have tattoos these days. But – what if I've struck gold?

Mr Abdul watches the girl walk away.

Then he starts to walk in the opposite direction.

Shit.

For a moment I'm torn, like Alice in Wonderland: which way, which way?

I swerve to the right, following the girl onto the Common – but she's moving too fast for me to keep pace without drawing attention to myself; so I do a U-turn and follow Mr Abdul instead. He is walking down towards the poorer end of town. As I follow him, my mind races ahead of itself. If Mr Abdul knows the blonde girl, does he know what she saw? What if he put her up to something? What if he's Mr White, he seduced Eva, and now he's intimidated this girl into silence—

Rational, I remind myself. *Dispassionate*. I mustn't get carried away.

Mr Abdul enters a run-down residential street and knocks on one of the houses. It's a pretty grim place, to be honest. I can hear a child screaming. One of the windows is broken and some pizza boxes have been taped over the hole, but the masking tape is flapping loose. There's a battered car squatting outside the overgrown front garden. Eggs thrown at the windscreen have formed gloopy flowers. As I walk closer, I'm horrified to see the word *MURDERER!* spray-painted in purple down one side.

And then I realise: this is Luke's house.

Ten minutes later, the front door opens and Mr Abdul emerges, followed by a woman who must be Luke's mum. Abdul turns and gives her a hug. Even from here, I can see she's been crying and she nods, drying her eyes, as he says something soothing to her.

She passes him a lead and he comes out with a dog: a brown mongrel with an exuberant spray of a tail.

'Hey!'

Mr Abdul has spotted me. I wave and cross the road to join him, a blush on my cheeks like a rash. I get the feeling that

I've not been as subtle as I'd hoped, that he may have guessed I've been following him.

'Want to help me walk Buster?' He offers me the lead.

We walk down the road, past some graffitied railings and a vandalised bus stop. Walking Buster helps me feel less awkward. He's such a cute dog; I always wanted a pet but Dad wouldn't let me, which is why I got into birdspotting instead.

'Is he yours?' I ask.

'No, he's Luke's,' Mr Abdul says. 'I've been walking him regularly, to help Luke's mum. She's struggling to look after him, between work and her other two kids, and the other day some lads turned up outside the house and started throwing things. Poor Buster got some glass in his paw, so I took him to the vet. She wants to move house, and the council are relocating her, but it's going to be a small flat. So I've offered to take Buster for now – until Luke's released.'

'You think he will be?'

'I think he should be.' Mr Abdul gives me a challenging look, as though expecting me to be my father's daughter and argue back. I say nothing. He talks some more about Luke: what a star pupil he is, how his artwork is some of the best he's seen in years. I listen hard and watch Buster snuffling along, taking such delight in the world, rapturous at the smells around him. Eventually I say: 'I bet Luke loved his dog', and Mr Abdul tells me that Buster howled for days with a broken heart when Luke was put away. I feel tears prick my eyes.

'If you want, we can go and visit Luke,' he says gently.

I can't help but flinch, wondering how my dad would react to that.

'Or you could write to him,' he goes on, as though sensing my thoughts. 'Luke loves receiving letters, they're the only thing keeping him going right now.'

I nod and we carry on walking in silence. Mr Abdul does have a way about him. You don't have to spend very long with him before you feel like you're with a good friend, someone who won't judge you; he makes you feel as though you can unravel your heart. The girl in me feels compelled to open up and tell him about how odd I feel right now, suddenly popular on the surface, but lonely in my core, unsure my new friends really like me, unsure I'll ever have a boyfriend. Resisting this urge is uncomfortable, and it strikes me that this is one of the difficult things about being a detective: staying cynical. I have to be on my guard all the time.

I debate all the ways I might bring her up and finally I decide to just be provocative: 'I was actually good friends with Eva ... I remember her saying once that she had a crush on you.'

Mr Abdul does a double take and blushes. Then he replies: 'You're right, she did, as a matter of fact. My partner says I get too close to my students, that I don't draw a line. But I believe I handled it well. Anyway, I'd better be going.'

We're walking so fast now that I'm having to jog to keep up with him. Buster senses the tension in the air and barks.

169

I wonder if I dare push him even further and ask about the blonde girl, but maybe I've set off enough fireworks for now.

In a perverse way, I'm pleased too. My suspicions weren't unfounded. It feels like a victory – *See, Dad, I told you I was onto something* – but I also feel sad that I'm having to do this all by myself.

Chapter 37

Eva's Diary: 2 September 2016

A few months after DI Jackson arrested Luke, the Dares started up again.

The half-term holiday was over and we were back at school. Our class timetable had been shifted and now Luke and I were in the same class for Art – just when I wanted to get away from him. I was dreading it. I thought that he'd spend the whole lesson watching me; I was surprised to discover it was the one time he had no interest. Once Luke picked up a paintbrush, his absorption in his art was almost religious. At the end of each lesson he'd look up and notice me with a start, almost guilty for having neglected me for an hour.

Mr Abdul was number 1 on my Older Man list. How could I flirt with him when I had an unwanted bodyguard by my side? Then came my chance. Mr

Abdul was reading out our grades from the week
before – the still life we'd been working on. I was top
of the class in my other subjects, but I didn't always get
my usual straight As for Art; too often I slipped to a B.
So when he gave me an A, I was delighted.

After a dramatic pause, Mr Abdul announced that
Luke had got an A+, declaring: 'This is the first time in
two years that I've ever awarded such a high mark.'

The whole class applauded. Luke was blushing like
mad. I couldn't stop grinning, even if I did feel taken
aback by the way Mr Abdul was looking at Luke, with
the tenderness of a father regarding his prodigal son.

'Today's lesson is a nude life drawing,' Mr Abdul
said, amused by our nervous giggles.

To be honest, the model wasn't that hot; she was
about 30, slender, with red hair, her skin freckled, her
arms bony and feet far too big for her body. I started to
sketch her and then made the mistake of looking over
at Luke's portrait. I felt so inadequate. Right, I thought
with a surge of competitiveness, I'm going to damn
well beat him. Then a more interesting thought came to
mind: what if I turned all this into a Dare? It was my
turn, after all. Luke was waiting for my comeback after
he'd dared me to shoplift a hairbrush from Superdrug.

I couldn't wait until the end of class for the Dare:
this one was too good to delay. So I texted Luke:

> dare: stay behind after class and tell Mr A you have
> a crush on him

I had to give Luke a kick, he was so engrossed in his painting. I made a signal for him to check his mobile. A few seconds later, his reply came back:

> Double dare.

'Okay,' I whispered.

The bell rang and as everyone trailed out, I saw Luke glance over anxiously. Finally, it was just me and Abdul. I was feeling much less cool than I thought I'd be.

'Everything alright, Eva?' Mr Abdul asked.

'Um, I was just wondering . . . if you could give me some extra lessons, after school?'

Mr Abdul looked taken aback. 'Eva, you got an A today, you're doing fine. I know Luke is your boyfriend and you can be quite competitive. But you don't need to be. You have an amazing gift with your ability to write so well.'

I felt both flattered and stung.

Competitive? Was that true?

'I heard that your short story won a Promising Young Writers Award,' he went on. 'Congratulations.'

I beamed, feeling a bit better. 'But, I want to be good at Art too. I want to be the best ...'

'Can't Luke help you? Wouldn't be that be a nice idea?'

'He's not actually my boyfriend, you know,' I protested. 'I mean, he's just a bit obsessed with me.'

'Oh, right.' Mr Abdul looked a bit disapproving, as though he didn't believe that his star pupil could behave like some kind of stalker.

'Besides,' I added in a seductive voice. 'I think he's a bit too young for me ...'

It could have been a sexy moment (I mean, when it comes to guys my own age, I have usually no problem luring them in), but like a clumsy fool, I twitched and knocked over a jar of water from the painting session. We both bent down to mop up. Mr Abdul cast me an uneasy glance and I felt mortified. Normally I deserved top marks for seduction; hell, I was an A+ student, but on this occasion I definitely deserved a D-.

Then his partner turned up. She was an Indian woman with long, wavy dark hair. She came in jangling her car keys and crying: 'Why's my handsome guy keeping me waiting?', then apologised when she saw me. You should have seen the look on Abdul's face: the shine in his eyes. As they left, I watched them kiss each other, chattering and laughing. I felt curious to see them so in love after presumably years of being together. Then I spotted Luke, waiting outside the studio for me with a scowl. Did I ever really love him? Have I ever really been in love? I'd been so convinced at the start. Now it felt like a fever that I'd recovered from.

Chapter 38

Luke

My cell has become a living hell.

I was finding it lonely and claustrophobic, especially after my lawyer dropped the bombshell about Eva's older lover. Over and over, I found myself scrutinising each and every date we ever shared, holding it up to the light, trying to work out when her affair might have begun.

Now I'd give anything to have the miserable space to myself again.

A few days ago, my new cellmate arrived. I'm not supposed to share with a convict, since I'm only on remand, but, ironically, the law doesn't seem to mean much here.

Meet Stuart: a skinhead in this thirties with a mean face and a livid scar running across his left cheek, branching into pale rivulets of puckered skin. He's boasted to me that he's in here because he committed GBH on his stepsister – '*She deserved it.*

She was a stupid bitch, always making my life a misery!' His temper is far worse than mine. He's challenged me to a fight twice, but both times he's backed off – thankfully I'm a foot taller than him.

Sleep has become impossible. You try dropping off when a guy in the bunk below you thinks he's a rapper and is trying to rhyme *whores* and *my cause*. The urge grips me to climb down and tell him to shut up, let him see *my* anger. No. I breathe out, telling myself to calm.

That's the trouble with this place. Everyone is so quick to solve everything by violence that it rubs off on you, becomes the norm. I used to like fighting, but only as play – pastel violence compared to the neon savagery of this place. Here, the fighting is nasty, and brutal; leaves scars. I need to protect myself. I need to make sure that when I get out of here I've not turned into some thug.

So I close my eyes and I try, try so hard to daydream myself back into the past, to a Luke who had a happier life, because it's the only way to survive here: the past is heaven, the present an impossible reality.

Just when I've given up all hope, the letter comes.

In the morning, the guard brings us breakfast – and, to my surprise, he gives me an envelope. I don't recognise the handwriting on the front.

I tuck it under my pillow and eat the crappy breakfast. Stuart has a nice habit of shoving food into his mouth, eating fast and then spraying crumbs everywhere as he speaks.

'Hey,' he says, 'if we put salt in the kettle and toss it over that git Craig when he comes back, it'll really sting like hell. My mate was in prison and he tried it.'

I stare at this psycho in disbelief.

'And why would we want to do that?'

He looks as me as though I'm the one who's mad for even querying him. I feel panicked. Oh God, this is what it's going to be like, day after day. I think of that quote – it's by a famous playwright but I can't remember who – *Hell is other people*. It's too true.

'I'll lose my privileges and you'll never get to Enhanced Privileges,' I point out, trying to appeal to his selfish side.

'Yeah,' he muses. 'I guess.'

It's been a while since anyone has written. Even Mr Abdul has gone a bit quiet, though his last letter did promise a visit soon. Impatience scratches at me and I fish out the letter from under my pillow. I can't see Stuart now he's back on the bunk below me, so I try to tear it open quietly, wincing at every rustle. I turn the letter over and check the signature at the bottom. *Carolina Jackson*. What the hell?

Her dad's face flashes into my mind, raw as a Francis Bacon painting. That victorious look in his eyes when they charged me and he put me away. I was never a human being to him, just a statistic, a gold star on his policeman's uniform.

But Carolina's letter isn't snide. It almost seems apologetic. She says she wishes we'd been friends at school and hopes it's not too late for friendship now. She says she's thinking of me. And this is the best bit:

I want you to know that I think you're innocent. At first I have to admit that I believed it was you, especially when the knife was found. But now I feel there are too many details that just don't add up. The whole Mr White thing must have come as a terrible shock to you. I hope you're not too upset. I have a couple of theories as to who he might be ...

'What's that?'

I'm so engrossed I haven't even noticed Stuart creep up on me. He grabs the letter from my hands.

'Hey!' I yell, jumping down from the bunk. 'You give that back.' And I start to swear at him.

Stuart laughs gleefully, holding the letter back, taunting me as I try to reach for it.

'You bastard. Give it back or you'll be sorry.'

Something in his face changes. He seems to realise I'm at breaking point.

I get the letter back but I'm still shaking.

'There are girlies out there who fall for bad guys in prison,' he says. 'Looks like you've got a groupie.' Even though he's sneering, there's a shade of admiration in his voice.

I climb back onto my bunk and smooth out the letter – it's ripped and crumpled. Suddenly I want to cry like a dumb kid. Nothing in this place can ever be clean and clear. Everything has to be dirty.

I read it through again, but I still don't know what to make of it. She ends the letter by saying she's planning to visit. Maybe it's a trick. She could be working for her dad. Perversely, this gives me hope. Maybe the case isn't as solid as I thought it was.

I sigh as Stuart gets up, unzips and tinkles into the toilet. Two strangers in a cell, being forced to listen to the sound of each peeing, shitting, sighing, burping, grunting, farting, like the animals we are in this place. Factory-farm offenders locked in our cages. I just pray that I can get a trial date and get out of here soon. I may be an innocent man, but the way things are going, Stuart may yet drive me to murder ...

Chapter 39

Carolina

I'm starting to wonder what the hell I'm doing here. I'm standing outside Wandsworth Prison. You wouldn't believe how grim it is, so grim it almost seems like an architectural caricature. With that grey stone and those arched Gothic windows, it could be used as the set for a horror movie.

Rob was meant to be coming with me, but he dropped out at the last minute. He said he had to get on with his Economics essay and he was really behind. Maybe it's better that I do this on my own.

I just have to see him, I tell myself. *I'll just stay five minutes. Then I'll know.*

Once I get into the prison, I'm taken to a Visitors' Centre where I have to sign in. I booked this visit last week. It was pretty simple: I just filled in a form online. I'm told I can't take anything into the hall except a bit of small change and my ID, which disappoints me. I shove my rucksack into one of the red lockers. Then there's security, like the type you get in airports, where I have to walk through a white arch with a warning beep. I hate being frisked; having a stranger's hands on me makes me shudder. I grit my teeth and pretend I'm in the woods with some blackbirds and then it's over.

The Visits Hall is a sunny place filled with tables. There's even a play area for kids. I spot Luke and give him a little wave, then hurry over to the coffee bar. I'm delaying, of course. I buy us two coffees and head to his table.

Okay, this is it.

'Hi, Luke,' I mutter, sitting down and passing him a drink.

His hands are in his lap. His shoulders are slumped and he looks as though he's suffering some kind of permanent and terrible hangover, bleary and puffy, his skin sallow.

'Hey,' he said. 'I got your letter.'

Is it my imagination, or does he look a little wary? He lifts his hands and I'm shocked to see that his left one is wadded in a thick white bandage.

'Luke – Jesus, are you okay?'

'It was one of the guys.'

I nod. I know prison isn't a holiday camp, but it looks like Luke is having a tougher time than I'd imagined.

Then all of a sudden, Luke opens up, his voice shaky, his words faltering.

'His name is Stuart. He got put into my cell. He's been convicted of GBH. He had this really nasty scheme – to chuck hot water at the guard when he came to collect our breakfast trays, but to make it really hurt he thought he'd add salt to the water. Extra sting, you see. I tried to stop him and whatever, but it ended up scalding me instead. I mean, if it'd been my other hand, my right, my painting days would be over, I reckon.'

I gaze at the edge of the bandage and see a flash of skin, red and raw, and I shudder.

'Oh God, we have to get you out of here,' I say.

He stares straight at me.

'Your dad seems very intent on keeping me in here.'

'I – I'm going to help you,' I say. 'I want to be a detective. This is my first case, that's the way I look at it. I'm not undermining my dad's work, I'm just – complementing him.'

These are ideas that have been simmering in my head all week. But as I speak them, they sound childish, like I'm some kind of wannabe kid from *Scooby-Doo*. I swear a dubious look flashes over Luke's face.

'I'm smart,' I snap. 'I'm good at spotting detail. I've learnt a lot from my dad. I can do this.'

'Sorry,' Luke says quickly. 'I really appreciate your help. None of my friends ever visit,' he adds bitterly.

I curse Rob for not coming today. I'll nag him when I get back.

'So,' I say crisply, hoping I sound professional. 'We have to think about possible leads. This older man that Eva was seeing' – I see Luke flinch and I wince, sensing how raw that wound must be – 'I was wondering if he might be a teacher. Mr Abdul, maybe.'

'No.' Luke's voice is firm. 'Mr Abdul has been my *only* true friend since day one. He's the only one who's visited me here. He wouldn't betray me.'

'My dad says—' I break off, swallowing, for every time I mention him, Luke winces. 'Well – it's just, it could be anyone, right? It could be the very person you don't want it to be.'

Luke folds his arms, and in his stubbornness he reminds me of my father. 'Abdul had an alibi that night. He told me that. He and his partner were over at a friend's house for dinner.'

I nod uncertainly. Alibis can be faked.

'Look,' I say, 'I don't know if you know about this, but when Mr Pieachowski and Siobhan were first searching for Eva in the woods, they were approached by a girl. She has blonde hair, she's small and waifish, and Siobhan mentioned a tattoo on her wrist. I don't know if she's familiar to you?'

Luke looks surprised. 'Nobody's told me about her.'

'She mentioned a film and implied she knew something – and she ran off before anyone could ask more. So, yesterday, I was watching Mr Abdul's house and I saw a waifish girl, with long fair hair, carrying a videocam as she left.'

Luke raises an eyebrow.

'Okay, I know there are lot of blonde girls out there – but I think I also saw a tattoo. It could be her.'

Luke sits up. 'Why don't you tell your dad? He could go to Abdul, get her details.'

'Um, he's not really in the mood to listen,' I admit.

'Because he's convinced it was me,' Luke says bitterly.

Great, now I'm making him feel worse: Luke's realising that his paranoias are justified. I feel a flicker of guilt, worried that I'm betraying my dad.

'Can't you just ask Mr Abdul who she is?'

'I did ... Yesterday after school. You know how friendly and open he normally is, but he got defensive and told me to mind my own business. I've never seen him behave like that before. But then again, he hasn't seen me behave like that before, either. It did sound like I'd been spying on him.'

I thought Luke would be pleased, but he still looks sad and sulky. He's biased too, I realise. He can't believe Abdul could possibly do any wrong; I'm not telling him what he wants to hear.

'Okay,' I carry on quickly. 'There's another thing. I know that the night Eva was murdered, another guy showed up on the CCTV in the early hours and my dad never really looked into him properly.'

'What!' Luke looks astonished. 'Your dad – my God – he really has got tunnel vision – he's out to get me—'

'No, no, listen,' I reply, 'I mean, he wasn't actually seen *in* the woods, he was on the road. He might have absolutely nothing to do with it all, but I still want to check the CCTV again. He might have heard something, seen something.'

'Okay,' Luke breathes out. 'So how are you going to find this guy?' Hope brightens his face, but it's immediately shadowed by doubt, as though he's scared to have faith in me.

'I have friends at the station,' I say. My voice becomes bolder. 'Luke, I'm going to get you out of here.' I feel strong as I say the words.

Then Luke's expression darkens again and he fiddles with his bandage.

'Why are you helping me?' he asks. 'I don't get it. Is this story that you want to be a detective some kind of bullshit? Is this a trap?'

'No! I just ... ' I bite my lip. I find myself echoing DC Okeke's words: 'I've watched my dad work on this case, and I know he's under huge pressure – I mean, before they arrested you, every day he was going into his office and the higher-ups were coming down on him to hurry up and find the murderer. National news, this sort of spotlight on the force, it's not good. So maybe something has been missed. I know you don't really know me, but I feel ... I just care about justice. I care about it so much.'

Luke smiles. 'You'll make a good detective.'

I feel an urge to hug him, but I hold back.

'D'you think you'll be okay with Stuart?'

'Don't worry,' he says quietly, and I'm relieved to hear a note of stoicism. I'm even more certain now that he's innocent. God, I'm so glad I came and didn't chicken out; today has changed everything.

Silence falls between us. I notice there's a smear on my glasses and I take them off, rubbing them on my jumper. His eyes flit over my features, drinking them in. He *notices* me. A blush sweeps across my face and I quickly shove my glasses back on and grab my coffee cup.

'Have you ever worn contacts?' Luke asks. His tone is light, his eyes playful.

'No.' I squirm in my seat. 'I mean, glasses are more practical and easy, so . . . '

'Sure.'

For a minute there, for the first time since I got here, it felt normal. We might have been in the outside world, in a café window, smiling and flirting—

Some commotion over at another table breaks the spell.

Luke reaches out as though he's going to hold my hand; I grab his and shake it briskly, as though he's my client. I stand up, say thank you and goodbye, and I promise I'll be in touch. The look on his face as I leave reminds me of that video of his arrest on YouTube; like a lost little boy who's been deserted by a parent. Halfway to the door, I feel I've been mean, even misunderstood him. Why would Luke flirt with me? Nobody ever flirts with me. He's probably so alone in here, he just craves the human touch. But when I turn, the guard announces that time's up, Luke rises, and it's too late to go back.

Back home, I go into the kitchen to make myself a cup of Breakfast Tea. It's shivery cold in the house, so I fiddle with the thermostat, and there's a rumble as the heating comes on. It's then I feel tears in my eyes. Each little choice I make seems like such a luxury of freedom. How can Luke stand it, not being able to control anything in his life any more, being trapped in that tiny space with some psycho? I pick up my mobile and start composing a text to Okeke, asking if he still has the CCTV tape, praying that he'll help me ...

Chapter 40

Siobhan

I'm sitting in the living room watching TV, when the doorbell rings. My parents are out at a yoga class, so I figure it's Rivka, who said she might drop by. I'm taken aback to find Sebastian on my doorstep.

'Hey,' I say, hugging him. 'It's been ages since I last saw you!'

In the living room, we settle down with iced drinks and chat about school for a bit. Then when the conversation runs dry, I find myself chatting away and I remember how Rob teases me for 'talking at people' when I'm nervous, so I shut up and start weaving little plaits into my hair.

Sebastian always was a bit of a funny one. I met him about a year ago. He goes to St Cuthbert's, a boys' only school over in Esher. They hold this fancy Christmas dance every year and invite St Martin's students to join in. Eva bought a ticket but had to drop out at the last minute because she had a virus.

I feel mean recalling this, but I was a teeny bit glad. When I was with her I was always second-best: the one boys went for when they realised they couldn't have Eva.

Sebastian was definitely one of the best-looking guys at the dance. Tall, blonde, suave and masterful, like something out of *The Great Gatsby*. I gave him the Eye and he asked me to dance. We kissed at the end, under the spinning disco lights, gold fake snow falling over us, and it was so dreamy. When I visited Eva the next day and showed her a pic of him, she said: 'Oh my God, he's hot!' and I felt a little thrill, knowing that I could also attract sexy guys.

We had one date. It went well at first; Sebastian took me to a fancy Italian restaurant and insisted on paying for a three-course meal. I drank far too much red wine and he kept on encouraging me. We ended up snogging in the back of his car and going oral and then he pushed really hard for me to have sex with him. He had no idea I was a virgin because I'd lied to him, thinking it would make me sound more worldly. So I said no, I wanted to wait. It was hard resisting him, though. He was the best kisser and his voice was hypnotic and cajoling – 'Oh Siobhan, you're so sexy, you taste so good, I want you so badly, don't tease me like this.'

Then he snapped. He yelled at me that I was a stupid prick-tease. *Ugh*, I thought, *I never want to see him again*. Then the next week he sent me a text apologising profusely. I decided I'd forgive him, but every time we planned to meet he'd cancel about thirty minutes beforehand, just as I was perfecting my make-up. In the end we went out for a few drinks and he suggested we should just be friends. He bought me a present, a little clay black cat, which he said was lucky, and it was so sweet and sexy of him that I have to admit, I wished we could be more than friends. But then he went quiet again, ignoring my texts for weeks. It isn't just that Sebastian runs hot and cold; the fact is, he is plain weird.

Sebastian is the only guy in the world who isn't on social media, so I can't look him up online and check his relationship status. Out of my gang of friends only Eva met him, and she didn't like him at all. She was always telling me to dump him. She had this paranoid thing that he didn't like her, even though they hardly knew each other. But who could ever dislike Eva?

'I saw your vlog about Eva, by the way,' Sebastian breaks the silence.

'Oh, cool, thanks,' I say.

My YouTube channel recently reached 500,000 subscribers. I feel chuffed, but it's kind of awkward – now I've said all I wanted to say about Eva the vlogs have become more about me, which makes me feel a bit guilty. The whole point of the videos was a way to remember Eva.

'I've been thinking,' I say. 'D'you think I should stop dyeing my hair and go dark again? I mean, it was Eva who said I should dye my hair . . . ' I trail off, realising that he isn't even listening. He's trawling through *Times* articles on his iPhone.

I fold my arms and sigh loudly. Every time I see Sebastian, I think how nice he is at first and then I gradually remember what it's like to get him on a bad day – how rude he can be, how unpredictable and disconnected.

My phone pings and I pick it up (making sure that Sebastian can see that he's not the one ignoring me, now *I'm* ignoring *him*).

'Oh,' I say.

It's a text from Carolina.

I'm a bit freaked out by how she's wormed her way into our gang. It's all Rob's fault. For some reason, he really likes her; I worry it's a crush. Rivka seems fond of her too, but I'm just not sure. She's got this brisk, headgirl quality and ties her hair back into a plait like she's about twelve. Yesterday Carolina texted me to meet because she had 'something urgent' she needed to discuss. Like what, I thought, geometry homework? The etiquette of birdspotting? So I didn't reply and now she's texted me again.

She's asking what sort of tattoo the blonde girl had, the one who approached me back when I was searching for Eva. I text back, **why?** wondering if she's working for her dad. She texts back saying she just needs to know, so I sigh and reply, **It's hard to remember.** I close my eyes, taking myself back to that day, that horrible day. I remember the rain in my hair, the smell of wet leaves, the forest looming over me, and I start to tremble. My memory keeps jumping ahead, to that awful moment. I try to rewind, slow it down, but the girl is a blur. I text back: **It was on her wrist. Maybe a letter S or a Z but maybe a K. Maybe a symbol, like Sanskrit.**

Carolina's reply comes back: **That's pretty vague.**

I get cross then and put down my phone.

'Who're you texting?' Sebastian asks, finally paying me attention.

'Carolina – she wants to find this girl in connection with Eva's murder. She made a film, we think.'

'What!' Sebastian comes and sits next to me. 'What d'you mean, a film of Eva's murder?'

'God, no, I don't imagine it's *that*,' I reply in horror. 'When we were searching for Eva in the woods, this girl approached me. She said she knew something about a film. And then she ran off, nobody's heard from her since.' I sometimes worry that she never even mentioned a film, that it was just what I *wanted* to hear back then when we had no idea what had happened and were desperate for answers.

'She might have filmed Luke killing her,' Sebastian says. 'Like a snuff movie.' I look at him in confusion. 'Have you ever seen a snuff movie?' I shake my head no. 'It's when someone kills someone and it's filmed. So it's like a crime film but for real. No fake blood, no actresses. And it's strange, because you're watching someone's death become immortal, captured on film for ever.'

'That's awful!'

We fall silent and I curse Carolina, because now my memories are all stirred up. My boots slipping on the squelchy leaves as I ran to the pit, that feeling of terrible dread ripping open my stomach. Sometimes I wish I had never seen Eva's body, that the police had just called and informed me of her death. I can't ever erase the image of her lying down there, cold and dirty and wet and dead.

I start crying. I can't help it. I try to hide it from Sebastian, but he hears my sob and pulls my hair back from my face.

To my surprise, he holds me close and strokes my hair. I blurt out in teary fits how much I miss my best friend and how I still go back to Mrs Lambert, and the uncanny connection with Eva's spirit and how I'm scared it's all my imagination. He doesn't even laugh at me. He says there are lots of cases of people communicating with their loved ones after they die.

I hesitate for a moment and then ask him if he'd like to join me in trying to contact Eva. I tell him that if I copy Mrs Lambert, light some candles, create an atmosphere, it might work. I worry he'll think I'm being silly, but he agrees.

Upstairs in my bedroom, we switch off the lights. I set a picture of Eva down on the rug, laying a circle of tea lights around her. Sebastian looks handsome with the candlelight soft on his skin. I take his hand and tell him to close his eyes. Silence. I whisper, *Eva, are you there?* Silence. *Eva, Eva.* Suddenly, there's a violent growling noise and I jump. Then I realise it's just the guy next door, mowing his lawn.

Sebastian gets the giggles. I feel a bit cross, because the mood's ruined now. I tell him I'm going to recite Eva's favourite poem, 'Whose woods these are I think I know'. I speak the lines as solemnly as I can. As I reach the end, he says: 'That was beautiful.' Silence stretches out. Then he reaches out and strokes my hair and says: 'You don't need to dye it, you know. You don't need to look like Eva. Your natural hair colour is beautiful.' I'd forgotten how powerful his charisma is, how transfixing. Now he's stroking my face. I shouldn't give in to him. I hear Eva's voice echoing in my mind. 'If he plays games with you, play them back even harder.'

So, just as he's about to kiss me, I pull back.

Smiling, he leans in again. And it's no good. I find myself kissing him back. We sink onto the carpet. I tell myself that I am in control, I don't have to do anything I'm not ready for, but there's nothing threatening about his caresses, which are delicate and tentative. Soon I feel starry with desire, and I'm about to undo his trouser belt when suddenly he jumps to his feet.

He says he has to go.

'*Now?*' I jump up, grabbing his hand.

'Sorry.' Is he just teasing me? He leans in and kisses my temple. 'I'll see you soon.'

'But – when?'

But he's already sauntering down the stairs.

Chapter 41

Carolina and Luke

18 November

Dear Carolina,

Thanks for your letter. I loved the bit where you said that your mum would have liked me – that meant a lot to me.

I know it's my turn for a confession, so here goes. I've had a lot of time to think in here and maybe I've got to know myself a bit better. This all goes back a long way. When I was about 8 years old, I started to realise that I was different from the other kids at school. I was playing footie when another kid shouted out, 'Hey, you've got a hole in your trainer!' I knew about the hole, all right. Whenever it was raining I had to sit in lessons with cold feet and squelchy soles. I just couldn't figure out why the other kids had nice fancy shoes and I didn't. Then, when I started to go to their

*homes after school, I got a shock. They had DVD players. X
boxes. PlayStations.*

*Something began to simmer inside me. One day it
erupted. I brought a friend home from school. James asked
me why I didn't have a DVD player, why my TV was black
and white and the image was shit. That night, at dinner,
I started to lay into Mum with that innocent cruelty kids
have. To my shock, she started to cry. I remember the shame
twisting in my gut. I quickly stood up, cleared the table and
made her a cup of tea, not even caring when I burned my
fingers doing it, feeling that I deserved punishment.*

*My dad came home, had a lottery win and suddenly we
had money. I was desperate to get James to visit again and
when he eventually did come, I showed him all the new things
as though I was a salesperson in an electronic goods store.
When Dad went, all the treats had to go to the pawnshop.*

*Then I got my scholarship to St Martin's on the basis
of my art work. My silly little scribbles showed promise,
apparently! None of us could quite believe it. I was rewriting
family history.*

*I remember being very wary at first. I made excuses
never to bring anyone home. It was only when I got close to
Rob that I let him know the real deal. I started to get a bad
rep because my temper was my weak point. It's taken me a
long time to understand this, it's only thinking it all over
in here that I've finally had some insights into my past. I'd
get into fights and be convinced it was never my fault – the*

other guy started it, he picked on me, I was only reacting. So I became the cliché – the bad kid, the poor kid, the kid from the wrong end of town.

I have to go now, but please write soon, Carolina. Now it's your turn to tell me a secret.

Love,

Luke x

20 November

Dear Luke,

I hope you're doing okay. Your confession was amazing and I really appreciate you opening up to me and telling me all about your life as a kid.

This is just a short letter – I'll write properly later, but I'm feeling upset because I just tried to visit and they wouldn't let me in. No explanation. I booked my visit properly in advance. Are you in any trouble? What's going on?

I wish you were out here with me – autumn is my favourite time of year. The birds start to migrate. Swallows fill the sky, swooping and undulating in flocks. They look like punctuation in the clouds. I've taken a few pics for you.

I hope I will see you soon, Luke.

Stay strong.

Carolina xx

Chapter 42

Carolina

I head down to the police station on the no. 47 bus. The evenings are getting darker and my breath makes chilly dragons in the air. I picture Luke in his cell, under a thin blanket, and I pray he's not getting too cold. Winter in jail must be the bleakest thing. I'm not allowed to visit him till next week. Luke explained to me that all visits have been put on hold because they had a serious outbreak of violence at Wandsworth. He wrote that it was all to do with synthetic drugs being smuggled in and making even calm prisoners go crazy; he says he's steering clear of all drugs, and drawing like mad instead. Art is his drug. I miss him, I really miss him – writing to each other has brought us close together with an intensity that feels different to anything else. I've been hanging out more with Siobhan, Rivka and Rob but, though they're fun, I find their company superficial by comparison.

I pull his latest letter from my bag and reread it, savouring every sentence. In the last exchange we discussed the Robert Frost poem from school that starts, *Whose woods these are I think I know.* It makes me feel sad when I read it and I've never sussed out why, so I was kind of awed when Luke came out with the insight: *I think the guy who's writing the poem is dying. He's noticing the beauty of the world and it's so sharp because it's his final hour.* He attached a beautiful sketch with it: of the man standing in front of the trees, a moon shining down on him, snow falling softly. In turn, I wrote back and told him all about my mum dying and how Christmas Eve is the anniversary of her death. These are things I've never shared with anyone at school before.

I'm scared, sometimes, by how much I look forward to the letters. Luckily the post comes when Dad's at work, so he can't see the postmarks. It's all a bit *Romeo and Juliet.* I think of Luke's blue eyes and firm lips and what it might be like to kiss him, but I catch myself: that's not what this is about. I'm here to get justice for Luke.

I'm heading to the station to meet Okeke. He finally caved in a few days ago. He agreed that he would work on Luke's case in his spare time, outside office hours. He said that he had joined the force to do good work and he needed to be sure the right guy was put away. Yesterday he stayed behind at work and secretly printed out the CCTV image of the mystery guy in the woods. It's too indistinct to be of much use, but we have got a plan to work out who he is. And it's going to cost.

Hidden in my rucksack is an envelope of money. I have a savings account, and every birthday and Christmas for the past few years I've put a bit away. Earlier in the week, I withdrew two hundred. I'm meant to be saving up every penny I can for uni. I've got an interview at Bristol next week and I'm barely prepared. Nothing feels more urgent or worthwhile to me right now than getting to the bottom of this case and helping Luke.

I get off the bus. Okeke's just finished his shift. My dad is seeing my Uncle Jarvis, who's flown over from the US for the first time in years. I cried off dinner, pleading a homework crisis, and Dad didn't seem to mind too much. Tonight is my only chance, the one night I can be sure that Dad, ever a workaholic, won't be visiting the office.

As Okeke comes out of the station, he pulls on a woolly blue hat and wraps a scarf around his neck. He gives me a smile that looks nervous – or maybe he's excited.

'All set?' he says.

I nod. We're about to set off, when someone calls out for him. He turns.

It's DS Hutton. She's an officer one rank above him. I've never warmed to her much. She's middle-aged, with a blonde perm and a stern face.

'Okeke. I've just had a call.' There's a Post-it hanging from the end of her finger. 'It's from Mr Weatherby. He says he's expecting you and can you come twenty minutes later?'

'Ah ...' Okeke shifts from one foot to the other.

'Can I ask, what case this is in connection with?'

'The, ah, the stolen Mercedes one,' Okeke improvises.

'And Jackson's authorised this?'

'Sure.' Okeke gives her a conciliatory grin. 'Anyway, Carolina here is freezing, so I'll see you tomorrow. We're just getting drinks before ... I head off to Weatherby.'

And he hurries off, before DS Hutton can interrogate him further.

'Shit!' he says, as soon as we're out of earshot.

We get into his car. It's a small green Fiat. Now I feel guilty. I didn't mean to get him into trouble.

'I *told* Weatherby to call me on my mobile, not work,' Okeke slams his seat belt into the clip. 'Now they're going to find out. All that stuff about the stolen car case, I made that up.'

'But we're not using police money,' I cry. 'Like you said, this is in your spare time.'

Okeke falls silent. I fret that he's going to call the whole thing off. I know he'd like a promotion, and investigating a case that my dad feels he's solved isn't going to put him in anyone's good books. But he starts up the engine, flicks on the radio and we set off.

Weatherby lives in South Wimbledon, a maze of suburban streets. We pull up outside his house.

'I think we have to do this,' says Okeke. 'Just to be sure.'

I breathe out. 'Twenty years is a long time for the wrong guy to be in jail.'

Okeke nods. We pass the time by listening to the radio. A news bulletin mentions Eva. Her parents are setting up a bursary for talented kids in her name. Okeke flicks it off and we head in.

The guy we're meeting is a police-approved expert, someone they hire and pay to help them with details of a case as and when they need him. Weatherby has special expertise in enhancing CCTV images.

I was half-expecting him to live in a shed, like a techno hermit. But his house is terraced and his lawn is neat, just like any other in this area. When he opens the door, we come face to face with a grizzly, bearded man. His squinty, kind eyes glint behind his glasses. We shake hands. I suffer a sudden nervy urge to laugh. I think: *in a few minutes, we'll know for sure.*

I am certain that guy from the woods will turn out to be someone from St Martin's. As Dad said, the killer is likely to be someone that Eva knows. Someone we've overlooked.

Weatherby's office is in his dining room. There's a plate on the table, scattered with toast crumbs, and a cold mug of half-drunk tea. The rest of the room is crammed with computers and three vast screens, the floor a snakepit of coils and wires. He sits down at one of the screens and starts typing on a keyboard, chatting to us all the while, rattling off terms I don't fully understand. Okeke and I exchange glances, afraid and excited, and then – then – the enhanced image flashes up on the screen.

'Oh,' I say.

The guy looks around eighteen years old, white, with high cheekbones and a full mouth. He's six foot tall, and the hoodie he's wearing hides his hair.

'I don't know him,' I say. 'He's not from St Martin's.'

What if he *is* just some guy who was walking through the woods that night? But in that case, why didn't he come forward when the police appealed for witnesses, anyone in the area at the time? What does he have to hide?

As Mr Weatherby passes a memory stick to Okeke, I take the envelope of cash out of my bag. Okeke looks sheepish. He offered to pay, but I know he's on a low salary and in debt. Besides, I wanted to do this for Luke. I insisted I cover the cost.

Back in Okeke's car, we reflect on where this leaves us. 'So,' he says, 'now you can start checking this image against the social media. Search Facebook, Instagram ... be methodical.'

I notice that he doesn't use 'we'. As badly as I want to prove myself as a detective, I'm so new at this, and having Okeke by my side makes me feel reassured that I can move things forward. I hope he isn't going to bail on me. But I nod and say I will do the best I can.

The next day Okeke texts to say he managed to run the image through the system but there was no match with any criminal. I text back: **are you in trouble with work?** He goes silent on me.

I only have classes in the morning. During the afternoon, I head straight home and start searching through Facebook. I'm just logging in when a text comes through from Rob, asking me to hang out with the gang later. I text back that I'm busy and carry on, scouring social media. Endless photos of parties, kids drinking, dancing, posing, flirting.

By 7 p.m. my eyes are burning. I slip a letter for Luke into an envelope and walk in the dark to the post box. I mutter a little prayer for him and post it.

Back home, I realise how hungry I am. I start cooking dinner and as I set a place for Dad at the table, I feel a flicker of irritation. Be rational, he's always said. Be objective. So why the hell didn't he chase this guy? Why ignore a loose thread?

I hear his key in the door.

'Carolina!' His face signals danger. Then the rant starts. He found out from Hutton that Okeke has gone behind his back. Hutton thinks I'm involved; Weatherby confirmed that I was at his house. I turn the veggie sausages in the pan, trying to stay calm. This is nothing compared to what Luke has to face in jail.

'Aside from the deception, it's a complete waste of police funds,' Dad says.

I can't land Okeke in it. I realise I have to come clean.

'Actually, Dad, I paid Weatherby myself.'

'What? How? Your savings? Carolina, that money is for university.'

'Sorry, Dad,' I say quickly. 'I didn't think you'd be mad. It's just that studying crime books isn't enough. I know that now, helping you with Eva's case. I roped Okeke in – please don't blame him.'

'Carolina, can I trust that you're not thinking of following up on this insane Luke-didn't-do-it angle?' he asks, calming a little.

Oil from the pan spits onto my wrist. I wince, then look Dad in the eyes and do my best fake smile.

'Of course. I promise.'

'If you want more hands-on experience, you don't need to go wasting Okeke's time and your own money. Come to me. I don't know why you'd go behind my back like that.'

I spear a sausage and let Dad rant away, getting it all out of his system. As I set down his plate, all I can think is, *Dad hasn't even asked to see the picture of this guy.* He's not interested. For him, it has to be Luke and that's it. Doesn't this suggest my dad is not being his usual rational self? Doesn't this imply he has tunnel vision? I've read about cases like this. Miscarriages of justice always occur when objectivity is lost.

I know Dad was under huge pressure to arrest somebody and arrest them quickly – but what about making sure he definitely has the *right* guy?

Dad sits down and tucks into his food. I notice how tired he looks.

'You know,' Dad suddenly interjects, 'Okeke's very ambitious. He wants my job, I can see.'

'He has a long way to go before he'd get to your position.' It would take him a decade, if not more.

'Just be careful,' Dad says. 'I think he'd love to take credit for solving this case, rather than me.'

For a moment I'm taken aback. I'd seen Okeke as a dear friend who was helping me out – but then again, why would he risk his career? He says he wants to do the right thing, but what if he's just looking for ways to undermine Dad's methods?

Back in my room after dinner, I sit on the bed, feeling confused. Then I decide that I don't need to get tangled up in police politics. Maybe that's what I can bring to this case – I can be the objective outsider. I open my laptop and carry on scouring through Facebook photos. I start adding more friends, people I only vaguely know; some of them accept me and some ignore me. I'll keep on looking. I don't care how long it takes; I have to find this guy.

The next morning I get up early, ready to go back and observe Mr Abdul's house. I pack my camera. This time, if the girl's there again, I'll be prepared. As I'm finishing breakfast Dad drops his bombshell. He's heard from the police warden at Wandsworth. Luke is going to change his plea.

He's going to plead Guilty.

Chapter 43

Eva's Diary: 7 September 2016

I remember the week I first met Sebastian.

It was the end of the summer term. School was busy and buzzy and I'd been nominated for headgirl, which everyone said I was sure to win. Yet I still felt restless. Once in Art class, Mr Abdul stood right behind me, observing my painting. All the little hairs on my back of my neck prickled, but I had no idea how to take things further. When I asked him for extra lessons he said I didn't need them, and kept suggesting that Luke could tutor me if I really wanted help.

Then I heard rumours about a really cool house party over in Esher, which was being held that Friday. Getting out of the house required a bit of scheming – my interview at Oxford was looming and Dad was being pretty strict about me staying home – but I told

208

him I was meeting Siobhan for a study session and promised I'd be home before curfew.

Luke picked me up in his car at the end of the road.

The crowd at the party were mainly from St Cuthbert's. Siobhan and Rivka had failed to show and I was sick of Luke being my shadow. We stood in the living room, barely speaking, the silence weighted between us.

'Why don't we do a Dare?' Luke said.

'Dares are for kids,' I said, sarcastically. Then I saw the desperation in Luke's eyes. Feeling mean, I offered to get him a drink, and that's when I saw Sebastian.

'I know him,' I whispered to Luke, pointing to a boy standing outside on the patio with a gaggle of girls. Like most of the guys at this party, he was dressed very smartly, in jeans and a preppy, pinstriped jacket. But he stood out nonetheless.

Luke looked sulky and asked if he was an ex. I explained he was meant to be Siobhan's man and I'd never met him before, but I recognised him from the pics she'd shown me on her phone.

From what Siobhan had told me he didn't sound like a keeper, though I'd held back from telling her to dump him. I mean, I got the appeal of a bad boy, but Sebastian was no rebel; he just sounded weird and erratic. I knew that there was a tension between us because if we went out on the pull, I always scored

the hottest guy. I didn't want to be one of those girls
who never have female friends, so I'd been positive
and agreed with Siobhan that maybe 'he'd just
been in a bad mood that night' and that he might
not be texting back very often 'because his mobile
was faulty'.

Now, the sight of him with his arm around another
girl made me furious. The trouble was, Siobhan could
be really naïve at times. When we were kids we used
to play a game where we'd try to draw what each other
was thinking, to prove we were psychic. Siobhan never
seemed to suspect I was cheating, sneaking peeks at her
poorly concealed drawings; she actually believed that
we had a special connection. I loved Siobhan with all
my heart, and I couldn't bear to see her treated badly
and taken advantage of.

'You're right, Luke, we have to do a Dare,' I said,
beckoning him up the stairs. He followed me into the
back bedroom of the house, rolling his eyes.

The big double bed was covered in coats from party
guests. I opened the window, staring down over the
patio. Now Sebastian was whispering into the girl's ear.
She was very pretty: willowy and slender, with long
dark hair that was obviously dyed.

'God, he is such a sleaze.' Luke echoed my
disapproval. 'Some guys just don't understand how to
treat girls.'

He gave me a look, as though I ought to appreciate how truly lucky I was to have such a caring boyfriend.

'Go on, then,' I said, goading him. 'What should we do?'

This was what I liked about Dares: it was a way to bring out the bad boy in Luke as he sought to impress me.

Luke smiled and withdrew the shiny little square packet from his wallet. 'I dare you to fill this condom with water and drop it on him.'

I grinned. It was a great Dare. That dick needed to be taught a lesson. My only hesitation was Siobhan. What if she found out? She'd been saying she wanted to introduce me to Sebastian for weeks.

'Double Dare,' I said.

'Fine,' said Luke. There was a sink in the adjoining bathroom and he turned the tap until the condom bulged like a beachball.

He came to the window and called down: 'Hey, this is a gift from Siobhan.' Then he dropped it.

Sebastian moved like lightning. The balloon hit his girl smack on the head. She jumped in shock and I jerked away from the window, grabbing Luke's hand and holding it tight. We both giggled nervously. The danger of the Dare had bonded us, but we were more like naughty kids than boyfriend and girlfriend.

When we crept downstairs I felt guilty. We'd got away with it but the girl was in tears, completely drenched. Sebastian was trying to dry her hair with a tea towel; dark henna stains bloomed on the white cloth. Someone said: 'God, it was just a *prank*. Sebastian's sister is totally overreacting.' His sister. I felt mortified.

Luke sensed how cut up I was. He said: 'Dare you to do some blow with me.' I'd done it before and really didn't like it, but I couldn't say no to a Dare. Once I took it, I felt fizzy and weird. I hate the loss of control; it seems like an ugly, selfish drug. I swore I'd never let Luke cajole me into taking it again. Then someone yelled over the thump-thump of a dance track, 'THE PIGS ARE HERE! EVERYONE CLEAR OUT!'

Luke and I were running and stumbling out across the lawn, laughing, when I looked back and saw DI Jackson standing on the patio. We sprinted away, jumped into Luke's car and shot off. I found myself half hoping we'd get away with it, but half longing for the sound of sirens too ... It was crazy of me, of course, one urine test and I'd be had, but I kept picturing him on the patio: his dark eyes, his electric charisma.

Thankfully he didn't follow us. But it seemed that this idea of an older man hadn't gone away.

Abdul or Jackson? I tossed them over in my mind like a coin, wondering whether to go for Heads or Tails.

Chapter 44

Luke

Carolina is waiting in the Visits Hall.

I see her before she sees me, her face bright and eager. My heart sings for the first time in days. As I walk towards her, she jumps to her feet. She's blushing – despite her brisk manner, she blushes at the slightest thing. It's sweet. Her curly hair hangs loose around her shoulders, rather than tied in its usual plait.

I'm now on Enhanced Privileges, which means I can wear my own clothes; it feels much better to be able to greet her in jeans and a T-shirt instead of that horrible uniform. The bandage has come off my left hand, though there's still a nasty pink scar that's healing.

Suddenly I act on impulse and pull her in for a hug. At first I feel her tense, but then she holds me back just as tight. It feels so good, I don't want to let go. I want to tell her she's my Guardian Angel.

She pulls away abruptly and sits down. I sit down too, anxious that I've made the wrong move. We both speak at the same time.

'I got your letter,' I say just as she says:

'My dad said you're going to plead guilty.' She crosses her arms, leaning away from me.

For a moment I'm confused, angry that her dad is spreading more lies about me, and then I realise what must have happened. 'Oh, I told Stuart I was guilty. He was giving me such a hard time, plus he's just joined a gang here, and I was scared he was going to turn them all against me. I just wanted to sound tough so he'd lay off me. So I put it about that I was guilty and it's kind of worked, they've left me in peace.'

She stares at me very intently. I'm being *assessed*. For a moment my temper flares, but then I picture how it might have been for her the last week, how she must have doubted, worried, wondered.

To my relief, she nods sharply.

'You shouldn't even have to put up with them – you're on remand, you're *innocent*,' she says fiercely.

Oh, thank God: she believes in me, still.

'I have a trial date,' I say. 'It'll be early New Year.'

'That's good news, Luke. Has your lawyer got any closer to finding out who Mr White might be?'

I shrug. 'He's says he's got an investigator on it, but I don't know ...'

'Maybe you should change your lawyer,' she says. An

awkward pause. 'I asked around. Mr Princeton, well, he isn't exactly your strongest bet.'

Great. Now Carolina's confirmed my worst fears.

'You know, when I first got in here I thought that my lawyer would fix everything. The lawyers you see on TV are shit-hot, really smart. You never see the lame ones who do sod all.'

'You need a new one,' Carolina asserts.

'One of the guys here warned me that changing so close to trial would mean starting from scratch – I'd lose time. I don't know.' I rub my temples. 'What about the CCTV footage? I mean, seriously, it was so kind of you to check that out for me.'

'I'm still chasing that up,' she says quickly.

'You can't ask your dad to help identify him? He's got all the resources.'

She shakes her head awkwardly.

'Your dad really must be determined it's me who did it,' I say, bitterly.

'Once he makes up his mind about something, it can be hard to change it,' she says, biting her lip.

I want her to say she hates him and to side with me completely, but whenever we discuss him she's always evasive, wavering, and that scares me a little. Everything feels so fragile. I'm worried he might be hiding some kind of evidence that he'll whip out at the last minute, crush her faith in me and stop her visits.

I open my mouth to speak when we're given the warning: visiting is up. She says quickly: 'I'll start looking at local hotels too, see if anyone remembers Eva and Mr White. I don't think my dad is pushing that angle either.'

'I don't think I could survive here without you,' I say.

It all goes by so quickly. Just a minute left, and she'll be walking away. I'm still stung by the way she sized me up earlier, that hard cold look of suspicion when she tried to figure out if I was guilty. I don't want her ever to look at me that way again. She leans forward, her eyes wide. I reach for her hand. The blood in her cheeks beats crimson and warm. I whisper that we should say goodbye. She nods. I lean in. Just an inch. My breath is shaky; it gives me away. And then, just as our breaths are mingling, I feel a sense of déjà vu, a shadow memory—

The last person I kissed was Eva. We were in the woods. She was telling me we had to break up, that I had to let her go once and for all, and I shut her up by grabbing her and pressing my lips to hers—

Panic rises in my chest. This is a mistake. I'm about to pull away, mutter an apology – but Carolina's soft hand touches my cheek and we kiss. The buzz and din around us fades away. I feel the bad memory dissolve. At first my lips move automatically, but then I taste the sweetness of her kiss and emotion floods through me, something I haven't felt for a long time: happiness. This place is brutalising, but she's made me feel human again.

'Oh!'

Someone wolf-whistles at us. Carolina pulls away.

We lock eyes and smile shyly. Her eyes are starry. I can see how much she cares for me.

Carolina's come into my life so suddenly, so unexpectedly, I can't help but wonder: is she just in love with my tragedy? Perhaps she likes the idea of me playing the martyr. Would she still like me if I *did* get released? An ugly urges comes over me to crush her sweetness, mock her faith in me.

She picks up on my change of mood. There's a confused look on her face. She gets up, says: 'Bye,' and hurries off.

I call after her but she doesn't look back.

I regret it, after she's gone.

Back in my cell, I pick up my pencil and start to sketch her face from memory. Drawing is the only thing that keeps me sane in this place, though I'm close to running out of paper and should ration myself.

Every time she visits, I feel glimmers of my old self again, that recognition of the Luke I used to be. Then the moment she leaves, I feel this place reshaping me again, hardening me, rot seeping back into my soul.

I'm desperate to keep sketching but I have to attend a cleaning class. Literally, how to clean floors. Last week I had to attend a compulsory literacy lesson that was so simple I wanted to cry with boredom. I was amazed to realise that half the guys in this place, even guys in their forties and fifties, can't spell and have no idea where to place a comma in a sentence. I'm starting to think that prisons are a place for those that society has failed, for the poor and mentally ill to be shuffled away out of sight, for those who might have lived completely normal 2.4-kids-and-a-mortgage, nine-to-five existences if only they'd had a better start in life.

As we fill our buckets with water, I feel despair wash over me. I was meant to be attending university interviews this month, but they were all cancelled. I pick up the mop. Is this all I can aim for upon release? Having been stuck in a Class A jail for twenty years, I then get to spend my days swishing a mop for the living wage? I picture myself, jaded and bitter, old in middle age, cleaning shit from school toilets. *Boy, thanks for giving me so much hope.*

I can't see Carolina hanging around for twenty years, then falling for a cleaner. Her crush would never last that long.

I'm so scared. I relive our kiss, recall the hurt on her face. What if she deserts me like the rest of them? The only thing this place has taught me is friendships are ephemeral, trust an illusion. *Oh God, please can Carolina find something. Please, God, please ...*

Back in my cell, I gaze out at the patch of sky. I've seen it change with the seasons, from a bright blur to skies of cloud and grey and darkening nights and paler dawns. I've been in this place too, too long.

I take the duvet cover and pinch it between my fingers. I tell myself that if it all goes wrong, I'll tear this into strips one night; they'll find me in the morning, a bloated corpse.

It would break my mum, devastate Freya and Matt, but some sick part of me can't help but picture Siobhan, Mr Abdul and everyone else who lost faith in me – then they'd all be sorry.

Tears sting my eyes. Knowing I've worked out an escape plan is the only way I can survive the present.

Chapter 45

Carolina

Luke and I are lying in the grass. It's a summer's day, the sky is clear blue, bees buzz around us and two dragonflies dart by in flirtation. Luke is whispering in my ear, private little jokes that make me laugh. His fingers trace over my lips, and then he is kissing me, his hand on the small of my back, pulling me in tightly—

'I think we should try the Antoinette Hotel first,' Okeke says.

'What?' My bubble bursts, bringing me back to the dark, cold winter's night.

'The Antoinette Hotel,' Okeke repeats, looking bemused at my lack of focus as we walk towards the car park.

'Um, sure – good.'

We reach his car and I get into the front passenger seat. It's deathly cold and he puts on the car heater, which emits sickly fumes.

As he drives on, my mind drifts back to Luke and our kiss. I've been kissed before. Okeke was my first – I glance at his profile, blushing at the memory – but that was years ago, when we were kids. Our kisses were a nervous experiment. Kissing Luke felt like the first time I'd been kissed properly, with passion ...

I know I shouldn't get involved with the guy I'm trying to help. It's so unprofessional. But then I think of his eyes again, and how long his lashes are, and the way his nose turns up, sweetly freckled—

'Here.' Okeke's car indicator makes a clicking noise as we turn into the car park of the Antoinette Hotel.

We get out and I tell myself to *focus*.

I'm so grateful to Okeke. It's a Friday evening and he's given up a night in the pub. Last week, I appealed to him about how lame Luke's lawyer is. He was meant to be checking up on the identity of Mr White and investigating hotels, but Luke's just found out that nothing's been done; it turns out his lawyer has been off sick for a whole month.

Okeke checked the records and saw that Siobhan had listed some dates she thought Eva could have been with Mr White. Dad had apparently checked out a few local places, but what if he had missed something? What if the staff he spoke to had missed something? I said it was worth checking again, and Okeke agreed.

In the Antoinette Hotel, I sit at the bar while Okeke goes to the desk. I watch him flash his badge at the receptionist and then ask questions. I want to be the one up there, doing the detective work, but they'd just write me off as a schoolgirl. I open my rucksack and pull out the letter for Luke I'm halfway through writing. A waiter comes up and asks if I'd like a drink.

I ask for a tap water. He frowns, but he's too polite to object, so he just nods and strolls off.

Okeke comes over and sits down with me.

'Nope – nothing. No Mr White here on those dates.'

He sighs. The waiter brings over my tap water. Okeke asks for one too; the waiter smiles thinly.

'Even if we do find Mr White, then I'm going to have to go back and convince the whole team too. They're all on your dad's side. They think Luke did it.'

'Dad wouldn't ignore you,' I say. 'He wants to know the truth.'

Okeke nods. 'You know, when I first joined the force, I made some massive mistakes in my first few months. One involved confiscating a drug from a teenager which I then pocketed.'

I blink in surprise. *Okeke is a dark horse.*

'I was just young and stupid,' Okeke says. Then, seeing my face: 'Yeah, older than you are now, I know – but you're a wise head on young shoulders, Carolina. Anyway, your dad found out, chewed me out, but then covered for me. He made me swear to be a clean copper and I took that to heart. I learnt to take pride in my work, respect it as a moral and ethical duty.'

I'm touched by his confession. If we can find Mr White I

know Dad will be pleased – I think of how happy he was when I found the knife in the woods . . .

We head out to three more hotels in the area, but each one draws a blank. It's getting late now and the next one on our list is further out, into the countryside.

'Shall we call it a night?' Okeke asks, looking tired.

'Just one more,' I beg him.

So we drive out through the winding little country lanes, to a small boutique hotel, the Hotel du Vin. We pull up in a car park surrounded by trees. Inside, the reception is white, with sprigs of dried flowers in vases everywhere. The bar adjoins, so I sit down and order a Coke whilst Okeke goes over to the desk. Ed Sheeran is playing in the background and my foot taps along.

I pick up my mobile, flicking to my WhatsApp. I do a search for my chat with Siobhan from a few weeks ago, when I sent her a picture of the blonde girl and asked if she recognised her as the girl she'd seen in the woods. I thought it would be straightforward, but – no. Siobhan sent me three replies. The first one was a yes, the next was a no, then the last a not sure if it's her. I'm close to giving up on that lead to be honest. Ever since I've been hanging around with the gang, I've noticed how vague Siobhan can be. Rob says he thinks she smokes too much pot and it's made her scatty. This makes me worry that the hotel dates she's given us for Eva might be wrong too. God, I hope not. If we can just pin down Mr White's identity, then it'll be a major breakthrough.

I look up. I'm aware that Okeke is still talking to the guys at reception. There's a deep frown on his face. I resist the urge to join them. I can't hear what they're saying over the volume of bloody Ed Sheeran, but his face says it all. He's found something.

When Okeke eventually comes over I leap to my feet.

'What is it?'

'Nothing,' he says in a flat voice.

He won't look me in the eye. He strides out so fast, I have to run to catch up with him.

In the car, I say: 'You were talking to them for so long – what about?' He ignores me, his eyes on the road, his hand shifting the gearstick in jerky, angry swerves. Finally I give up, fold my arms and sit in a sulk. We're supposed to be a team, working the case together. Why would he hide something from me? I recall my dad telling me how ambitious Okeke is.

'Look,' I say, as he pulls up near my house. 'If you want a promotion, and you want to be the one to tell the force – fine. I'll keep it secret.'

Okeke flinches and gives me a wide-eyed look. 'It's not that . . . it's just – nothing. Go to bed, we'll talk in the morning.'

I sit in his car for five more minutes, whilst he fobs me off with monosyllables, before I give up and storm off, slamming the door behind me.

Chapter 46

Carolina

Okeke, please tell me what u know. We have to work together, C. It's the fifth text I've sent him since last night. Maybe I'm being too pushy. Maybe I need to give him more space and then he'll come to me.

It's a Saturday. I just tried to have a nap but I'm too hyper. I get up and pull on my DMs. Then I make a decision: I will go to the Hotel du Vin myself. I might not have a police badge or a warrant or anything except my charms – if indeed, I have any charms to speak of. I hesitate, wondering if I really can sweet-talk a member of staff into telling me anything. Well, if I'm going to become a detective, I need to develop those skills, so I may as well give it my best shot.

I check the journey on Google maps. The train, bus, bus and walk is going to take me at least two hours. I stuff a spare jumper into my rucksack, along with my notebook. Dad's in his study, as usual. I open the front door and step out onto the garden path. A flashing light blinds my eyes. There's a small crowd at the front gate. I swing in confusion. Who are all these people? One leans in, trying to shove a mike in my face. The gate squeaks forward. A few slip onto the lawn. That's trespassing, I try to say, but my voice is lost. They're asking me questions. About Eva. My dad. I back up, open the front door and just manage to slam it shut. I stand in the hall, back against the door.

Dad is in the hallway, looking anxiously through the window, though all we can see through the mottled glass are ominous shapes. He says: 'I think it's better that we face them together, Carolina.'

'What?' My mobile's in my pocket and I became aware that it's vibrating non-stop, with a barrage of texts.

'Come on.' Dad guides me to one side so he can open the front door. 'We'll face them down, then they'll go. Otherwise they'll be here all afternoon.' His voice is cool and matter-of-fact, as though we're negotiating with a salesman.

'But – I don't get – what?'

'I'll do all the talking. Just be by my side.' Dad opens the front door and the noise hits us again.

The press have gathered on the lawn. Someone shouts: 'When did your relationship with Eva begin, Detective Inspector?'

'Okay,' Dad says. 'I'll just say a few words. That's all. This is my statement.'

He puts his arm around me. I feel as though I'm floating above myself in confusion. Dad is never tactile; I nearly shrink away from him.

'Eva Pieachowski was a school friend of my daughter Carolina. I can assure you that my relationship with her was *never* inappropriate. Since her tragic death last month, I – and the rest of the Metropolitan Police Service – have dedicated our lives to finding her killer. The diary that you have in your possession is a fake, a fabrication, and I will be seeking legal representation regarding the lies that are appearing in press articles online. I have nothing more to say on this matter.'

I know I'm doing a good impression of a goldfish now. Dad rests his hand on my shoulder, squeezes. His smile is manic.

'Dad,' I hiss.

'Keep smiling,' he hisses back.

The press aren't satisfied. They fling questions at us like stones:

'But the handwriting in the diary has been verified—'

'Have Eva's parents been in touch with you?'

'Carolina – did you know about your father's affair with Eva Pieachowski?'

'ENOUGH!' Dad guides me towards the door. A photographer leaps in front of us, his camera flashes, Dad roars, pushes him, and then we're through the door, Dad slams it shut and the noise is muted.

I turn to him in shock.

'Dad! What the hell's going on?'

227

Chapter 47

Eva's Diary: 10 September 2016

A few weeks later, my plan finally came to fruition.

One evening, I was surfing on Facebook when I saw a link to an article. It was about the burglars who'd been targeting Wimbledon Village; some arrests had been made. The article said that DI Jackson had led the investigation. The photo of him was so sexy that I Googled him and even saved a few photos in my pics folder.

Then, by chance, I was walking down the corridor at school with Siobhan when we spotted Carolina. We were quietly taking the piss out of her and Siobhan said: 'It's hard to believe her dad is that DI.' And I was like, what? Suddenly everything clicked. It felt like fate had smiled on me.

The next weekend I followed Carolina. She was

going to the woods, her weekly birdspotting trip. It was funny, watching her; she walked with hunched shoulders, as though she was perpetually walking against the force of a fierce wind. I pretended to bump into her just as she was trying to photograph the lesser spotted warbler or whatever. To be honest it was pretty clumsy, but she seemed grateful to have my company.

Easy as that. Over the next few weeks, I kept popping over to her house for homework sessions. It wasn't much of a chore, to be honest. Doing homework with Siobhan is hard, cos she always gets restless, puts on music or shows me her Instagram. I could sit at Carolina's table in companionable silence and indulge my geeky side. I even felt a bit embarrassed by insisting we had to keep our friendship a secret. She wasn't as bad as everyone said, but it would've been social suicide to tell anyone.

The problem was, DI Jackson was never bloody in. Carolina said he was the biggest workaholic. I was beginning to get fed up when I came up with a plan. I was meant to be meeting Luke one Saturday but I sent him a text crying off with a period/headache and went over to Carolina's house instead. I knew she'd be out birdspotting.

I rang the bell and there was no answer. I couldn't believe how bad my butterflies were. I wondered if I'd

ever been this nervous in my entire life. I rang again
and I was just about to give up when he answered.

I thought he'd recognise me after the reckless
driving, but if he did, he certainly didn't show it. At the
very least, I hoped he might notice my outfit. On my
walk over, I'd had boys catcalling, wolf-whistling and
honking their horns all the way. But he merely sighed
and said Carolina wouldn't be back for an hour and
wasn't I expected later?

'I really need to chat to her about a homework thing.
Could I wait in the kitchen or something?'

He sighed again and muttered: 'OK.'

He didn't even offer me a cup of tea. Just left me
in the kitchen and went off into his study, which was
next door. I sat there for fifteen minutes, willing him
to come out, even if just to go to the loo. But: silence.
I very nearly chickened out at this point, but I forced
myself to get up, to go to his study door and knock. No
answer. I sidled in.

'Can I take a look at your gun?' I asked.

When I saw his shocked expression, I felt
triumphant. Now he was paying attention.

'I mean, all cops have a gun, don't they?' I said. 'I'm
just desperately curious.'

All of a sudden, he noticed me. I saw it happening –
he took me in, cool, discerning, intrigued. I felt a surge
of confidence.

'Didn't I once pick up your boyfriend for reckless driving?'

Oh. That's why he was looking me over. My confidence waned. 'Um, yeah, that's kind of embarrassing ... I mean, he's not my boyfriend now. I was just hanging out with the wrong crowd then.'

'It's probably best that you steer clear of him,' Jackson agreed.

'So, can I?' I insisted. 'See your gun?'

He frowned, then unlocked a drawer in his desk and took out a black pistol. He stood up and I came a little closer, trying to hide the excitement trembling all over me.

'Carolina likes looking at it as well,' he said. It was the first time I'd ever seen him smile, and he looked so different. It was another shade of sexiness; he was no longer a dangerous black panther but playful, his eyes crinkled and sparkling.

'This is where you put the bullets in.' He showed me the empty chamber.

'Will you show me how to shoot it?' I said. I was about to add that I was joking, because he looked so very stern, when he cut in:

'You ever seen someone who's actually been shot by a bullet? Who doesn't just get up like they do in the movies, but ends up in a wheelchair, disabled for life?'

I felt sheepish.

'Hey,' he said. 'Sorry if I'm being too heavy. I see kids who carry knives in to school for a laugh. Their innocence is so dangerous. They get themselves in a fight which would normally have just been a tiff and then in the heat of the moment ... ' He trailed off, looking sad. 'I've seen lives ruined.'

I felt then that DI Jackson could never be indifferent about anything. Suddenly I was overwhelmed. I reached for the gun and I deliberately let my hand brush against his. He jumped, gave me a strong look, then quickly put the gun back in his top drawer and locked it. He stood there, staring at the desk, his hand still in his pocket where he'd lodged the key. The tension in the room was palpable. He could feel it too, what was happening between us, but he didn't know how to handle it. I waited. Minutes passed and he just stood there. So I went to him.

I curled my arms around him and pressed my lips to his. For one nerve-racking moment he didn't respond. His lips remained a thin line. Then he groaned, a visceral sound that thrilled right through me, and his hands were in my hair and he was kissing me like he wanted to devour me. His aftershave was subtle, expensive, not like the cheap stuff Luke slapped on. His stubble was harsh on my cheek. I had never felt so turned on by a kiss before ... but I was a bit shocked when he ran his hands over my body. It was our first kiss and it seemed so forward compared to the boys at school. I thought: how far is he going to go? What if he wants to have sex, here, over the desk? It was a bit like being in the middle of a Dare. Half of you wants to run and half of you wants to play and the coin of emotion tosses over and over. I knew I had a right to say no, but I wasn't sure if I wanted him to stop. I felt like a girl and a woman all at once—

Then he pulled away. He was breathing hard and he gave me a stern look and said: 'Is this even legal?'

'I'm seventeen,' I said incredulously, but I felt like a kid. I wanted him to see that I wasn't some silly teen, that I was so much more than that.

'I'm too old for you,' he said. 'What would your dad think of this?' And he gave a funny, sad laugh.

'I like older men,' I burst out.

He laughed again, but now I felt that he was mocking me. He shook his head.

'You want to try new things out. I was the same at your age. You want experience but, I don't know, maybe innocence is worth more.'

'I'm already experienced,' I cried, and then bit my lip, wondering if I should pretend I was a virgin.

He frowned. I sidled up to him again and he put a hand on my wrist, like a cuff, warning me to stop. I did something very full-on then. I put my hand right on the front of his trousers; I could feel him responding against me. He gave me a look that was appalled but thrilled. Then we were kissing again – and parting too quick. There was a sound in the hallway. He hurried out.

'Carolina!'

'Hey.' She blinked when she saw me come out of his study, but she was so pleased to see me that she didn't pick up on anything.

We did our homework. Her dad went back into his study, but not before he'd given me a look that blew me away in its intensity. I interpreted it as: to be continued. When Carolina went off to the loo, I grabbed her phone, scrolled down her meagre list of contacts, found DAD and stole his number.

I texted him that night. No reply.

I texted him again the next, even though I was on a date with Luke. I made an excuse, went to the bathroom, texted him and prayed.

I texted him every day for a week. Each time I felt more foolish and more reckless; it was like, I've embarrassed myself so much now I may as well just carry on. Finally, at midnight, the buzz of my phone under my pillow brought his reply:

> Please don't text me. This isn't appropriate now, is it? Thank you for your respectful co-operation.

Fuck. *Respectful co-operation?* I lay back in my bed, feeling punched in the stomach. Tears filled my eyes. Shame, anger, disappointment, self-hatred. I stared through the gap in the curtains at the smile of the half-moon. I reminded myself of our kiss and I remembered his groan and I thought, *I am not going to give up.* He wants me, I want him – and I'm going to get him, one way or another.

Chapter 48

Siobhan

When Sebastian says he's going to drop by on Saturday afternoon, I'm convinced he'll cancel at the last minute. It would be just like him. After last time, when we had that amazing kissing session in my bedroom, he's regularly texted me saying **I want to see u again**, but then when I reply asking **when**, he ignores me. I guess he lives a long way away, over in Esher, and it's a hike to come here.

So I try not to get excited about seeing him, but my body doesn't listen. My stomach is all skippy. My parents have been planning a trip into town to buy some new curtains and they were amused when I asked if they could go this afternoon. I showed Mum a pic of Sebastian on my phone and she got it in an instant. 'He's a looker, Siobhan!' I sit in the living room and wonder which way things will go. Heads: charming, sexy Sebastian. Tails: moody Sebastian. I have some good news to tell him – my vlog is doing so well now that an agent has approached me about a possible book. My parents are so proud, and I'm hoping Sebastian will be impressed.

When I hear the bell, I jump up, breathe out slowly and then stroll to the door.

It looks good: he's smiling and his eyes are bright. Before I can even tell him about my vlog, he says: 'Have you seen the news?'

'No – why?' I smile as he leans in to kiss my cheek.

'Aren't you going to offer me a drink?' he demands, taking off his coat and coming in.

'I was just about to.' I roll my eyes and go and get him his favourite lemonade but he says he wanted a Pepsi. So I go and get him his Pepsi, feeling fed up now, but when I pass him the drink, he gives me a soft kiss and my irritation melts away. He pulls me onto his lap and passes me his iPhone.

'Look!' he says.

So I look at the article from *The Times*.

DETECTIVE WAS LOVER OF MURDERED GIRL.

I nearly drop the phone in shock.

I swear out loud.

I swear out loud again.

Sebastian laughs, his face suddenly boyish and soft.

'They're making it up!'

'But Eva told you she had an older guy.'

'Shit! You really think it was Jackson? But how did they ever even meet . . . Oh.' And just like that it all falls into place.

I get up from his lap, my mind burning, and I pace the rug. 'So *that's* why Eva became friends with Carolina. I never got it, but now ... She must have done it to get to Jackson. She had a plan all along.'

Sebastian is acting odd: he keeps breaking into giggles, as though he thinks the whole thing is really funny.

'But ... Luke ... what if Jackson just pinned the whole thing on him?'

'He could have,' Sebastian chuckles. 'I mean, they were love rivals, right?'

'Or this could all be bullshit,' I say, looking at the link once again. 'After all, it says here that the story did break in the *Daily Mail*. I mean, it was only last month that they were saying Eva had been secretly planning a sex change and her dad made them print an apology.'

Suddenly Sebastian sobers up. 'Well, they have a sample from her diary.'

'That explains it!' I shout. 'It was stolen from my locker! I mean, Eva asked me to look after her diary for a bit, to keep it safe, so I stashed it in there. It must have been taken by a journalist.'

'That figures,' he agrees. 'They must have had the hand-writing checked and verified properly. They'd be sued to hell if not.'

'Yes.' I sink down into my armchair, sucked in by the old brown leather. I feel raw with grief again. I think of my best friend, sneaking into a hotel room with Jackson, him taking sleazy advantage of her. Why couldn't she tell me? A dark thought crosses my mind: maybe Carolina and Jackson groomed Eva together, invited her over, set up a seduction, lured her in. I've got to know Carolina recently and she's much more together than I'd ever realised. She might be a geek but she has her own quiet energy, a kind of outsider's charisma. *I'm so sorry Eva. You should have told me. I should have made you.*

'Jackson was so nice to me!' Each time a revelation hits, a violent fizz of shock surges through me. 'I mean, when I went in to tell him about Eva's older man, he didn't give a thing away. Man, that guy is such a creep.'

'He'll be fired,' says Sebastian, downing his Pepsi.

'Maybe Luke will be freed. Maybe they'll restart the investigation.'

Sebastian frowns. 'Maybe,' he says. 'But I'm pretty sure Luke did it. I saw him at Rob's party.'

'You were there?'

'You invited me!' he says in exasperation. He makes a twisty 'You're mental' sign with his finger against his temple and adopts a singsong: 'Someone's been smoking too much po-ot.'

'Okay, that's enough. I left the party early cos I was feeling ill. You probably came after me.'

'Well, then. Anyway, Luke was watching Eva all night, like he owned her. If she so said so much as two words to another guy, he looked like he might hit him. The thing was, you could *tell* he didn't have her. He was trying so hard, but she was a free spirit. He was going to either have her or kill her.'

Sebastian goes quiet after that, doodling on the notepad Mum keeps on the table for To Do Lists. *Oh Eva*. I look at her photo on my phone and her smile seems as impenetrable as the Mona Lisa. Suddenly I feel like I'm drowning in loneliness. Maybe I'm delusional; maybe Carolina *was* her best friend. After all, when we went to see Mrs Lambert, Eva's spirit never once mentioned Jackson.

'Sebastian, d'you think we should try to contact Eva again?'

He raises an eyebrow and I blush, worried it sounds like a come-on after what happened last time. As much as I want his kisses, Eva is more important right now. 'We didn't do it properly last time ...'

'I'm really sorry,' he says, getting up, 'I have to go. I have to see my mum, she's sick at the moment.'

'Oh, right.' I'm taken aback, cos Sebastian never mentions his family or friends to me; he's cagey like that. 'She's like got the flu?'

Sebastian ignores the question. 'You know, when I was a kid, my grandfather died, and for a few nights after, I'd wake up in the night and hear a tapping noise. He was into Morse code, he'd taught me a bit, and when I listened to the taps I realised that he was saying goodbye to me. I think that if Eva is going to get in contact with you, she'll find a way.'

I'm touched by his confession; I've never heard Sebastian open up like this before.

For a moment, I'm scared that he's humouring me, but he leans in and gives me a tender kiss goodbye.

After he's gone, I sit out on my patio and smoke a cigarette, watching smoke slowly curl towards the silhouettes of the trees at the bottom of my garden. *I'll never forget you, Eva*, I assure her. *I'll always think of you, every day. I hate Jackson. How can we know if anything he's done in this investigation is even legit? What if he planted evidence? What if he ignored things? What if he—*

Then I realise.

Oh God, Eva.

Was it—?

I mean, did he—?

Did Jackson pin all this on Luke because he wanted to cover things up?

Was Jackson the one who killed you, Eva?

Chapter 49

Carolina

> St Martin's
> *Independent School*

I stare at the sign. I've passed it countless times on my way in and out but I've never entered these gates feeling quite so nervous before.

Outside school, I feel powerful: a detective, making things happen, fitting together puzzle pieces. Back here, I feel more and more lost. As I enter the class for registration, everyone falls silent. Twenty pairs of eyes fix on me as I go to my seat. My face is the colour of a rosebush by the time I sit down. I pull out my Chemistry textbook and pretend to be engrossed.

The first catcalls start – *'Your Dad's a sleazy peedy ...'* etc. as though we're back in primary school, for God's sake. I just keep my head down.

Rivka walks in. I look up, knowing she'll come and sit

next to me. Instead, she walks right past me and sits down by Siobhan. I turn to look at them, and suffer twin glares.

Then Siobhan starts to sing 'What I've Done' by Linkin Park. They keep looking over, waiting for me to react. I refuse to give them the satisfaction. I've spent enough years putting up with this; I know how to retreat deep inside. But my heart is breaking to feel it happening all over again.

Where's Mr Abdul? It's almost nine. Why, today of all days, does he have to be late for register? If Rob was here, he'd stick up for me and tell the girls to back off, but his seat is empty; maybe he's off sick.

I feel something hard hit my shoulder. Rivka has thrown a pen at me. Next, a rubber goes flying off my cheek. Laughter from the others. Everyone waiting to see when I'll snap. I keep on staring at my textbook, the words *Bunsen burner* huge before my eyes. Then something white and wet splatters across me and I jump up in shock. Rivka has tossed her Tipp-ex at me. The lid isn't screwed on it properly – half the bottle has glooped over my arm, across my jeans and the rest on the floor in a pool.

'Oops,' Rivka says, mock-repressing a laugh.

Enough.

I leave the room to the sound of the whole class jeering. My white footsteps stain a trail through the corridor. In the playground, I walk at a furious pace.

Why didn't I just turn around and tell them where to go? Why didn't I defend Dad? Why didn't I tell them it this was all bullshit – Dad's exact word? He swears so rarely around me that I felt relieved by the strength of his assertion. He said the so-called journalists were bastards who had built him up and now they wanted to knock him down. It was just a weekend's gossip for them, but for him the damage might never be undone.

He managed to get rid of the press pack at the weekend by calling DS Hutton. She came over from the station and threatened to arrest them all for trespassing, and my dad reiterated that he would take legal action. Finally, they trailed off. DS Hutton came in for coffee. She told Dad that the constabulary were behind him and nobody believed the slander. She kept patting him on the shoulder.

'Carolina,' she said, 'you've got to be strong for your dad.'

I cooked his favourite veggie shepherd's pie for dinner. We ate it in silence.

I desperately want to believe Dad, but I can't help thinking about Eva. How sudden our friendship was, how she just happened to be in the woods that day. How I'd turn up at my house to find Eva was already there, early, chatting to Dad. Then there were those nights that Dad was away, staying in hotels, saying it was for work. Did I sense that Eva was attracted to him? Of course. I'm not stupid – anyone can pick these things up easily enough – but it didn't seem a problem at the time. I know he's attractive. He's always had women's attention. I noticed it even more after Mum died ... I felt weirdly proud that she found him handsome.

I never thought that anything would actually *happen* between them—

I hear myself moan.

How *could* he? I think of the photo that sits on the desk in his study, the one of him and Mum with their arms around each other. For years I've been scared that I might end up with a wicked stepmother. To my relief, no matter how many women flutter around him, he's never shown any interest. I always thought this was because he was still in love with Mum, a love that ran so deep he'd die a widower. But – *Eva?* A *seventeen-year-old?* A girl *my age?* That practically makes my dad a peedy, a disgusting, lying, cheating peedy.

I think I know now why Okeke suddenly clammed up in the Hotel du Vin. I think he *did* find out who Mr White was – and he couldn't face telling me the truth. I think it's why he's ignoring my texts now. He's shellshocked.

And what the hell am I going to say to Luke?

I'm in love with him. I don't understand how or why it happened. It just did. I guess it springs from an affinity – he's an outsider too, someone who doesn't fit in, who's nervous in a group. The letters he's sent me have revealed a guy who is so funny, clever and kind. He is also a very good kisser. That makes me blush. He said in one of his letters that when he gets out he wants to make love to me, *with the sun and the sky bright above us.* I've read that line about fifty times now and it still makes me shiver. I've told him things in my letters that I've never told anyone. We've both scribbled down plans about what we'll do if he gets out. How we'll go travelling next summer, backpack around Europe, sleep under the stars, adventure together.

But is it all over now? How can Luke ever feel the same way about me? Surely he'll never forgive this?

I hate my dad. I hate him.

Sleazy peedy.

I'm just storming out of the school gates and onto the main road, when I see Mr Abdul's car.

I stop short. The girl with the blonde hair is in the passenger seat next to him. They're arguing vehemently. I step closer and she lifts her hand to sweep her hair back from her face. I see a tattoo, clearly visible, on her wrist; a little stencil, like a *Z* or an *S*, just as Siobhan described.

It is *the girl who Siobhan saw in the woods.*

Oh my God.

I raise my phone to snap a pic when a horn sounds loudly. Mr Abdul is slowing down and the car behind him, a red sports car, honks impatiently—

Mr Abdul looks up, spots me, and there's a panicked look in his eyes—

I take the photo—

The blonde girl tugs his sleeve—

The sports car swerves around them and—

.Oh God.

The sound of Abdul's car hitting the wrought-iron post of our school gates. The shimmer of flying glass, an arc of shards raining across the road. The metallic screech as the car slides back along the tarmac, as if clawing hold for dear life. The crunch as the rear of the car crashes into the wooden school sign by the entrance, mutilating the italic swirl of the words *St Martin's*. The sign collapses onto the roof and then come the soft noises of aftermath, of tinkling and of steam and hissing. I run over to the car. Mr Abdul has been flung against the steering wheel and blood is pouring down his face. The blonde girl is whimpering; her pale hair is decorated with red flowers.

I find my fingers tapping my phone and my breath sharp in my ears.

'Police, ambulance or fire?'

Chapter 50

Eva's Diary: 11 September 2016

How to get him? Jackson was all I thought of, day and night. Things with Luke were becoming unbearable. I guess I was playing a coward's game – the thought of dumping him felt so daunting that I tried to provoke him into dumping me first. I kept making excuses to not see him. I had my period about three times in the space of one month. The trouble was, he didn't react like a normal guy would and play it cool. If he texted and I ignored him, he would just send me 6 more texts. When I did eventually try to break up with him, he insisted that I should feel assured of his loyalty and devotion, and that we were destined to marry. For the time being, it was just easier to go along with him.

Then one night we went to a party and on the way back, Luke pulled up on a random street and tried to kiss me. I closed my eyes and pretended he was Jackson, but I couldn't sustain the fantasy. I felt angry when Luke ran his hands through my hair, a sad echo of how it had been with Jackson. My body only wanted Jackson's touch.

Siobhan was always going on about signs and destiny, and most of the time I was dubious. But when I looked out of the window and saw the man himself, coming out of the newsagents opposite and climbing into his police car, it seemed as though I'd somehow conjured him there by the sheer force of my will. *Look at me, look at me*, I thought desperately, but he just drove away.

I was overwhelmed with yearning. I looked at Luke. I couldn't be angry with him any more – all I felt was compassion. He felt about me the way I felt about Jackson. I realised how hard it must be for him. But I thought that this had to be a sign. Jackson and I were going to happen.

That's when I had the idea.

I was sitting in Starbucks one evening. Siobhan had stood me up, the scatty moo; she was so disorganised these days. Then I happened to notice that her so-called boyfriend was sitting at a nearby table. Over the last few weeks, Siobhan had been hoping to introduce him to our gang, but he always stood her up at the last minute. Now I knew why the willowy girl standing behind the till looked familiar – she was his sister. She'd dyed her hair again; this time it was vivid tomato.

Sebastian put down his latte and blew his sister a kiss. She smiled back shyly. It all seemed a bit creepy to me. Then he noticed me and his face darkened. He got up and came over.

'Hey, you're that girl from the party, aren't you? You threw water all over my sister, didn't you?'

'No,' I replied quickly.

He stared at me. He really was very handsome; amazing bone structure and his slate-grey eyes. I could see why Siobhan had fallen for him.

'I think it was you,' he insisted. 'I think you're a liar. Hey, maybe I should just throw my latte at you now. Wouldn't that be funny?'

'Don't be such a jerk. You've confused me with someone else,' I said. I felt annoyed and bewildered too, as guys normally fall for my charms.

Sebastian sauntered back over to his table, where his sister was hovering with a panini. He gave her a radiant smile, turned his back on me and then started to eat.

I sat there, cross and unsettled. Then it came to me. Wouldn't Siobhan call this a destined opportunity? I went into the toilets and I called up DI Jackson. He was a bit suspicious at first, but then I faked tears, sobbed that I was terrified and in danger, and he promised he'd be right over.

When I came out of the bathroom, Sebastian was still shooting me obnoxious glances whilst he chewed his way through his snack. He even held up his phone and snapped a few pics of me, so I picked up my phone and snapped a few back. He looked taken aback at that.

I didn't even care this time if Siobhan was upset. She deserved so much better than this loser.

You should have seen the look on his face when Jackson came striding in with another, younger, man in uniform.

'Where's the guy?' Jackson put a hand on my shoulder and I was electrified by his touch. 'You OK?'

I nodded and pointed at Sebastian, who was wiping his mouth with a napkin. He protested when they approached him, of course, but Jackson was so cool. He didn't bat an eyelid, just informed Sebastian that an accusation had been made against him and he needed to come to the station immediately, to be questioned. Then he told me I should travel with him. In the car, I felt weak being next to Jackson. I tried to speak but he put up his hand, said we should wait until we got to the station and follow official procedure.

It was only at the police station, sitting in an interview room, that I began to panic. DI Jackson

went off and the other cop, a young spotty guy, made
me a cup of tea and said I had to make a statement. I
thought, this has gone too far. I told him that Sebastian
had been trying to blackmail me about a video that
had nothing to do with me, hyping it up to the point
where I had felt threatened. The cop frowned and asked
me when the actual assault had taken place. I chewed
my lip and said Sebastian had tried it on with me,
and I'd fobbed him off, so it wasn't *an actual assault*
as such ... The cop pointed out that we'd been in a
public place. I said Sebastian had followed me into the
toilets – then I shook my head. I said I wanted to drop
the charges, that I was so traumatised by what had
happened that I was confused.

The policeman stood up and gave me a long look. He
said he'd speak to DI Jackson.

I waited and waited. My palms were damp; I could
feel sweat around my scarlet nails. I thought of all the
ways I could play this. I could start crying and say
they weren't taking me seriously. I could get cross, say
I wanted to call my father and accuse the young cop of
negligence. Either way I'd been stupid. I shouldn't have
exaggerated so wildly, nor lied so recklessly. I should
have just kept it real – but then Jackson would never
have come to the rescue.

Finally, he entered. I looked at him defiantly,
steeling myself.

'We let Sebastian Banks go,' he said. 'I'll give you a lift home.'

In the car, Jackson gave me an icy glance and then: 'What kind of bullshit are you trying to pull?'

'Oh my God, that's sooo unfair. I'm the victim here, you could get into serious trouble for undermining my story and–'

'Listen. I've dealt with real victims of abuse and I know what's what. We both know what this is about, Eva. I'm not stupid. You wanted my attention and so you acted like a three-year-old and made up a story. Has it occurred to you that while you waste my time with tall tales, there are real crimes going on? While we're busy dealing with you, there's a burglary or an assault that we miss?'

I felt completely crushed. 'I'm sorry,' I said weakly. Tears began to slide down my cheeks and I wasn't faking. I realised how selfish I'd been, so wrapped up in it all that I hadn't stopped to think things through. I wanted to fling my arms around his neck and beg forgiveness, but that would be pathetic.

He turned into my road. I was dreading what my parents would say. I was sure he would want to tell them, but he pulled up at the row of evergreens (ironically, the very place where Luke normally waited for me), and said more gently: 'I'll drop you off here, okay?'

'Okay,' I said meekly. 'Thank you.'

'And no more games. You promise? You'll end up with a record.'

I nodded, unable to look at him. 'I'm sorry. I promise, I swear, I won't ever do it again. I know I went too far, I know it was dumb. I was just so desperate to see you again. But I'll leave you alone.'

He reached out and clasped my face in his hands, gently wiping away my tears with his thumbs. I looked at him then, through the blur, my heart thumping.

'You're a very beautiful girl,' he said.

'Please,' I whispered. 'Please just kiss me one more time.'

He leaned in and gave me a very gentle kiss – but broke off before it could deepen. I crumpled inside, fearing it was much too fatherly for my liking. He carried on stroking my hair, though, and I felt comforted; he stared into the distance, as though he was thinking very hard, or struggling with himself. Then he said: 'I want to trust you Eva, but it's hard. If we do this, how could I know you wouldn't just go and tell your friends? I'm a man who the whole community looks up to, you understand? And I do take my job very seriously. How could I know?' He looked despairing. 'I'm a fool. Every man who's ever been here has come undone.'

'Oh, but I would keep it secret, I swear I would,' I

said. I reached out, wanting to kiss his mouth, but he was still staring at the distance, so I ran a stream of little kisses across his cheek and down to his neck. He groaned and pushed me away.

'It will be on my terms. I'll text you the time and place,' he said. 'A hotel. You'll do exactly as I say and you won't tell a soul. Agreed?'

'Okay.' I blinked, shocked. There, just like that, I had him.

Chapter 51

Luke

Dear Luke,

This is the third letter I've sent in the last ten days. I hope they've been reaching you.

I just wanted to say, once more, please don't be mad at me or Dad. I know it must be tough for you, with all this new coverage, but the press are printing lies. They just want to keep writing about Eva. They know the story sells so they'll find whatever they can to spin it out until something better comes along. The best scoop will be the one that reveals your innocence when the real killer has been caught.

Mr Abdul is in St Anthony's hospital, just twenty miles away. I can't go and see him yet, because he's only allowed visits from friends and family. As far as I know, the girl who was with him wasn't seriously injured. I called the hospital to find out her name and was given a short lecture about patient confidentiality. One thought consoles me: this story is bound to turn up in the local paper, any day now, and I'm certain they'll mention her by name. Then I can speak to her and see what she knows.

I don't have DC Okeke on my side anymore. He's not responding to my texts. So I'm on my own now but I'm not giving up. I'm still searching for the guy on the CCTV camera.

You know you asked me, a while ago, where I'd like to go if we went travelling together? Well, I've found a place. I really want to go to the Outer Hebrides, the islands on the West of Scotland. The population is tiny and you can see the most amazing birds, like kestrels and falcons, and the Whooper Swan. It sounds like paradise to me.

Love, Carolina X

I read her letter over once more and feel a sob rise in my chest. Then the anger erupts, and I rip it into shreds, scattering them across my cell floor.

Chapter 52

Carolina

I'm on my way over to Rob's house tonight. He's been my guardian angel recently. Thanks to him, things are much better at school. He's the only one who's had my back. Yesterday Siobhan produced a big Get Well Soon card for Mr Abdul for everyone to sign. Rob told her in no uncertain terms that I should be allowed to sign it too – 'She was the one who saved the day and called for the ambulance.' Though Siobhan looked sulky, she agreed. It hasn't changed my 'unfriended' status on Facebook, though.

When Rob sent a text:

want to come over tonite and chill? X

I jumped at the chance. Home's a nightmare at the moment because Dad is so bad-tempered. Last night he had a massive go at me for nothing – for getting a tiny smudge of mud on the carpet after I came in. I was nearly in tears, he was so cross. Then he rubbed my arm and said sorry, something about stress, it would all blow over soon. I know his colleagues are standing by him now, but I'm scared that they'll lose faith any day and fire him. Dad has asserted that the diary is a fake; he's even hired a lawyer to defend him and threaten the tabloids with libel. Some of the more serious newspapers have taken his side, pointed to my dad's great track record, and said it's all a terrible smear. I write letters to Luke that assert his innocence, but deep down, I'm haunted by uncertainty. I keep thinking: *If – IF – if it is true, then maybe it wasn't his fault.* Eva loved male attention, so maybe he resisted her and she got frustrated. Maybe she tricked him into going to the Hotel du Vin; maybe they just met for a drink and it got late and he booked a room and ... Oh God.

Now, sitting on the bus, I try to forget about Dad and focus on my detective work. I'll visit Mr Abdul next week and then there's the CCTV suspect. Despite flitting through a thousand Facebook profiles, I've still not found a lead.

Rob lives in a fancy house not far from where Eva used to live. As I climb the stairs to his bedroom, I can't help imagining her and Luke walking up the same staircase, hand in hand. I glance into the hallway and picture them in a dark corner, sharing secret kisses. The image hurts and I push it away. I get so mixed up about Eva. I still feel broken by her death, yet sometimes I hate her because I'm scared Luke's still in love with her ghost. And I can't bear to think that she just used me to get to Dad. A part of me even feels triumphant that I've stolen her boyfriend – isn't that petty?

Hanging out with Rob is making me feel much better. We're up in his bedroom, sitting on his bed, Mozart playing in the background. It's only when I start to unwind that I realise how tense I've been these last few weeks . . .

Rob's avoiding the topic of my dad – thank goodness. Instead, we've been watching Siobhan's awful vlog. Rob mimics the one where she gives a guided tour of her wardrobe until I nearly cry with laughter. Then he sighs and says he misses Luke because this is just the sort of thing they'd do together.

'I feel really bad – I've not visited him in ages,' Rob says wistfully.

'You should go,' I say tentatively, because I know everyone's tired of me nagging them to visit.

'I know – I just – I'm going to be called up to the stand in that trial to testify as a witness. I'll have to say that yes, Luke did drink, yes he took drugs and yes, the way he behaved with Eva was pretty obsessive.'

I blush. Rob has no idea of what's gone on between me and Luke, of course.

'I just worry that Luke might try to – that he'll feel betrayed by me. I just feel our friendship has been wrecked. I can't win.'

He sighs. 'Luke and Eva and I, we used to make these videos all the time. We'd do our own remakes of famous scenes from movies. I still have some on my phone.'

'Show me,' I say.

He gives me the handset and I watch them act out *Reservoir Dogs*, all in black suits, waving plastic guns. Then another video starts. Eva, Luke and some others from school are in Rob's kitchen. There's a party in the background and Eva is making a cocktail. I'm struck by how fresh-faced Luke is, with his hair flopping over his forehead and his boyish grin. Prison has aged him by about ten years.

'Hey,' Rob cries, suddenly defensive. 'That video – it's kind of secret, I meant to delete it.'

'Wait, just let me see!' I spin away from him obstinately, watching more. My heart is beating very fast as I realise what I'm seeing. 'Rob – this is – you've done it – this guy!' I jab the phone. 'You've found the killer, now we can save Luke.'

I press PAUSE, freezing the video. Rob stares at me in bewilderment. 'What d'you mean?'

We sit down on his bed and I restart the film. I show him the blonde guy in the edge of the frame, sneering as he watches Eva.

'Him! He's the one who's on the CCTV tapes, who was near the woods too that night! I've got an enhanced image – and it's HIM!'

'What?' Rob looks bemused and euphoric at the same time. He reaches over, grabs his guitar and twangs a chord several

261

times, then thumps it back down on the bed. Then his face falls. 'Maybe you should see the other video.'

'Wait – do you know who this guy is?'

'Let me just show you this one too.' Rob is insistent now, as though he's been wanting to share this with someone for a while. He presses PLAY and passes me his phone. Picking up his guitar again, he plays whispers of songs, snatches of chords with the tips of his fingers as I watch. It was made the night that Eva died, Rob tells me. It's a film of Eva, Luke and Rob in the bathroom, enacting a scene from *Psycho* – *God, the timing is unfortunate*, I think. I wonder who made the film choice. I can't help noticing that Luke watches Eva with such love and lust in his eyes. *Obsessive*, Rob said. Does Luke ever look at me with that intensity?

'Please don't tell your dad, or any of the police,' Rob says. 'The only people in the world who know it exists are you, me and Luke.'

'Rob, it doesn't matter,' I reply, though I'm not as sure as I sound. 'Look, the video looks bad, but you were just messing around, weren't you?' *Weren't you?* 'I think you're right not to show it to anyone yet. They'd probably just twist it and take it all the wrong way.'

Rob looks bright with relief.

'I can't tell you how many sleepless nights I've had over that video,' he says. 'You've made me feel sooo much better.' And he lifts his hand. 'High five!'

I slap his palm and we both grin at each other.

'But you never answered my question. Who is the guy?'

'I think Siobhan might know him? He's definitely not from St M's,' Rob says. 'Or Rivka. I'll find out, I'll get you a name tonight.'

'That would be amazing. Maybe we *can* save Luke.'

I feel exhilarated. I don't even have to worry about that tattooed girl any more. This is it.

Rob gives me a tight hug goodbye. As I pull away, he pulls me back in for a double. I'm surprised, because I doubt I'm Rob's type; I feel a flicker of disloyalty. Rob is handsome, clever and kind, but no: I can't. Luke has taken a special place in my heart and there's no room for anyone else.

As I head out into the night, I realise time has flown. It's nearly nine o'clock – no wonder my stomach is grumbling. *I can't believe I've found him*. I check my mobile. My dad has sent me about six texts, demanding to know where I am and what to do about dinner.

I almost text **piss off** and then I stop myself. Instead, I save it to drafts and tell myself to calm down, but all the way home I argue with Dad in my head. I yell at him and accuse him, refusing to let him tell me off. *How dare you*, I shout and point out that I'm not a little girl and I'm tired of being his emotional punchbag.

Back home, I find Dad at kitchen table.

'Where were you?' he snarls.

'I was at a friend's.'

I go to the fridge and get a bag of carrots out and suddenly I can't stand it any longer, it's all been churning inside me, and I have to ask, I have to, and I turn and cry: 'You slept with her, didn't you? You did. You slept with Eva.'

'I – no,' he says, but I hear the uncertainty cracking open his voice.

I stare at him and he stares back. There is fear in his eyes; I turn away in shock. I peel and chop the carrots savagely. My Dad. And Eva. *Chop. Chop. Chop.* It's true. I know it's true.

I hear a noise and when I turn around, I realise that he's crying. I tell myself to go and give him a hug, but I have a sudden vision of Eva in his study, flirting with him whilst I was next door doing my homework, and such a sense of disgust comes over me that I can't bear to touch him. Instead I take the kettle and fill it with water. I make him a cup of tea, in his favourite owl mug, the one I bought him last Christmas. I add his three sugars and set it down next to him. When he wipes his eyes, he looks like a little boy.

I sit down.

'Carolina,' he says. 'I know it sounds bad. I can't tell the truth because I'll lose my job. But there is a little – there is some truth in the rumours ...'

I'm scared he's going to make a big confession. I want to know everything, but at the same time I don't want to know anything. I don't know if the day will ever come when I can cope with knowing the details.

'Dad, Luke is in jail,' I say.

'Because he's guilty!' Dad sets down his mug and the liquid spills onto the table. He is defiant. 'This changes nothing.'

'Of course it does! You always said to me, a good detective should be rational and stay unbiased!'

'I saw how that boy treated Eva. She turned up one time with bruises after they'd been "play fighting". He is violent and abusive and guilty as hell.'

I'm shocked by the emotion in his voice. What he says doesn't sound like Luke at all. Fleetingly, I think of the video Rob has on his phone, the way that Luke wielded the knife, all part of his game, but that *was* just playing.

'Dad,' I say, my voice very firm, 'you have to listen. My friend Rob just showed me a video that he made at his party. There was a boy in this video, at that party, who knew Eva. I recognised him – he's the same guy who showed up on the CCTV tapes that night. The guy you never bothered to properly identify. I know you said he wasn't important, but it's too much of a coincidence to pass over now. He knew Eva and he was passing so close to the woods that night. That has to mean something.'

I wait for him to argue with me but he doesn't. His conscience is troubling him. He looks washed out and defeated; suddenly he seems like he could be my grandfather. He says in a quiet voice: 'I'm certain we have the right man. But we could take another look ...'

Silence. I check my phone and see there's a new text from Rob. 'I have his name,' I say. 'He's called Sebastian, Sebastian Banks.'

Chapter 53

Astra

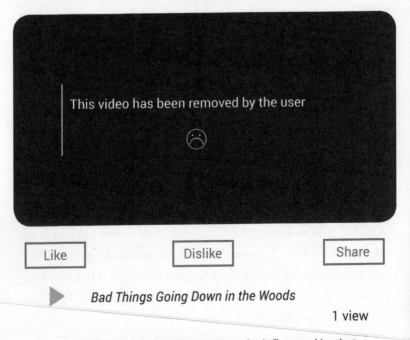

This video has been removed by the user

| Like | Dislike | Share |

▶ *Bad Things Going Down in the Woods*

1 view

Comment: Hey this film seems to be influenced by that Eva killing, it's kinda bad taste, don't u think?

I told him that the videos would be part of my film project but he said he'd kill me if I didn't take them down. Why can't anyone see what's staring them in the face? Why can't they see this is fact, not fiction?

Chapter 54

Eva's Diary: 18 September 2016

The first time DI Jackson and I met for a date, I was terrified. I dressed up in a new black dress and heels. I wanted to look as adult as possible, and when I walked into the lobby of the hotel, our secret meeting place, I was relieved when the receptionist treated me with polite respect. I went up to room 301 and there he was, sitting on the king-size bed, waiting for me. When I entered, he said: 'Wait!' I thought he was going to stop and search me or something, but he just sat there, savouring me, and I smiled, slowly drawing off my coat. He told me he'd ordered room service and poured me a glass of fancy wine.

'How was your day?' he asked, which made me want to laugh, because it was as though I was his wife or something.

We sipped wine and he asked me some questions about school and stuff. He pulled me onto his lap and stroked my lips with his fingers.

Then he went weird on me.

'Maybe this is a terrible mistake,' he said, swallowing. He looked as vulnerable as a kid, but I wanted him to be manly and strong again. 'Maybe we should stop, before it all ...'

And I thought: now? Now I'm sitting on your lap in a sexy dress, in a hotel room? So I said: 'I swear I will never tell anyone, I swear.' He stared at me all the while and I saw that look I loved return – that look of starry lust that made me feel beautiful, powerful, wanted. I realised I didn't need to say a word more. All I needed to do was lean over and kiss him.

Then all doubts were forgotten. All of a sudden, he got very frenzied, tearing off my clothes, unzipping his trousers, making love to me without even undressing. It was fast and furious and I was excited but overwhelmed. It was much nicer the second time, when he took it more slowly, touching me gently, tenderly, making me feel special. Afterwards, we lay in a sleepy haze and talked quietly. When I looked at him, he was imperfectly perfect – the deep lines around his eyes, the scars on his hairy chest, the slight sag of his stomach. Every inch of his body seemed hard with wisdom, with life experience. I gazed into his dark eyes and he leaned down and gave me an Eskimo kiss of affection.

'I think I'm falling in love with you,' I said.

A moment of weakness. I should've played hard to get. He looked a bit shocked.

We were saved by the buzz of my mobile. I'd been vaguely aware of it going off all evening but had been too engrossed to care. He said: 'Who the hell is texting you that much? Is your dad wondering where you are?' A look of guilt clouded his face.

'It's, um, Luke,' I said. 'The guy you arrested for reckless driving, the night we first met.'

That was a good move.

'That dick. I can't imagine why a girl like you would be hanging around with a guy like him. So, he's your boyfriend?'

'No, no,' I protested quickly. 'He's just a guy I went on a few dates with and now he's kind of obsessed with me.'

I felt a bit mean, given how devoted Luke was to me.

'Just cut him off. Don't take any nonsense,' DI Jackson said briskly.

He leaned in to kiss me.

'You've exhausted me already,' he said, his lips against mine, 'but I just can't stop wanting you.' I laughed in delight as he began to stroke me again.

In the morning, things went weird again. I wanted

to make love, but he pushed me away and got dressed. I felt him withdraw from me; felt my power was lost now that his lust was satisfied.

'If I find this all over Facebook later today, I'll kill you.'

I felt as though I was going to cry. He quickly softened and apologised, kissing me on the forehead. And I had to do the big *I swear, I swear, I swear I'll never tell a soul*, all over again.

On our third date at the hotel, he said I should call him Peter. But it felt too odd so I carried on with DI, for short, like a play name, and he seemed to find that amusing.

I wanted to see him every night but he was always working. We met every ten days or so. He wanted to keep me at a distance, which puzzled me because he was so eager whenever we did meet. I sensed he had trouble trusting me, but I had faith that it would come with time. He had to see that I wasn't some schoolgirl who'd blab all over the place.

Sometimes even a fortnight passed and I'd go mad with frustration and he'd text me something like: Patience is a virtue, Eva, like he was my dad. On the days we were due to meet, I found myself quivering, unable to concentrate in lessons. It was the way he looked at me when we were making love that got me; he would say: 'Keep your eyes open' and then he'd stare into me, searing my soul.

He said something that made me laugh too – 'They say Helen of Troy launched a thousand ships, but you'd launch a million, Eva. No, I'm serious. Look at me, look at what I'm doing, the risks I'm taking ...' He buried his face in my hands. 'I try to stop,' he whispered. 'Every time, I try to stop myself ...'

My heart was racing. How could he say that? Whenever I came out to see him, I was ravenous with anticipation.

'But I can't,' he continued. 'I can't stop. I can't. You're just so beautiful ... I'm hooked.'

And so we kept on meeting. Things got more and more intense. The trouble was, he rarely stayed the night. We'd have four or five hours together and then we'd leave the hotel separately. It was a weird kind of dating. I sometimes fantasised about us living together, but the thought of us in one bedroom and, well, Carolina in the next, like our daughter, felt odd. I found out he was fifty-two. 'So there's a thirty-five-year age gap between us,' he said, looking appalled. He frowned when I said age didn't matter.

He got funny if I ever mentioned the word love. He said we should just keep things secret and simple. He said that a lot. *Let's keep it simple, let's keep it as it is.* But I knew how much he loved me; I could see it in his eyes. Once or twice, after we had sex, he'd open up to me. He'd tell me about how stressful he found his job.

He told me he had a bad back from so much overwork –
I would massage it for him and he would look like he
was in heaven.

On one special night, he told me about his wife,
Mary. He wept tears as he confided that she'd died
of lung cancer five years ago. I was the first woman
he'd been with since. (I can hardly believe he's been a
monk for so long!) He told me he'd been feeling like a
dried husk, denying himself any love, any pleasure,
out of loyalty to his lost love – but he'd found me so
irresistible, he couldn't hold back.

We had a rule that if I came to his house to see
Carolina, I mustn't make the slightest slip. To be honest,
there wasn't really any need for me to be friends with
Carolina any more. When Siobhan found out I was
doing homework sessions with 'weird geek girl' as she
called her, she was incredulous. But I'd grown fond of
Carolina and I loved going over there on weekends,
writing an essay, knowing he was in the study next
door. Sometimes I'd hear him coughing or pacing about
and I'd have to bite back a smile.

Siobhan guessed I was in love; she knows me too
well. In the end, I told her I was seeing an older guy but
I refused to say more, no matter how much she begged
me. She was excited, but said I should dump Luke. I told
her I was trying. Siobhan didn't seem to quite get how
hard it was.

Chapter 55

DI Jackson

'Good luck today, Dad,' my daughter says, passing me a cup of morning coffee.

Is it my imagination, or is there a barb in her voice? She used to look up to me. Now I catch her watching me with guarded eyes. I've been knocked off my pedestal; I'm no longer the Perfect Dad, the Perfect Detective.

'You *will* interrogate Sebastian properly, won't you?' she asks.

'Of course I will,' I reply. 'That's my job!'

She rolls her eyes as she turns away, and I feel sadness fill me.

I head out to the car, put the key in the ignition. I dread the drive to work. I dread what might await me. I'm hanging on to my job by a thread. How long before the Superintendent calls me into her office for the last time ... How long can I survive? I have the sudden urge to rev up the engine, put my foot down on the accelerator and smash into a shopfront, accelerate my fall from grace in one glorious insane finale.

I knew from the very first moment I kissed Eva Pieachowski that she would be my downfall.

I thought I was in control of the situation.

As I've often warned Carolina, life is a game of chess. Talent, looks, intelligence, can only get you so far; it's the strategies you employ, the moves you make, that determine your course. From the moment Eva turned up in my study, asking to see my gun, I knew I wanted her. But I also knew I had to be very careful, think through every detail.

The first night we went to a hotel, before I laid a finger on her, I made sure that she deleted my number from her mobile (the little minx must have stolen it from Carolina). Then I gave her a new number – I'd bought a separate phone specifically for her texts and calls – and I made sure that she stored it against a fake name in her list of contacts. We chose the name Mr White. She sulked about it, but I kissed her and said it was necessary if she wanted me to open up to her.

Then there are the receipts for the hotels we visited. Fourteen nights in all. I tried to change the locations but the Hotel du Vin fast became her favourite place and I liked to indulge her. I made sure that we were never on the hotel CCTV together; we always went to the room separately, and we always left separately. In the week after her death, I was dreading that a member of the hotel staff might remember seeing her and come forward to the police, but nobody ever got in touch. Thinking about it, they probably never made the connection – Eva would always turn up to see me wearing provocative clothes and too much make-up; looking twenty-five not seventeen.

When Carolina asked me about my nights away, I said I was working. I always felt terrible, lying to my daughter. Those lies made me feel as though I was committing adultery; before I left the house, I would open the drawer in my study, take out the wedding ring and say a silent apology to Mary's memory ... But I wanted Eva so badly. She was a drug that I couldn't stop drinking; her beautiful body was all I thought of, night and day.

Most of us have two impulses ribboning through our personalities: the impulse to flourish and the impulse to destruct. Freud had some fancy names for those drives; I can't remember what he called them, but he was right that they exist. I see the darker urge in criminals, day in, day out. They steal and fight and graffiti and wreck lives not only to lash out at society, but also to hurt themselves. Often, they want to be locked away; they want to be punished. They are driven by self-destruction. Was it obsessive lust for Eva that drove me to start our affair, or was it some desire for punishment? Did I feel so disloyal to Mary, my former wife, that I wanted to be found out?

The agony of it all. Of having to wear a mask. Having to nod and comfort her parents with platitudes, watching them cry whilst I was biting my lip to stop my own tears flooding out. I wanted to keep the phone Eva messaged me on but I knew I had to get rid of it; I allowed myself the indulgence of listening to her beautiful voice just one last time before burning it and scattering the charcoaled remains between various bins.

From the start, I knew that Luke was guilty. Eva once turned up at the hotel room covered in bruises, saying she and Luke had been play-fighting. Every time I sat with him in those interrogations, I wanted to punch the daylights out of him. The way he kept changing his story, muttering, making up lies, swearing and stuttering. The sick bastard. It drove me mad that I never got a confession out of him.

Whatever happens now, at least I have one consolation. At least the right man is in prison. I can't believe this Sebastian lead will yield anything. We'll see.

Sebastian Banks sits opposite me in the interrogation room.

We pulled the kid out of an A-level History class at St Cuthbert's school. He was calm and polite; he agreed to a DNA test; but as he opened his mouth for a swab, I noticed a little twitch in the corner of his mouth. And it's still there now. For all his cool, the boy looks under pressure.

I knew he looked familiar. Hutton passed me a file this morning, noting that he'd previously been brought down to the police station. He's the boy Eva told me assaulted her, until she confessed she was making the whole thing up. No charges were made; in fact, we had to apologise to him that night. I don't believe it's a significant connection.

I had to fight to sit here in this seat. I'm no longer leading this investigation, but I'm still involved. Superintendent Birch argued that it might be best if I stepped to one side and let another officer interrogate Sebastian. I pointed out that the tabloid slander shouldn't prohibit my ability to do my job. I also pointed out that I was planning to sue the damn papers who fabricated the diary and printed lies (a fudge). Finally, she relented.

DC Okeke, Hutton and the rest of the team are watching through the one-way glass. Okeke muttered something about charging the wrong guy, and I reprimanded him sharply. After he went behind my back, tried to get my daughter involved in a sideline investigation, I am determined to erase all doubts in his mind. But, as I switch on the recorder, I note a faint tremble in the tips of my fingers.

And so it begins.

'So, Sebastian,' I ask. 'Can you tell us where you were on the twenty-third of September?'

Sebastian leans back in his chair. He's dressed in his posh school uniform: black trousers, white shirt, zebra tie.

'Yes, I was at Rob's party,' he replies in a cool, middle-class monotone. 'Eva was there. She spent the entire night with Luke.'

'Did you have a good night?'

'Sure.'

'Did you drink?'

'No, I'm teetotal,' Sebastian says. 'Drugs, drinks – they're not my thing.'

'You don't like losing control?' I ask.

'I prefer not to,' Sebastian replies.

He's not giving much away, I muse. He's polite, but guarded.

'Did you see Luke and Eva leave the party?' I ask.

'Oh yes, I was standing in the garden, getting some air. I watched them leave together and walk into the woods.'

'Did you feel that Eva was leading the way, or Luke?'

'Oh, definitely Luke. He knew where he was going, he had his hand on her back and he was guiding her to the right. Then they disappeared into the trees and they were – gone.' Sebastian waves his hands like a conjuror wafting smoke.

Well, I think, *even if Sebastian isn't involved, he can certainly boost the case for the prosecution*. We don't have anyone on record who actually saw Luke guiding Eva away. All the other kids had been too drunk, high, confused, blurry.

'And were they arguing?'

'I don't remember that, but they both seemed in a bad mood.' Sebastian laughs. 'Clearly, Luke was in a *very* bad mood.'

I smile too. It's a good strategy. I want Sebastian relaxed, off guard, lulled into a false sense of security.

Next, Sebastian asserts that he left the party around midnight, by car. He drove home sober, checked on his mother and went straight to bed.

'Why did you check on your mum?'

'She has lung cancer,' he says, his voice a shade flatter. 'She's been given six months to live. They put her on a drug called Everolimus, it worked for a while but then it stopped.'

I frown, blinking, thinking of Mary, of the cancer that stole my own wife away. I look down at my notes; suddenly, I've lost my thread.

Is that a glint in Sebastian's eye? As though he thinks this is all a game?

'I see,' I say. 'And what time did you go to bed?'

'I didn't go to bed. Sometimes my mother can make a lot of noise at night – when she has bad dreams or if she's in pain. That was one of those nights, so I decided to go for a drive. Sometimes I like to take a walk.' For the first time, his expression becomes vulnerable, childlike.

'You were walking on the road by the woods at one-twenty a.m., according to CCTV. Did you enter the woods?'

Sebastian shakes his head but replies: 'To an extent, in that I was on the outskirts.'

'So, you were, in fact, *in* the woods.'

'Doesn't it show up on the CCTV that I was?'

'The CCTV cuts out before we can see whether or not you entered,' I say. 'Perhaps you knew that. Perhaps you calculated the spot.'

'How on earth could I know that?' Sebastian asks incredulously. 'What, you think the average eighteen-year-old has access to CCTV screens?'

'You weren't far from the pit where Eva's body was found. I find it hard to believe you didn't hear anything.'

Sebastian is quiet, his hands a steeple beneath his chin. Finally: 'I did hear something, as a matter of fact. I heard a distant cry.'

'Why didn't you say anything at the time?'

'What good would it have done? She's dead.' Sebastian shrugs.

Now the boy sounds like a sociopath. I let out a faint yawn. I watch Sebastian, waiting for the usual echo, a classic sign of empathy. But there's none.

'So you heard someone cry out in the dead of night and didn't think to call the police?'

'To be honest, when I heard them I hurried away as fast as I could,' Sebastian says firmly. 'I thought the cries might be kids playing about, or a gang having a fight. I didn't want to get involved.'

He just states facts. There's no remorse or regret in hindsight. Or perhaps his response is justified. It is natural to run.

'You and Eva didn't really get along, did you?' I ask.

'I hardly knew her, to be honest,' Sebastian shrugs.

'Earlier this year, on the twenty-eighth of August, Eva called our station from a local Starbucks and claimed you had assaulted her.'

'No charges were made against me,' says Sebastian, though he looks a little prickly. 'We were just messing around. You were there that night. The whole thing was a farce. I remember you apologising to me.'

'You say that you hardly knew Eva. Now you're saying you knew her well enough to mess around with? Bit contradictory, don't you think?'

A pause.

'Aren't you the one who knows Eva intimately?' Sebastian gets cheeky.

I was waiting for that to come up. I'd like to throttle him for going there, but I keep my cool. 'You're the one under arrest, so I suggest you take the situation seriously.'

'Maybe you and Luke were in cahoots,' Sebastian muses. 'Maybe you plotted together.'

'Please answer the question.'

'Look.' Sebastian suddenly pulls out his iPhone and shows me a video. I ask that he hold it up to the camera, so that it can be recorded.

The video shows Eva in the park. She's passing something from her bag to a friend with blonde hair. Then the video cuts to show Sebastian's face and Luke appears in frame, threatening him, shouting abuse and waving a knife.

'Eva was in the park with Luke one day and I happened to hear her shout for help. I went over and saw Luke was getting heavy,' Sebastian says. 'When she saw me she *told* me to film it – I guess so that she had some evidence? As you can see, that's when Luke started to lay into me too.'

'But I thought you were against intervening in dangerous situations.'

'On this occasion, I felt I had no choice.'

I feel terrible sadness. I recall that Eva called me that day. I'd thought she was playing games for my attention and I told her off, refused to listen. It was a classic case of Cry Wolf. What did she say that day? I wish I could step out of this interrogation, give myself the luxury of time and space to think. Then it comes to me. I hear her voice, breathy, catching with tears: *'Sebastian was trying to blackmail us.'* 'Us' – or was it 'me'? I can't quite remember.

Blackmail: it doesn't fit with the video Sebastian has just presented to me, does it? Unless Eva later calmed down and felt she wanted to protect Luke? It does show him waving a knife.

'You're sure this video hasn't been edited in any way?' I ask.

'No,' Sebastian says, but he hesitates a second before he replies.

'We'll need to download it from your phone. We'll be able to see if it has been edited.'

Sebastian remains silent, cool.

'You're sure Luke wasn't mad because you were attempting to blackmail him, perhaps?' I needle him. 'Is blackmail your thing, Sebastian?'

Surprise on his face, as though I've caught him unawares.

'Probably ... not.'

'Why would you blackmail someone, Sebastian? Why would you be in need of money?'

'If you investigate my life, you might be able to create some kind of story. My mum's sick. My dad doesn't live with us anymore. And my half-sister, she's gone back to live with Dad's ex. So we don't have much money and it all goes on my school fees. You could therefore conclude that I might want to blackmail someone, but actually, no, I just wanted to help Eva. I happened to be in the right place at the right time to do that.'

We release the kid thirty minutes later. I gather the team together. We'll send Sebastian's DNA for testing. In the meantime, everyone's got a different opinion on him. He is a slippery character for sure, but the evidence against him is circumstantial at best. Luke, meanwhile, has *concrete* evidence against him, as well as a clear motive. I can see my team coming round; I was always good at persuading people.

Just then, Superintendent Birch interrupts. She wants to see me in her office.

Birch is one of those people who make up for their small height with tremendous energy and presence. Her arms are folded, her mouth a terse line. She's always been my biggest champion, promoted me up through the ranks, but this time I know she's bearing bad news.

'You were compromised back there,' she says. 'The tabloid poison has seeped in everywhere. At one point, the suspect was making fun of you. We're supposed to be the ones setting a good example to the public, Detective Inspector.'

'As I have said, this so-called diary is pure fiction. Either Eva did write it, and they were her secret fantasies; or some other fantasist, perhaps in cahoots with Luke, is trying to undermine the case.' How many times have I said these words? Maybe fifty, maybe more; they're becoming frayed and tired.

'I believe you.' She gives me a direct look. 'But we will need you to take a break. I've suggested it before, and now I'm going to insist—'

'No!' I hear myself say.

'You will be welcome back,' she asserts. 'This is not a suspension, it's just extended leave. Just until the trial is over and justice is done. Then, when things have quietened down, you can come back.'

Chapter 56

Carolina

I'm sitting in Caffe Nero, waiting for Okeke to show. We're finally back in touch, though our texts have been awkward and brief. At least he's started sharing details of the case again. I still feel hurt that he cut me off, but now I understand why. Dad was no longer his hero. The man who had once warned him about rule breaking had himself broken every rule in the book. Well, at least we see eye to eye on that.

When he comes in, he flashes me a jerky smile hello, buys himself an orange juice at the counter and sits down opposite me.

'Hey,' he says, 'how are you?'

'Good,' I lie. 'You?'

'Great,' he says in a flat voice. Then he pulls his iPhone out of his bag. 'Look – the Big Bad Blog's been updated.'

'Yeah, I've seen it,' I interject, but he carries on telling me all the same:

'"The BBB has learned of new evidence in the ongoing investigation into Eva Pieachowski's murder. A well-known pupil at St Cuthbert's, Sebastian Banks, was in the woods on the night she was killed. Banks claims he heard screams – or was he the one who made Eva scream?"

'And if you Google his name another, bigger site comes up. It replicates the BBB story and has one of those voting panels at the bottom.' Okeke shows me:

WHO DO YOU THINK KILLED EVA? VOTE NOW!

- SEBASTIAN
- LUKE

'That's pretty crass,' I wince, though I find myself longing to see the results of the survey, and which way opinion is going.

'Luke's on forty-four per cent, Sebastian's on fifty-six.' He puts down his phone and looks at me with tender eyes. 'Look, Carolina, things are hard enough for your dad at work ... and you writing the Big Bad Blog isn't helping.'

I gulp down my drink too quickly and then suffer a coughing fit, until tears pinch my eyes and Okeke has to clap me on the back. When I first set up the blog, I dreaded being found out, and then, when nobody guessed, I got complacent. Now, all of a sudden, I feel as though Okeke has whipped out a pair of cuffs and slapped them on my wrists.

I could deny it, but then I'd be as bad as my dad, lying my way out of everything.

'How did you find out?'

'There are too many confidential details. Things that only the police know. Things that only you know. Yesterday, I texted about Sebastian claiming he heard cries in the wood that night. Now it's all over the net. That was confidential. I took a risk, sharing that with you.'

'But people should know the truth! Like Wikileaks.'

'No, Carolina, it's not the same at all!' Okeke notices an elderly couple at a nearby table glancing over at us. He leans in and lowers his voice. 'Don't you see that neither Luke nor Sebastian can have a fair trial with half of the case already in the public domain?'

'What – what d'you mean?'

'How can you be so naïve? Look, imagine the jury. They turn up to court and they've already read half the case online and they've got all sorts of prejudices, their minds are half made up. That's just one of a hundred problems with you writing this blog. God, your dad's in enough trouble as it is, what with being on leave and under investigation by the anti-corruption unit. Our Super has always supported him, I know she'll want him back on the force as soon as the fuss dies down – but do you want him sacked?'

'No!' I might be mad with my dad, but I don't want to punish him. Losing his job would break his heart. 'I just started it because I was lonely and curious and I just put it out there and then it took off. I had no idea that would happen. And then I wanted to help Luke.'

'I know,' Okeke says softly. 'I know you wanted to do the right thing.'

There's a brief silence between us. I sense Okeke is about to get up and leave, so I ask him quickly: 'When we were in the Hotel du Vin, you found out about Dad then, didn't you? That's why you went so weird on me.'

'Yes,' he sighs. 'I found a Mr White there a few days after the date Siobhan had given us. I ran a check on the credit card. It was registered to your dad's address. I'm sorry I didn't tell you. I didn't know *how* to tell you . . .'

'So I had to find out when the press came to our front door,' I cry, reliving that awful moment.

'Sorry,' Okeke says quietly.

'If . . . Look, Dad is still denying the affair. If you show your seniors the credit-card receipts, they'll know he is lying. Then he really will be sacked.'

'I . . . I don't know what I'm going to do,' Okeke says.

'My dad is a good man,' I insist, but I can see from Okeke's expression that he's no longer certain of this. 'Look.' I pull out my phone, desperate to rebuild things, reignite his interest in us as a team. I show him a shot of the blonde girl with a tattoo. 'She was in the car with Mr Abdul the morning of the crash. I saw her, Okeke, and I think she's the girl who approached Siobhan in the woods.'

'Carolina, I can't do this any more. It was risky enough

before, but now, if anyone found out that I was the source of the leaks ... '

'I'll shut down the Big Bad Blog. Please trust me ... '

'I can't,' Okeke insists.

'What about Eva's diary?' I ask desperately. 'Was there anything about Sebastian in there?'

'There are pages torn out of the diary, the later entries have been burnt and we're not sure it is hers. It can't be used as evidence.' Okeke touches my cheek. 'Look, we – the police – we're in charge now. We'll sort it out.'

'But I can help, I know I can.'

'You already have played a big part, Carolina. You found the knife, and that has been the most important evidence in this case so far.'

'Yes, and it put Luke away,' I say, feeling even worse. Maybe Okeke is right. Maybe I'm causing more harm than good.

Okeke says goodbye and leaves me sitting in the café. Despite the buzzy crowd around me, I feel very alone. I pick up my phone and scroll despondently through the blog. The earlier entries are such an embarrassment – salacious and biased against Luke. I realise that I was simply ventriloquising my dad back then; I was determined to condemn him. Maybe I should take it down, but I *want* to keep it up, because it presents a gradual change of heart, and maybe whoever is reading it will find their sympathies changed in turn. I'll never tell Luke I was behind it, at least not until much later. The tide is turning. We have another key suspect and I am determined to see Luke's name cleared.

Chapter 57

Eva's Diary: 22 September 2016

I was getting sick of the Luke situation when
something terrible happened. It was a week ago
today, a Thursday. Siobhan had asked me to look after
her weed for her. Her parents had started to notice
the smell and they'd been lecturing her. She'd been
denying ever having inhaled an illicit substance,
but it wasn't working. Now she was scared that they
might check her bags. The deal was that I'd give her
the eighth or whatever before school. I was pretty mad
at her, to be honest, but she was my best friend, so I
went along with it. We met in the woods by the edge
of the park to do the swap. Just then, Jackson texted
me. I told Siobhan to go ahead to the library for study
period and that I'd follow on. She smirked, said, 'Oh,
the OAP's in touch, is he?' in a sing-song and then

ran off laughing. I was texting Jackson back when a
shadow fell over me.

I turned around. It was Sebastian. I froze. He stood
there, arms folded. Then he held up his phone and
pressed play. The video was of me passing the pot to
Siobhan. It made me look like some kind of dealer!

'You bastard,' I cried, trying to grab the phone.

He held the phone at arm's length and made me try
and reach for it like a primary school bully. Then, just
when I was sick and tired of his game and about to
stalk off, he slammed me up against a tree trunk.

'No. You're not going anywhere,' he said. 'You
messed with me and now you get to see the
consequences of that.'

I stood there, sweating in the daylight, staring into
his cold grey eyes. It was impossible to tell if he was
psycho-serious or just messing with me. He tried to
blackmail me. He told me I'd have to pay him to get the
video back. Five hundred pounds, minimum, in cash.
Then, all of a sudden, Sebastian was on the ground.
Luke was standing over him and yelling, 'What the hell
d'you think you're doing to my girlfriend?' He got his
knife out and Sebastian tried to film him. Luke roared.

Within a minute Sebastian was up on his feet and
making a run for it.

I turned to Luke and grabbed him in a tight
hug, overwhelmed with gratitude. I loved him

then, for what felt like the first time in months. He was my hero.

I called Jackson, tried to tell him what had happened, but he wasn't having any of it. 'Oh sure, Sebastian. The guy you tried to set up in Starbucks. Don't start that game again, Eva.' He hung up on me.

I was furious and decided that it was over with Jackson. I would stay with Luke. At least he gave a damn about me. I couldn't seem to get rid of Luke and I was so tired of fighting. Part of me was relieved at the thought of giving in.

Then, two nights later, I met Jackson again. I was so mad at him that I turned up half an hour late and refused to let him kiss me. When I explained the whole story, he told me I was stupid to ever carry drugs, even for a friend. Then he asked if I ever took drugs. I admitted I had, once or twice, but only because Luke had persuaded me. Did I want to lose my looks and career and throw it all away for the hollowness of addiction, he asked. On and on he lectured me, until I was ready to scream. I said something about already having one hectoring father and not needing another. Then he backed down and apologised. We had make-up sex, which is just the best sex ever. Afterwards, he held me close, stroking my hair and I fell in love with him all over again ...

The Sebastian thing continued to freak me out. Normally guys liked me so much they forgave me when

I was bad, but Sebastian seemed to have some kind of vendetta. What if he kept trying to blackmail me? What if he found out about Jackson?

It felt like we were at war.

So I went back to Starbucks, where his sister worked. I thought of how simple it had been to befriend Carolina. If I could do the same with Astra, it might help to smooth things over.

Nothing went according to plan.

Astra was serving, so I sat down at a table covered with dirty cups, so that she'd have to come to my table to collect them. I said 'Hi' and she replied in a wary voice. I asked if she had time for a chat. She said she had five minutes' break and sat down.

Then I saw the scars on her wrist: a pale pink medley of criss-crosses. She saw that I'd seen, so I quickly said, 'Oh, I love that tattoo on your wrist.' She smiled and said it was a gift from Sebastian.

'I'm pretty worried that I've pissed Sebastian off,' I confided in her.

She just shrugged. 'Sebastian likes to play games. He does like to toy with people, and it's never a good idea to get on the wrong side of him.'

'Then what does he do?' I gulped, thinking of his psycho eyes and the way he had pushed me up against that tree.

'Just be good to him,' she emphasised. 'Sebastian

293

is also one of the kindest people I know. When we were kids ... well, we had a difficult time and he protected me.'

I was intrigued. When I put my mind to it, I can be a really good listener and I know how to get people to tell me their stories. 'When I was a kid, my dad used to burn me with cigarettes.' I felt sheepish at the lie, but I hoped it might encourage her to share.

'Our dad did a lot worse,' Astra said. 'If Sebastian hadn't been there ...'

'Is your dad still around?'

'No. Thank God.'

'But,' I pressed her, 'what did your dad do?'

Suddenly I saw the change in her eyes.

'You want my confession? Are you recording this on your phone, as some kind of joke, so you can get back at Sebastian? God, you're so manipulative!' She stood up. 'As if your dad burnt you,' she scoffed, looking at my bare and admittedly flawless arms.

I opened my mouth to bullshit some more, but something in her eyes warned me not to push it.

'You know what's so funny about this?' she hissed. 'When we were kids, I tried to tell people and nobody ever wanted to listen. Not even our own mother. Nobody would listen. Nobody.' She stormed off.

I told Jackson about it but he wasn't interested. He told me I was only picking at a wound; instead, I needed leave it alone so it could heal. Still, I can't help feeling that Sebastian and Astra are seriously weird.

As for Jackson ... I still don't feel as if I really, fully, have him. He still insists on secrecy. We never meet in public, still use the secret stupid phone, and he has made it very clear that if I so much as hint at our relationship to anyone, he'll kill me.

Last week I got him to cuff me to the bed, just to keep things spicy. It was hot, but afterwards I had bracelets of red on my wrists. Siobhan noticed. I quickly made up a story about my Older Man being adventurous, and she looked anxious. I think she's worried I'm dating some kind of contract killer.

That's the trouble with my situation – so many lies, all stacking up like a house of cards. I know that one day it will come toppling down on me ...

Chapter 58

Luke

The letter from Carolina arrives and I'm not sure if I want to open it.

It's been a week since she last visited. I've had three letters from her since then. I have wanted to sit down and reply, but I feel lost for words. What the hell can I say to her? *Well, Carolina, it's been interesting to find out that your dad was the mysterious Mr White who was screwing my girlfriend. That he decided to oh-so-coincidentally pin the blame on me. And did you happen to know anything about it?*

I thought I'd be released at once when the Jackson revelation came out. But no: it turns out that the police and the law stick together. Apparently my arrest still stands, even though the guy who instigated it was sleeping with the victim. My Eva.

I sit in my cell, on my bed, and listen to the sound of a bird outside my window. In her last letter Carolina said she'd made a phone recording for me of some birdsong blended together, which I can hear the next time she visits. The idea sounds terrible and I have no sodding interest in the noise a blackbird makes, to be honest, but the tenderness of her intention touches me. She's also said, in letter after letter, that she *swears* she didn't know about her dad. That's she's shocked, dismayed, disgusted, reeling, upset, angry.

Maybe she deserves another chance. After all, it's not like I get a lot of other visitors. Even Mr Abdul stopped turning up, sometime before the accident. I want to send him a Get Well Soon card, but I feel too angry that he deserted me. He even stopped looking after Buster and gave him back to Mum. She still comes, but as much as I crave my time with her, I find her visits depressing; she keeps saying I'm doomed, I'm my father's son, and I should prepare for the worst.

Rob and Siobhan used to write, but their letters have dried up. The last I heard from Rob was just a brief note telling me that he had an offer for Cambridge.

Carolina is all I've got now.

I open the letter.

Hey, Luke, I hope you got my other letters. I just wanted to share some good news with you. I got accepted for uni today – I'm going to be studying Chemistry at Bristol.

Something tightens in my chest at the thought of her being miles away in another city, moving on, living her life without me.

Then:

And the other amazing news is this – Sebastian's DNA was also found on the knife after a retest. I guess my Dad still has some friends at the station and he found out. So there we go – Sebastian has as much evidence against him as you do, if not more, cos you're a good guy and he's a complete weirdo.

I actually feel weak, and then a surge of adrenalin bubbles through me. I leap over to my window and look out at the December sky, ice-blue with cold. It no longer taunts me. It makes me feel something like – hope.

Sebastian. Of course. He was there that night at Rob's party. I remember that Eva and I steered well clear of him, because of the trouble he'd caused a week earlier. He'd been filming Eva with Siobhan's drugs in the park. He'd threatened her, attempted to blackmail her, and I'd hit him. I'm such an idiot for not mentioning him to the police before. I was so busy defending myself I never stopped to think about anyone else. I didn't *want* to pin it on anyone else. For a moment I feel angry, knowing he's been willing to let me take the fall. Then oddly, I feel sorry for him, because I know that in a few weeks' time he'll be living like this.

I've spent months shouting, protesting, pleading, and I've been met with deaf ears. Surely now they will have to start listening. I grab my pen and write down everything I know about Sebastian Banks for my lawyer.

I love you, Carolina, I love you for saving me.

298

Chapter 59

Carolina

New Year, New Year. Soon it will be 2017. Luke's will be the first trial of the year and he'll be released and then, finally, finally, we can be together. I see us cuddling in cafés and cinemas; I see us messing around in the snow, building snowmen; I see us in the park as the spring blooms, lying under a tree, sharing sunshine kisses. This is our future. I want to fast-forward Christmas and rush through New Year and start living properly, living a life with Luke. My first boyfriend; my first love.

I'm also keen to get away from home. Last week Dad was ordered to 'take extended leave' from his job. The press are going crazy, saying that he should be fired; they think locking him up for life is the only fit punishment. We've had to change our home number because of all the hate calls.

He's been mooching about the house in a foul mood. For a workaholic like him, it's hell. He's taken up smoking again, which I hate. He's back on Luke again, too, with a new kind of vengeance. He is certain they'll be 'begging him' to come back after the trial delivers a Guilty verdict. I've found it so unbearable that I stopped cooking for him and take my meals to my bedroom. God knows what he'd say if he knew where I was going today . . .

At Wandsworth I go through all the tedious security procedures and weave through the visiting desks towards Luke. When I see him shock shrills in my stomach: *Oh God, not again.* I sit down opposite him. The black eye is all I can see. The lids are swollen lips, his eyelashes flecked with dried blood, his pupil a feline slit.

'Hi,' he says. 'No need to compliment me – I know I'm looking wonderful.'

The joke relieves the tension. I laugh, a bit too loudly.

This is the first time I've seen him since all that stuff about Dad. I've sensed Luke pulling me away from me at a distance – can I blame him? Even now, his arms are folded and he's biting his lip.

'Cheer up,' I blurt out stupidly, and give him his Christmas present. I had wanted to spend some time with him first, get used to being in each other's company before giving it. But I'm desperate to lighten the mood. 'Sorry I couldn't wrap it – but the guards wouldn't have let me take it in.'

Luke's face warms with emotion.

'Oh – oil paints – perfect!' he says. 'Hey, this is a really expensive brand. You shouldn't have.'

'I wanted to,' I insist.

He looks at me and I feel all the uncertainty between us dissolve.

He leans in. Small, tender kisses at first; kisses that promise forgiveness. He puts his arms around me and the kiss becomes deeper, longer. When we pull back, we're both flushed and Luke's eyes sparkle. I'm shaking with a sweet ache; I want more. Luke's looking just as frustrated. If only we could kiss in private, without this noise and din around us and people flicking us glances and the guards smirking. He grabs my hand and squeezes it tight. I love the way he reacts to everything with such intensity. Nothing is pastel in his world.

'Thank you. I don't think the guards will let me keep this in my cell, though ...'

'I'll look after it for you,' I say quickly. 'After the trial, when you're out, I can give it to you then.'

He nods and I ask him tentatively what happened to his eye. He shrugs and says he doesn't want to discuss it and spoil the mood. I feel sick. The people in here seem so damaged that they can't bear any to see hope flourish; they have to destroy it. Luke doesn't belong here.

'Did you find out anything more about Sebastian? I take it they arrested him? My lawyer's rubbish, I haven't seen him for days.'

'I know he's been called in for questioning three times now, so I imagine it's likely.' I only know that from Facebook gossip. Now that Dad's off the force and DC Okeke has cut me off, I feel lost. 'Also, Mr Abdul will be allowed visitors from tomorrow. I'm going to see him and get the lowdown on this blonde girl once and for all.'

'Maybe she doesn't matter – Sebastian's the one who was clearly *there*.'

'But she might have seen something. Maybe she's holding back from fear.'

'Man, I feel like I'm in the dark – even that blog has gone AWOL. I used to check it out, even if it was a load of bull.'

'Yeah, I shut it down,' I say without thinking.

Luke stares at me. '*You* ... had something to do with it?'

Oh shit. I start to panic. I wasn't planning to tell him until he got out. I've practised speeches in the mirror, imagined us lying in a secret place together, confiding quietly.

'It was *your* blog?' Luke presses me. I laugh, look away as he continues. 'I don't think this is funny. You're – you got me put away in here.'

'No!' I cry. 'I know I got it wrong at the start, but when I realised—'

'Got it wrong?' Luke's voice rises; some security officers have noticed and are looking over. Luke is oblivious. 'This is my life we're talking about. That blog started all the dirty opinions and rumours against me – it probably gave the police the idea to go after *me*.'

'Luke, they went after you because you were the last person to see Eva alive,' I fire back. 'It was just a blog, a stupid mistake – and I'm sorry, okay, nobody could regret it more than I do.'

'This is a conspiracy. You and your dad – you're in this together. Did he get you to set it up, did he make you write it?'

'Of course he didn't,' I say. Now Luke is totally out of order; I'm not going to stand for this, no matter how upset he is. 'I am sick of people making me and my dad into one person. I can think for myself. I set up the blog because I wanted to and now I regret it. End of story.'

'You are such a stupid bitch,' he cries. 'You ruined my life!' His fist is coiled. I recoil in shock.

Guards run over and try to grab Luke. He wrestles them away, knocking over the visiting table. I jump up, backing away. All around us, people and inmates watch on. Finally, they manage to control Luke, handcuffing his wrists tight behind his back. He's still glaring at me as though he wants to kill me. I notice his oil paints, fallen on the floor; I pick up the palette and stuff it in my bag.

'Yeah, go on, just rob it, take it away from me!'

I hurry away, shouting echoing around the hall as Luke refuses to go back to his cell.

Chapter 60

Siobhan

A few weeks ago, I went to the police station to change my statement about what happened on the night of Rob's party.

It was the paper that triggered it. I mean, how weird is this? I was down in the living room when I suddenly found this random piece of A5 paper which had fallen down between the sofa and the little table our phone sits on. Scrawled on it, *in Eva's handwriting*, in blue ink, were the words: *Luke took me into the woods to kill me.* The same line repeated on a new line, six or seven times.

That night I dreamt about Eva. The next evening, I arranged to see Mrs Lambert. I texted and asked Sebastian to come, but he's gone AWOL as usual. I thought about taking Rivka but decided it was better not to; she thought the whole thing was silly and her sarcastic looks and glib remarks would spoil everything.

When I told Mrs Lambert about the writing, she said she thought that Eva was trying to get in touch. Now, I have to admit that even I hadn't been 100 per cent convinced by her before. I had wanted to believe, so I always argued that she was for real – but I had my doubts. That night, however, everything changed. Mrs Lambert lit a candle and prayed to the angels to help put Eva in touch. All of a sudden, the candle flickered. Tears streamed down her face. She said she was crying the tears of Eva, that Eva was in distress. Eva wanted us to let her rest in peace. And then she told me what Eva was saying: *Luke took me into the woods to kill me.*

That's when I realised that it was necessary to change my statement.

Chapter 61

Carolina

I'm on the bus, on my way to the hospital. I have no idea if Mr Abdul will be willing to speak to me, but I'm going to try.

The fight I had with Luke is still upsetting me. I picture the monstrous look on his face again. Have I been in a bubble these last few months? Who was that version of Luke? The thought arises, no matter how hard I try to swerve away from it: *Was it like that for Eva, that night in the woods?* The sudden change, the flare of his temper? Yet again, I wrestle with doubts about Luke. I don't want to be this person – scared and sure of his guilt one minute; sentimental and certain of his innocence the next.

My dad has always said: *People have so many sides to their personalities, Carolina.* I remember us watching a show on TV about theatre, how actors create credible, three-dimensional characters for the stage. And he said, *People aren't 3D, they're*

10D. They're baffling. You can know someone for years and not know them at all.

I can't bear this constant confusion. I find myself thinking of Rob and the video he showed me where Luke was messing with a knife, the video the police still haven't seen. I wish I could conjure up every piece of evidence and lay it all out in front of me and examine it with cool reason. I pick up my mobile and text him:

> Do u still have that video of Luke? Could u email it to me?

Suddenly I feel a flash of compassion for Dad. I didn't like the video Rob showed me and so I trivialised it. It's hard to be objective. Something will always slant our reason, colour our judgement. Our bias makes us blind.

I head into the hospital, its labyrinth of corridors full of busy nurses and doctors and patients in wheelchairs and lifts that take hours to arrive. I am about to get out of the lift at the fifth floor when a girl hurries in. I step aside to make room.

'Thanks,' she says breathlessly.

It's her.

She presses for the ground floor. I notice her tattooed wrist as she reaches for the button. I stay in the lift, nodding as though I too need to go down.

The doors slide shut. The floors pass away from us ... four ... three ...

'Um, do you have the time?' I ask her.

'It's two thirty.' Her voice is hard to catch and she's too shy to look me in the face; her gaze hovers uneasily around my collarbone.

'I'm here to see my teacher from school,' I say breezily, pretending I'm one of those nattery types who love to share their lives with strangers. 'He was, like, in this terrible crash.'

'Mr Abdul? He's my dad,' she says.

'Your *dad*?' My voice sounds squeaky and I quickly frame it with a reassuring smile.

'Well, not by blood – I don't see my real dad any more, or my real mum – but he's my foster-dad. He lives with my real dad's ex. I've just started living with them. By the way, you're going the wrong way, he's up on level five, on Crocus Ward.'

She gets out at the ground floor, frowning, and I call out a cheery goodbye. As the lift climbs back up again, I feel almost disappointed.

So that's that. There is no big conspiracy, except – why didn't he tell me about her when I asked him? And did she really see something that night? For a minute, I want to stop the lift and shoot out after her, but she'll hardly confess to a stranger. So, I get out at floor five and I go on in to see Mr Abdul.

Chapter 62

Carolina

I'm half-expecting Mr Abdul to tell me to get lost, so it's a relief when he gives me a crooked smile. He's lying in bed with a bandage around his head and cuts on his face and one of his arms is in a sling.

'Hey, Carolina,' he says in a frail voice. 'How are you?'

'I'm great.' I sit down gingerly on the plastic chair by his bed, noting the Get Well cards and grapes on his table. I should have brought something. 'I hope you're doing okay?'

'I've never been better,' he says.

We both laugh, and I feel a bit less awkward.

'I – I just saw your um, foster-daughter in the lift,' I say casually. 'She was going as I was coming. She seems nice.'

'Astra? Yeah, she came for a bit,' he says. 'So, how's school? Rob came the other day and he said you were having a tough time, with your dad and everything . . . '

309

'Oh God,' I groan. I know he's trying to be sympathetic, but I wish he hadn't brought it up. 'Uh huh. It's grim. Dad's been suspended and he's kind of hanging around the house, drinking a lot and being really *angry* . . . '

'I'm sorry Carolina – I can't imagine how hard it is for you. It will get better. You just have to try and brave it out right now.'

Even from his hospital bed, wrapped in bandages, he's a wonderful listener. But I'm meant to be the one getting him to open up, not the other way round.

'When I saw Astra in the lift just now—' I steal one of his grapes without thinking and he smiles and tells me to go ahead. I laugh awkwardly, then carry on. 'So we chatted very briefly. She seemed a bit – upset.'

'Astra.' He sighs. 'It's very tough for her. She moved in two months ago. She was at St Mary's but she'll transfer to St Martin's next term. It's complicated. My partner used to live with her dad. But now Astra has chosen to come and live with us. We hope that one day we'll be able to legally adopt her. It's taking time for her to trust us. Her mother's sick and dying, but they've fallen out. I tell Astra she ought to patch things up with her. She'll regret it if she doesn't. She doesn't get on very well with her half-brother, either.'

'That's so sad.'

My heart is trembling and I'm trying to think of what I can say next to get him to tell me more.

'Have you seen Luke recently?' he asks. 'The trial's not far off, is it?'

310

'Yes – yes – I only went last week.'

'You've been visiting him a lot recently, have you?'

I nod uncertainly, wondering if I should confide in him about the fight. I've been dying to tell someone. I've held back from telling Rob. It still feels disloyal, when Luke has so few allies left.

'Just be careful, Carolina.'

'I thought you liked Luke!' I say. I lean in; I sense that he's debating whether or not to tell me more.

'He has been charged with murder,' he replies at last, 'and you should never forget that, Carolina.'

'Luke told me you gave him a copy of *The Upanishads*, that you think there's been a miscarriage of justice.'

'In most miscarriages of justice, there is very little evidence tying the suspect to the murder. But Luke was the very last person to see Eva alive, they went into the woods together, the knife used to kill her was his, his DNA is on the knife. I fought the evidence at first, but in the end . . . it is really rather overwhelming.'

'Does Astra – does she know something?'

'She – does,' he says at last.

'What?' I frown.

'I'm going to share this with you on the condition that you keep quiet, Carolina. It's not something I want to get out, but I'm worried about you.'

'Okay,' I whisper. 'I promise.'

I'm really not sure I'm ready to hear this, but I force a smile and nod in encouragement.

'Astra loves making films – she loves David Lynch and Kubrick – pretty dark stuff. She wants to make a stylish horror, so she's been going to the woods, filming after dark. I worry about her, so I try to make sure she has a friend with her.' Abdul's voice is laced with pride. 'She didn't go to Rob's party – her brother did, but I think she felt nervous about being with so many strangers. Instead, she went into the woods with her camera. Her brother had offered to meet up and walk her home at the end.'

'She caught something, didn't she?' I'm gripping the edge of the bedsheet.

'I saw a bit of the footage. Luke was running through the trees and there was blood. Look, Carolina, I'm just telling you what I saw. After that, how could I believe in Luke's innocence? Think about it, Carolina – even if someone else *had* taken his knife, *had* murdered her, what about the blood? If Luke found her after the stabbing, why didn't he call the police?'

For a long moment I am mute.

Luke and I have never discussed that night in detail. I did try once or twice, but he clammed up, and I thought it was unkind to push him.

'But there *could* be an explanation. He could have cut himself. That would explain why his knife was dropped in the woods and someone else could have picked it up,' I add triumphantly. 'Did she have any footage of the murder?'

'I don't know. She won't show me the whole film, and she

won't tell me what she saw. I've told her to go to the police, but she won't. She just bursts into tears and says she can't – she says he *threatened* her. She is scared that she'll be seen as an accessory to the crime. I don't want to see her in trouble or any more distress, so I'm keeping quiet. The girl's been through enough.'

I'm shocked. I always thought that Mr Abdul was an honest man, who believed in doing the right thing. 'I mean, you really should have told . . . '

'Astra is very vulnerable right now,' he says. 'If she was mistakenly charged as an accessory, if she was arrested too, it would destroy her completely. I love her as though she was my daughter, and I will not put her through that. I will not see her suffer for Luke's crime. That boy is so desperate, it wouldn't surprise me if he tried to pin it all onto her. Astra's not strong enough to fight back.'

I've never heard seen Mr Abdul like this, so fierce and full of conviction. He'll do everything in his power to protect his daughter.

Then he softens, reaches for my hand. 'Look, I found all this out a few weeks after Luke was arrested and remanded in jail. I knew he was going to be charged anyway. There's no doubt he's going down. Carolina, are you okay?'

I can't look at him; instead I focus on the grapes, on a slightly bruised one; I pluck it off and put it in the bin. Mr Abdul watches me.

I've been waiting months for this knowledge. And now

I've bitten into the apple and tasted the truth, I just feel sick. I can still feel Luke's blue eyes caressing me, his soft lips against mine, his hands curling up into my hair, his letters, his *I love you*s.

'I stopped visiting him,' he says, very gently. 'I thought it was best. Luke can be very persuasive, you know.'

'Yeah,' I say, 'tell me about it.'

'I told you all this because I want to protect you, Carolina.'

'Thank you,' I whisper, nodding sadly.

I check my mobile again. Rob's replied to my text; he's sent over the video of Luke in the bathroom.

I think of my dad, abandoning all his morals for the highs of sex with Eva. I think of Mr Abdul, hiding evidence in order to protect the surrogate daughter he loves. If there's something I've learnt today, it's that people who seem so sure of their principles can never hope to live up to their own ideals. They have their weak spots too; maybe that's what makes them human, but it also makes them hypocrites. I can't be like them.

I don't even stop to think it all through. I just obey my conscience, do my duty and text the video to DC Okeke.

Chapter 63

Luke

Dear Carolina,

I've started this letter a thousand times, ripping it up and starting again.

I'm sorry. The words sound so flat on the page but I really do mean them.

I can't make excuses for losing my temper with you. But I can tell you how terrible it is in this place night and day, day and night. It's like I'm in a constant storm and I'm trying to throw down an anchor and hold on until the blue sky comes.

You've often asked me whether I still love Eva. It's been there in your letters and I can see the question in your eyes. I want you to know that the love I feel for you is so much stronger than anything I ever felt for Eva. My relationship with her was based on trying to fit in, I can see that now.

When Eva became my girlfriend, I finally felt as though I'd made it. I'd become one of them. I'd escaped my past and the future looked bright.

Then all this happened, and it was like I'd slipped all the way back to square one. I turned out to be the loser my mum had always feared I'd be. Worse, the precious thing I thought I had with Eva turned out to be a sham. I still don't know what to think about her and your dad. Knowing I meant nothing to her. How useless our relationship seems, such a waste of time – and all for this. A cell and my life as good as over. Every day that I spend in here, I feel I become smaller, as though my soul is being slowly stripped away.

When you told me about the BBB, I was afraid because it looked like history repeating itself. I can't bear to think I was just some good cause for you to take on. Maybe I've got it all wrong, the way I did with Eva, I don't know. I felt paranoid that you were using me, laughing at me. I can't trust my judgement anymore.

I forgive you for the BBB. We weren't even friends when you started it and who can blame you for seeing me the same way everyone else did? My trial is tomorrow and I don't think I can face it without you. I've enclosed a sketch with this letter, a portrait of you, drawn from memory. I hope you can look at this picture and see all that I feel about you . . .

With all my love,
Luke x

Chapter 64

Carolina

Today is the day.

I'm walking through the woods on Wimbledon Common. It's freezing cold. I thought that being outside in nature would console me. Instead, I only feel lonely, the birdsong a lament, the trees forlorn with winter stark. I check my watch. It's time.

Today is the day of Luke's trial.

I thought I'd wake up feeling too sick or too angry to contemplate going, but I don't. I just feel numb. I've been lonely for most of my life, but this isolation has been on a whole new level. In the past, I never knew what it was like to have a proper boyfriend; I had no idea what I was missing. Being in love made everything heady and hopeful. Losing that has been rawer than anything I've felt before. Now I've learnt how loneliness shadows the future – nothing to look forward to, nobody to spend it with.

Worst of all, I know that my first experience of love was with a boy who killed his girlfriend. A psycho.

And yet. Luke's portrait of me is still a square in my inner pocket, the edges so creased the paper is on the brink of tearing. A part of me, no matter how silly, still hopes that today I'll hear something that takes away this terrible feeling. I want a reason to believe in him again.

It ends with you, Luke, it all ends with you.

Chapter 65

Luke

Now it begins.

I'm standing in a smart suit, the knot of my tie tight against my Adam's apple. My hands are cuffed behind my back. Two officers in black trousers and white shirts lead me through a door marked 'PRISONERS ENTER HERE'. I'm taken into the dock and I sit down between them; they undo my cuffs and I rub my wrists and flex my fingers, savouring the freedom to move them.

The courtroom is like something out of a film; it feels surreal, make-believe. The judge in her horsehair wig, the prosecutor on one side and my defence on the other. A jury of twelve people.

Everyone is looking at me. At first all I see are hostile strangers. Then I spot a familiar face. My mum. She's wearing her best lilac suit, the one she only ever wears on special occasions. She's got that look of deep sorrow and pessimism, as though my guilty verdict is inevitable; I wish she'd just try to be more positive.

More faces: Rob, Siobhan, Mr Abdul. Mr Abdul's looking confused, which makes me uneasy. But Rob, Rob stares at me fiercely as though he's filling me with strength, and I'm so moved I could cry.

Then I see Carolina.

Carolina is the only person in this courtroom who isn't looking at me.

A sadness seeps into me.

Then I notice Eva's mum and dad. You'd think I was Jack the Ripper, the way they're staring, and for one crazy moment, I nearly laugh from sheer nerves. Mr Pieachowski looks thunderous. I realise that a smile must have ghosted across my face, like a psycho leer.

It seems safest to look at my shoes. There's a scuff of dirt on the rim of one, which I've got the urge to clean, but I'm terrified that anything I do will be interpreted the wrong way. I sit so still I feel cramp hardening in my muscles.

By the end of this trial, they'll look at me differently, I tell myself fiercely. When my Not Guilty verdict comes through, Mr Pieachowski will shake my hand. Carolina will run and fling her arms around me. Mr Abdul will rub my shoulder and smile. We'll weep together over Eva and then I'll walk out of this place and into the winter sunshine and breathe the sweet apple air.

Chapter 66

Luke

The trial kicks off. The judge makes a speech and then the prosecutor stands up and addresses the jury.

'The man that you see before you today is eighteen years old. I use the word man rather than boy to remind you not to be fooled by his youthful appearance. He is a mature male who knew exactly what he was doing when he took Eva Pieachowski into the woods on Friday 23 September. This man, Luke Jones, was the very last person to see her alive. The evidence that you will see over the course of this trial will illustrate just what sort of boyfriend Luke was. He was a man obsessed, a man who could not bear to let Eva break up with him, a man who refused to let her live a life without him. This is a man who knew of her other lovers, who was driven by jealousy and rage. This is a man who we will demonstrate was volatile, prone to fits of temper and unpredictable behaviour.

This is a man who carried a knife not for protection but for show – the very knife that Eva Pieachowski was stabbed with, thirteen times. A horrific crime that ended in tragedy.'

Holy shit. Everyone has dark and light in their personality, but I feel as though he's taken every element of night in me and pretended there's no day. I'm so shocked that even when my defence lawyer stands and makes his case, emphasising my youth, that I am innocent until proven guilty, that they can only convict me if this is proven *beyond reasonable doubt*, I can't digest his words.

I'm itching to take the stand. I want to go into verbal combat with that bastard and bloody show him how wrong he is.

But I have to wait my turn.

The prosecutor begins to make his case, calling Eva's friends and family to the witness stand one by one.

Mr Pieachowski is up first. A picture of Eva flashes up on a screen, blonde and beautiful. I look away. He has to identify her and answer some simple questions. Then they get onto the subject of me.

The prosecuting lawyer's harsh Scottish accent rings out: 'Mr Pieachowski, were you aware that Eva and Luke were boyfriend and girlfriend?'

'Not really,' Mr Pieachowski says. His tone is flat; his manner cold. 'Eva mostly kept their romance a secret.'

'And why do you think that Eva kept it secret from you?'

'She knew that I wouldn't approve. Luke – he seemed, well, rough and a bit unsavoury.'

I bristle, hearing the clichés that have been pinned on me my whole bloody life.

Then my lawyer cross-questions.

'Why did you think Luke unsavoury?'

'I don't know.' Mr Pieachowski falters. 'It was just a general impression.'

'Did you ever meet Luke? Speak to him?'

'No.' Mr Pieachowski frowns. 'Well, once, very briefly. He was from ... the other end of Wimbledon, the poorer end.'

'So this is an issue of class and prejudice. Luke is not from a middle-class family or neighbourhood and you make an assumption that he must be a criminal.'

'My Lord.' The prosecuting lawyer jumps up. 'I must object to this line of questioning. My learned friend is putting words into the mouth of my witness.'

'I agree,' says the judge. 'Change your line of questioning.'

Rob's called up to the stand next. He talks about me as though I'm actually a human being, describing me as a loyal friend and a loving boyfriend to Eva.

Siobhan is up next, biting her lip and pulling her sleeves over her wrists. When asked to comment on how I treated Eva, she says:

'Well. He treated her well, but too well. He seemed obsessed.'

Obsessed? That's a pretty strong word, isn't it? I loved her, plain and simple. Now everyone wants to twist that into obsession.

Finally, I'm called to the stand. When I have to place my hand on the Bible, my fingers are trembling. I leave a sweat stain on the Good Book.

Then the questions begin.

Chapter 67

Luke

This is his first question:

'How did your relationship with Eva Pieachowski begin?'

'Um, Eva texted me.' I'm careful to avoid mentioning that she saw me fighting in the playground – my lawyer advised me not to flag that up. 'She said – that she – um, she liked the look of me.' Damn, I need to be more articulate; one of the jury is raising an eyebrow.

'And how long did you date each other for? Can you give me the exact dates?'

'From 16 February 2016 to 23 September 2016,' I reply.

'I'd like to refer to an email that Eva sent to her friend Siobhan O'Hara, which describes how she felt about your relationship,' he says.

I steel myself.

'*My relationship with Luke was becoming unbearable,*' he reads. '*He was completely obsessed.*'

'Hey,' I protest, 'our relationship wasn't like that at all.'

The judge tells me off for interrupting. I say a meek sorry and shut up, but I'm hot with confusion. How could she write those things, exaggerate so much?

'When Eva said that she wanted to end your relationship, did you refuse to respect her decision?"

'Well, she didn't seem serious,' I say. 'It didn't make any sense.' I've rehearsed this with my lawyer but now, on the stand, my mind is suddenly a blank and I start to panic. 'Um, I don't know.'

'And Eva's parents – what did you feel about Eva lying to them about your relationship?'

'It was necessary,' I say, 'or we couldn't be together.'

'So you encouraged her to lie?'

'No-no – well – yes.' I shrug uneasily.

'So you did encourage her to lie?'

'Um, yes. We couldn't have dated otherwise.'

'On 18 August, Eva records that you drove – against her wishes – to Oaks Park. A text to Siobhan reports how, when she expressed her wish to end your relationship, you threw her from your car, and drove off, leaving her alone in the woods.'

'I went back for her!' I cry. I'm aware that I'm clenching my fists and I quickly shove my hands into my pockets. *Stay calm*, my lawyer warned me. *The prosecutor will do what he can to wind you up.* 'I went back and picked her up. She was fine.'

'But you didn't allow the break-up that night?'

'She was the one who changed her mind – she said she wanted to go to a Rihanna concert with me, she asked me to get the tickets. To be honest, I was confused myself.'

'On 1 September you sent Eva a total of sixteen texts in the space of one hour. Some of the texts include lines such as: *I love u and I will love u forever. I know u don't feel ready for marriage yet but give it time*. She didn't reply to any of them. How did that make you feel?'

'Um – I was curious. Surprised. I wondered why.'

'Would you say you were obsessed with Eva?'

'No! I was in love.'

'And when did you learn that Eva had another lover, an older man?'

'I was – on remand, in Wandsworth. My lawyer told me. It came as a shock. More so to find out that this man was the very detective who put me away,' I add quickly, determined to get that in.

'Really?' The prosecutor gives me a long look. 'When Eva specifically told you she wanted to break up and end your relationship, you didn't suspect at all that she might have another lover?'

'No.' Then I fret that makes me look stupid. Will that undermine everything else I say? 'I guess it was at the back of my mind that maybe there was someone else.'

'So when you went into the woods with Eva on 23 September, the night of her death, you were thinking – *at the back of your mind* – that perhaps she had another lover. Maybe you had heard rumours at school of an older man, and that may have governed what followed?'

'No!' I say. 'No, it wasn't like that!'

My lawyer stands up and cries an objection; the judge agrees. And then Mr Prosecutor throws me a curveball.

'When did your relationship with Carolina Jackson begin?'

My lawyer springs up again: 'My Lord, I believe that my learned friend is bringing up matters that lack any relevancy to this case!'

The prosecutor appeals to the judge: 'I need to paint a picture of how Luke reacted after Eva's death.'

The judge says she'll allow it.

When did I first meet Carolina?

Did we ever kiss on her visits to my jail?

How could I forget Eva so quickly if I loved her so deeply?

My face is throbbing with heat. I've not even told my mum about Carolina, not Rob, not anyone. That's our secret and now it's being turned into a soap opera.

'So, you were devastated by Eva's death and yet within two months you had another girlfriend?'

'It is possible to love two people at once,' I cry, remembering some advice Mr Abdul once gave me.

'So you love Carolina?'

'I – I don't know.'

'But you did love Eva?'

'Yes.'

I step down from the stand trembling. I know it went badly, but my head is spinning too much to pick it apart right now. I go back to the dock and slump into my seat. I never want to go onto that stand again.

Chapter 68

Siobhan

I'm weaving little plaits in my hair like I always do when I'm feeling nervy. This morning I filmed a vlog of me preparing for court. I wasn't allowed to say anything, for fear of influencing the case, so it was just about me picking my outfit. I got two hundred comments within five minutes, all wishing me good luck.

I was shiny with confidence when I left the house this morning, but the moment I enter the courtroom it vanishes. I feel as though I'm about to take an exam, and I've never been very good at those.

Eva hasn't left me any more messages. The paper is still folded in my handbag. *Luke is the one who killed me.* Every time I look at it, I know what I have to do.

The prosecutor asks Rob if Luke encouraged Eva to take drugs. Rob looks very uncomfortable, fingering the collar of his shirt. He should be the last person to sweat under pressure. He has a two-E offer from Cambridge. He's not going to miss out.

'No, Luke actually wanted Eva to avoid drugs,' says Rob. The prosecutor reminds Rob that he is under oath. He frowns and then says more loudly: 'This is truth, as far as I knew – Luke never put Eva under pressure to take drugs. He gave up smoking to be a good example, so she might calm down.'

'I'd like to show the court a video,' the lawyer says.

I sit up in surprise.

It's the *Psycho* video Eva told me about, the one they shot in the bathroom. To be honest, I'm not that disturbed by it – we filmed all these crazy videos all the time – but I can sense the shock in the courtroom. This isn't good for Luke.

'This video was filmed on your phone?'

Rob squirms and looks over at Luke.

For the first time, I nearly feel sorry for Luke. His face is raw with betrayal.

'Yeah,' Rob whispers.

'Can you speak up?'

'Yes,' Rob says, more loudly. 'But it was just a joke.'

'Were you not disturbed? Seeing Luke waving a knife at Eva?'

'No.' Rob stands up straight now, his voice ringing with authority, doing his best audition for PM. 'Luke loved Eva. It was just a dare. A silly video we made for fun.'

Rob stands down.

Now it's my turn. The lawyer kicks off by asking me the same question he asked Rob – did Luke ever pressure Eva to take drugs? Luke's pleading look claws at me, but then I feel a surge of anger. Even now, he's trying to manipulate me.

'Yes,' I say. 'Luke was her bad boy and she wanted to impress him.'

The courtroom stirs. The prosecutor looks pleased. *Oh Eva, I know this isn't strictly true, but we have to get justice. You'll never be able to rest until we do.*

'And how do you think that Luke demonstrated that pressure?'

'Eva told me that if she refused to take drugs, he would threaten her.'

Stirs and rustles and shocked glances. I have to force back a smile; the impact is exciting.

This isn't perjury, Eva. I'm just bending the truth as is necessary.

'When did you last see Luke in possession of his knife?'

'The night of Rob's party. Before they went into the bathroom, I saw him flashing it about. I'm sure I overheard Luke saying that he wanted to film *Psycho*, and Eva looked scared, to be honest.'

I'm aware of Rob frowning fiercely at me, but I quickly look away.

'And do you know whose idea it was to go to the woods? Eva's or Luke's?'

'I'd left the party by then, but Eva sent me a text saying Luke wanted to go for a walk but she wasn't very keen on the idea. So I figure he must have made her. And she never came back.' Tears sting my eyes. *Oh Eva . . .*

Now Luke's lawyer fires questions at me. He tries to make out that I'm exaggerating because my story differs from Rob's. I point out that I was much closer to Eva than Rob, and we all show different sides of our personality to different people, right? I reckon he's underestimating me because I'm a girl. But I won't be bullied. I stay strong for Eva and I refuse to back down.

I leave the courtroom feeling glorious. When I get home, Mum is waiting for me with tea and bickies, ready to be supportive. It's almost embarrassing to be in such a good mood. Then something crazy happens.

I'm sitting in my armchair. It's a bit of an anticlimax and I almost wish I could go up on the stand again. I don't think I've felt such exhilaration since I was in the school play way back in Year 9. Then I spot the phone pad on the table next to me. *It's covered with Eva's doodles and scribbles.* I'm so freaked out that I call Mum. She looks at it too and spots a name – *Sebastian.* She says: 'Hey, remember when your friend Sebastian came to visit – back before Christmas? He was sitting there doodling on that pad.'

How come Sebastian's handwriting is exactly the same as Eva's?

I sit there feeling very confused. He must've seen Eva's handwriting before, maybe even while he was here – her silly notes are pinned up on the fridge. I can't bear to get rid of them. He saw her handwriting and echoed it, maybe deliberately or maybe subconsciously. Could Eva have possessed Sebastian? Maybe she worked through him . . .

It's all a muddle. I feel very tired and tell Mum that I need to go and lie down.

Chapter 69

Luke

When I head out to court today, I feel strangely calm. I catch Rob's eye. He looks sorrowful and I give him a nod to say: *I forgive you.* I know the video can't be his fault; the police must have found it on his phone.

Mum is still crying and Carolina's not even able to look me in the eye. I feel more and more remote from them. This is out of my control. So many voices, statements, slants, white noise. My life has been shattered into kaleidoscopic shards. A little bit is in the hands of every witness on that stand. The jury will listen and decide. There's so little I can do.

Things kick off with the prosecutor calling a new witness to the stand.

Sebastian Banks.

He's wearing a fancy grey pinstriped suit and his voice, when he speaks, is smooth as silk.

'You saw Luke and Eva leave the party,' says the prosecutor. 'Can you describe in your own words what happened then?'

'Of course. I saw Luke lead Eva away from the party in the direction of the woods and then I overheard him say, *I'm just taking you out here to stab you.* Those words exactly.'

What a bastard! It is . . . well, it is true, I did say those words, but I was only joking. We'd been messing about with our *Psycho* film in Rob's bathroom, so I was just riffing on that. It sounds terrible out of context so I'll have to make that clear when have my right to reply.

My defence gets to his feet to cross-examine and I feel a surge of anticipation. The opposition stripped me bare on that stand; now it's Sebastian's turn.

'So, if you heard Luke say he was going to stab Eva,' he fires at Sebastian, 'why didn't you intervene? It's quite shocking to think that you just stood there and watched them walk away.'

'I do regret that,' Sebastian says. 'But Eva seemed fine and willing, so I assumed she had the situation under control.'

'And how do you account for the fact that your DNA was found on the murder weapon?'

'Luke threatened me with the knife on 15 September,' Sebastian replies. 'At one point he held it against my throat and I was trying to grab the handle to yank it out of his hand. I presume that is why my DNA shows up.'

'Why did he threaten you?'

'I was trying to help Eva. I knew her vaguely and I happened to see them in the park, arguing, so I attempted to intervene.'

'Liar,' I hiss, shaking my head.

'And what happened when you tried to help her?' the lawyer asks.

'Like I said, Luke went crazy and brandished that knife. I was trying to stay calm, use words to pacify the situation – but he was only interested in speaking with his weapon. The moment he physically threatened me, I ran.'

Bullshit! Complete and utter bull!

'Leaving Eva in a potentially vulnerable situation? You didn't think to call the police, if the situation was that troubling?'

'I agree – I should have done more to help. I felt intimidated and genuinely scared that if I interfered any further, Luke might come after me.'

Come on, I think, *what about the time he threatened Eva in that café? What about the fact that he filmed her and tried to make out she was some kind of dealer?*

'How did you feel about Luke's relationship with Eva?'

'I didn't really know much about it,' Sebastian shrugs.

'You weren't jealous? If you were watching them so keenly at the party, as is evident from the footage, it could well imply a keen interest.'

'No.' Sebastian sounds surprised. 'I just happened to be in the right place at the right time.'

A few more questions and it's over. And I'm thinking, *Hang on, what about the café, why not ask about that?* I could kill that lawyer.

I watch Sebastian step down from the dock. As he passes me, his expression jolts me; his smile is sad, apologetic, as though he had no desire to testify against me. I watch as he makes his way to the back of the courtroom.

They call my name.

I have to be calm and coherent. I mustn't let Sebastian derail me. I can't let him distract me.

This is the big one. We're going to go into the detail of the night of 23 September. I've gone over this night so many times now it's like a horror version of *Groundhog Day* . . .

I try to echo Sebastian's smooth style, but it's useless. I put my hand on the Bible, just as terrified as I was on day one of this nightmare.

My last chance. Sebastian isn't going down for this crime. I am my only last hope. All there is now is my version of the truth. It's up to me to tell people what really happened during that final night with Eva . . .

Chapter 70

Carolina

I tell myself that I'm a detective and my prime suspect is on the stand. He will confess and I'll have played a major part in wrapping this case up once and for all.

Luke hasn't been doing too well on the stand. Sebastian was born to be under the spotlight, but Luke's suffering stage fright. He stammers, swerves, stumbles, shifts. Every word he speaks condemns him further. It's obvious that he's guilty – so why drag it out? I'm sitting next to the Pieachowski family today. Rob is mad at me for passing on the *Psycho* video to the police, so I'm *persona non grata*. The Pieachowskis are cocooned in sober silence. They can't move on with their lives until they know what happened to their daughter. How can they contemplate forgiveness if they don't know who is to blame?

I want to shake Luke hard. I want to scream at him to confess.

'So, you went into the woods together. You claimed in your statement that you couldn't remember which direction you were walking.'

'That's right,' Luke says. 'It was dark and Eva was in a bad mood, so I was preoccupied. I wasn't really paying attention to where – where we were going. I only remember looking at her.' His eyes are cloudy with wistfulness.

Who was I to Luke? *I don't know*, he said when asked if he loved me. The kisses, the letters, the secrets shared – was it all just an act? Did he ever really mean it?

I feel the rustle of Luke's portrait, folded in my pocket, a tickle against my ribcage. I'm confused: there was love in the way he drew me, a tenderness in the pencil strokes. I can't help but notice how handsome he looks in his suit, his hair escaping his best attempts to tidy it for the courtroom.

A handsome killer, I tell myself.

'So you went into the woods – near the pit?'

'Oh – no.'

'But you could see the pit?'

'Ah, yeah,' Luke says. 'I think I did catch a glimpse of it, yeah.'

'How far away from the pit were you when Eva told you she wanted to break up? Two feet? Five?'

'Um, maybe three, I guess. Three, four.'

'And you argued?'

'We had a discussion,' Luke says firmly.

'About breaking up?'

'Yeah.'

For once Luke looks in control, able to handle himself.

'And you became enraged?'

'No. I was just upset. As you would be when someone dumps you.'

'If you were only upset, why leave Eva in the woods? You'd done this before at Oaks Park. You said it was a joke but having seen the distress this caused, why do it again? You were thirty minutes away from the party – that's a long walk.'

Luke looks lost. I sense the waves of tiredness around him, as though all the weeks he's spent on the stand have started to grind him down.

'I was upset,' he says, so quietly that I can only just hear.

'Would you say that you were devastated?'

'Yes.' He takes a sip of water from the glass on the stand.

I feel as though the rest of the courtroom fades away, and there's just me and Luke in this room. He's wilting: surely he's going to crack, any second . . .

'And did you berate Eva about the man she was leaving you to be with?'

'Yes.' Luke's eyes are glassy. Then: 'No, wait—'

He didn't notice the tripwire in the sentence and now it's too late, the lawyer is already onto the next question.

'And what did she say when she broke up with you?'

'She taunted me.' Luke seems lost. 'She said she was sick and tired of me and that it was time for me to stop clinging and let her go. She picked some bark off a tree and she flung it at me.'

'How did you react to that? You were angry, weren't you?'

'Ye-yes.'

'Did you threaten her?'

'Yes – I did – I was angry—' Luke rubs his temples. He takes another sip of water, his hand jerky, spilling some on his suit. 'I just – I didn't—'

'Answer the question,' the judge corrects him sternly.

'I had my knife and I was joking—'

'So you did have a knife at this point in the evening? You had a knife and you threatened Eva with it?'

Luke's eyes enlarge, swim, as he realises what he said.

'No – I mean. Earlier. I had it earlier.'

'At the party?'

'Yes.'

'So, you did not, in fact, lose the knife a few weeks prior to the party, as you previously claimed?'

'No – but I did – I did lose it. I lost it in the woods after when I was running away,' Luke stutters.

Oh God. I want to bury my face in my lap and put my hands over my ears.

'Why did you run?'

'She slipped into the pit and – I was angry – I wanted – I just – I want to tell the truth.' Luke looks despairing.

'Of course, Luke. Tell the truth.' The prosecutor is gentle now. I feel as though there's a pit opening up right here, in this courtroom, and Luke is being softly coaxed towards it. He's going to fall, oh God, I can feel it; he's going to fall—

'I did – I did wave the knife – but just to scare her – we had this game of Dares – she liked Dares, she liked it when I went too far – she liked me bad – I never meant to do anything – but then – then she was in the pit . . . '

'Were you in the pit, Luke? What did you do to her?'

My head swims; my heartbeat is frantic. He's going to confess. He's going to confess.

Chapter 71

Luke

I'm in the woods with Eva. In the cold and the dark. The knife is in my hand. The anger I feel seems foreign, beyond me; as if it's possessed me. She's laughing at me: 'Go on then, just stab me, that'll solve everything.' So I do. I swipe out and I injure her shoulder. I don't mean to slice hard; I just intend something light as a paper cut, but beneath her white top a thick red line appears and starts to thicken and swell and stain.

The look on her face. The shock. Triumph booms in my heart. For weeks she's been putting me down, jeering, saying I'm too nice, too boring, too lame. The kind, sweet Eva I once knew and loved seems to have gone for good. Her face is taut now and she's crying out – well, she can't say I'm Mr Nice Guy any more. She loses her balance, feet slipping on the wet leaves, and then there's a wail as she falls back, slithers down into the pit. She cries out my name. I stare down into the dark. There's a flash of light as she waves her mobile upwards. She says her ankle hurts. The knife is in my hand. It feels like power. I feel the wind on my face and I feel the darkness of possibility. It woke up when I used the knife. It whispers in my ear, go on, you could do more. You could go down into that pit and you could finish her off. Show her. Show her who's in charge.

Then I come to my senses. What the hell am I thinking, what the hell am I doing? I drop the knife, revolted. My fingers are sticky with red wetness. I call down to Eva that I'm going and I'm never coming back. It's over between us. She'll never have to see me again. She yells, 'Good, just go then, leave me and go!'

And then I'm running, running through the forest, and all the while that poem races through my mind to the rhythm of my heartbeat:

> Whose woods these are I think I know,
> His house is in the village though;
> He will not see me stopping here
> To watch his woods fill up with snow . . .
>
> The woods are lovely, dark and deep . . .

Chapter 72

Carolina

Luke is sobbing now and so am I. Tears slide down my face. I lift my glasses and smear them away. Mr Pieachowski gives me a furious look. He doesn't understand. Luke isn't a psycho. I've demonised and caricatured him over the past few weeks because it was the only way I could cope.

But no: Luke is not a cold-blooded killer. This is a crime of passion. Luke is only human. In English, we learnt about the concept of a fatal flaw, that crack in a person's psyche. For Luke, it's his temper, and on that night, in one dreadful moment, he crossed the line and went too far.

'You went back,' the prosecutor says. 'You went back for the kill ...'

'No,' Luke insists. 'I went home.'

'You went back. It was a job half done, and you were still angry, you still weren't satisfied. You knew Eva had hurt her ankle, you knew she'd be down there, weak and cold and terrified, and you went back to kill her.'

'No,' Luke swallows another sob. 'I drove out, I admit, but I just went to a service station and got some Coke. It made me feel sickly.' Luke's voice breaks. He sniffs, wipes his nose on his sleeve without thinking. 'Sorry. I'm sorry.'

'Please answer the question in full,' the judge goads him.

'I just sat in my car, looking into the woods. I thought that I should go back and check she was okay. I knew that was the right thing to do, but I felt so scared and ashamed. I was so in love with her. In all the books and movies, love is shown as redemptive, but with Eva, all it seemed to do to me was make me crazy.' Luke laughs through his tears, shaking his head, lips trembling.

'And you went back into the woods, didn't you? You were crazy, you say, so you went back to the woods and you killed her?'

I see Luke rise and find his strength.

'No,' he says firmly. 'Like I said, I just sat there. I was numb and in a state of shock. I couldn't believe what I'd done, how I'd behaved, the low I'd hit. I listened to this song, "Cry me a River" by Justin Timberlake. Eva once played it to me. It was like saying goodbye. Then I drove home.'

'So who do you believe picked up your knife to stab Eva, if you didn't?'

'My Lord!' Luke's lawyer springs up to object, but the judge overrules him.

'I don't know,' Luke says, shrugging. 'I honestly don't know.'

Chapter 73

Carolina

I'm standing in a stall in the Ladies by the courtroom, blowing my nose on a piece of tissue. I want to be angry with Luke. He chickened out of his confession and left us all unsatisfied. Yet, seeing him on that stand, going through every shade of emotion, I think I understood.

He couldn't face what he did. His mind had to shut the door and lock it tight and throw away the key. I close my eyes and picture the reality of it, of plunging his knife into Eva, the blood warm on his skin, wet on his face. I feel as though I might be sick; now I have to shut the door on it too.

All of a sudden, I have a strong urge to be back home. It's not the most fun place at the moment but today has reminded me of how short life can be, how we should value the people we love, because we never know how much time we've got with them. I want to make up with Dad. I've been so angry with him these last few months, but I have to learn to forgive him. He has been proved right in the end; he did arrest the right guy. I'll cook him his favourite meal. Maybe we can watch a movie together afterwards. We have to heal together.

I can look up the verdict online. I don't need to stay for the circus.

As I'm rinsing my hands, I glance into the mirror and gasp.

Astra. I watch as she goes to wipe her hands on a paper towel.

'You – had a video about Luke,' I burst out. 'Why didn't you just pass it over as evidence? You should have. Even if he threatened you – it would have saved all this – lying – the trial would have been over like that.'

She pauses for a long time before replying.

'It wasn't Luke,' she says, with her back to me. 'Luke wasn't the one who threatened me. All I had was a video of him in the woods with some blood on his hands, running ... '

'What? But Mr Abdul – told me that you said that Luke threatened you!'

She turns to me, tears in her eyes.

'Mr Abdul.' Her voice is raw with sarcasm. 'The teacher famous for listening to students. But does he ever really listen, or does he just have a store of platitudes that he churns out? It wasn't *Luke* who threatened me. He just assumed that, I never told him any names. I guess the video did make Luke look pretty bad ... ' She trails off.

'Who threatened you, Astra?'

'Nobody ever listens,' she whispers.

'I'm here,' I tell her firmly. 'I'm willing to listen. So ... was there more to the video than Luke?'

She nods, still not looking at me.

'You saw someone else?' I pause, knowing that I must play a softly softly approach. 'Someone else maybe ... hurting Eva?'

The faintest of nods. My heart is beating very hard.

'What happened to that video?'

She shrugs. 'I don't have it any more.'

'But – you have to come clean.' I've been keeping my voice controlled and neutral, but I can't sustain it anymore. 'You have to show Mr Abdul! You can't let this happen!'

In a flash she runs out of the bathroom. I follow her into the corridor, my hands still wet. It's busy with people milling around before the final verdict.

She's with Sebastian. *Her half-brother.* I see now. Their handsome features, the slant of their lips, the colour of their eyes.

Sebastian, whose DNA was on the knife. Sebastian, who was in the woods that night, helping Astra with her film. Sebastian, who must be the man on camera, who must be the one threatening Astra, who has such a hold over her that she's too afraid to come out and say it—

He takes her arm and she smiles at him; her expression is sunny. She is so good at putting on an act. Sebastian nods, his face grim, as though sealing their pact.

Arm in arm, they stroll out together.

There's an announcement as the court reconvenes.

I file back in slowly with crowd. I spot Mr Abdul and take the seat next to him.

'Astra, your Astra – she said it wasn't Luke,' I hiss.

'What?' Mr Abdul asked.

'It wasn't Luke who threatened her.'

'What?' Mr Abdul looks shocked. 'What do you mean?'

I feel my lip trembling, bite back tears and swallow. I open my mouth to tell him everything but the court is reconvening, the verdict is in, and we're all told to stand.

I look over at the jury, those twelve strangers, and wonder: do they have any idea who Luke is?

Oh God, I think as we rise for the judge, *what have we done?*

Chapter 74

Luke

I don't want to listen to the prosecuting lawyer as he sums up the case. If I do, I'll go mad, I'll jump up and I'll shout out. I feel cleansed by my confession. I unravelled and I told the truth, but surely they can see that I held nothing back? Yet his words ring around the courtroom and I can't shut them out. *A web of deceit . . . a man who encouraged Eva to lie to her parents . . . manipulated her . . . threatened her with a knife . . . forced her to take drugs . . . discovered she had another lover . . . and then took his revenge . . .*

Chapter 75

Rob

I am sitting in between Mr Abdul and Luke's mum. The defence lawyer is a good man. He's making a speech about how brave Luke was today. Brave enough to tell the truth. A boy who loved a girl who told him she loved him one day and played games the next. A girl who deliberately toyed with his temper. But Luke knew when to stop. He went home and he cried himself to sleep. This isn't a game of Cluedo, he adds, there will be no black envelope with a card which you can pull out and find the murderer. The jury must decide, and they must *decide beyond reasonable doubt* ...

Chapter 76

Luke

My legs feel weak.
The foreman for the jury stands up.
The judge asks if they have come to a decision.
The foreman says that they have reached a majority verdict.
The charges against me are read out.
And the foreman says: 'Guilty.'

Chapter 77

Carolina

This can't be. The judge is sitting there and talking about Luke as though he's a cold-blooded killer. She's saying that his crime was brutal and disgusting. She's telling him he'll be locked away for twenty years. I watch Luke bow his head, accepting his fate with quiet dignity. Isn't he going to object? Isn't his lawyer going to say something? Mr Abdul looks white. Luke's mum is crying audibly. Mr Pieachowski and his wife are holding hands. I stand up and cry out: 'No, you can't, you've got it all wrong!' and the judge tells me to get out of her courtroom before I get charged as well.

Chapter 78

Luke

I'm ready now. I feel at peace. I strip the sheet from the bed in my cell and rip it into frayed lengths.

My calm surprises me. This must be the right thing to do. I was half-expecting something dramatic to happen: something to indicate that the world, that someone or something benign that might be called divine, cares about me enough to stop this. All there is ... is this. I have to accept my fate. Even if I could survive twenty years in this place, the man who walked out of here would be a dried husk.

A bang at the door – my guard. I quickly shove the make-shift ropes under my pillow, though there's no danger of him seeing. He slides a food tray through the large letterbox in the door.

Tea. Toast. My mundane last breakfast. I want to laugh. Then I see the letter.

My heart flips. Anger fills me. Suddenly my calm feels fragile. *I won't open it*, I tell myself. *I'll carry on.*

So I start to tie the strips into tight knots. There'd be nothing more farcical than it snapping halfway through. When it's done I place the noose around my neck. I swallow. Still calm, just.

On impulse, I grab the letter and tear it open. I can't stop myself.

It's from Carolina. The compassion in her words shocks me:

I'm so sorry, Luke, I can't believe that I played a part in all this. I know I've made this promise to you before but know that this time I mean it, that I will pour every drop of my energy into making this happen: I will get you out of there, I swear. We will appeal. We will set you free.

That's it.

Violent tears shake my body. As I sit down on the bed, I realise the calm was an illusion, hysteria turned up to such a high pitch I couldn't even feel it any more. Anger shakes me again, the fury that I've been trying to lock down, because it's too much to bear day by day, for Mr Abdul, Rob, Jackson, all those bastards who judged me and put me in a box and made me their scapegoat, ruined my life so that they could go to bed and sleep every night thinking justice is done. The weeping is also a release. I look at the letter again. It feels as though life listened to my pleas. Life cared enough to send me a sign that

I might be loved, even just a little, by someone willing to help.

I look up at the patch of blue sky in my cell window and slowly, I undo the cotton noose from my neck.

Just one person is enough to save a life.

Chapter 79

Carolina

It feels weird, standing on the doorstep with Rob at my side, waiting to enter the house I've staked out so often.

'Carolina! Rob!' Mr Abdul opens the door and welcomes us in. His partner, Apoorva, calls out a cheery hello from the kitchen.

He shows us into the living room. I'm slightly disappointed. It's all so suburban, with a leather sofa, 50-inch TV, framed pictures of them both on every surface.

We sit down, nibbling crisps from a bowl, while Mr Abdul goes to the kitchen to get us some drinks. It's a Saturday night. Rob looks a bit uncomfortable, but he is flattered. It's not every day your teacher invites you to dinner. As for me – I have my reasons for being here.

Immediately after Luke's verdict, I thought there was still hope. Mr Abdul assured me that he would speak to Astra and try to persuade her to let him see the video in full. I admit that I got impatient. I went back to stalking his house that weekend, without much success. Mr Abdul spotted me hovering and took me for a walk on Wimbledon Common. As we crunched over the frosty grass, he told me that nothing had worked. He'd tried to cajole Astra and she'd clammed up. In the end, in despair, he had called the police. They'd taken away her videocam, checked the videos, found nothing. Nothing on her computer, either. Astra had been so distraught, she'd stopped speaking to him, packed a small bag and gone back to live with Sebastian.

'As much as I love Astra, I know she can be a fantasist,' he said. 'She had a very difficult childhood and she's learned to cope with it by hiding herself in movies and film-making, in the world of her imagination. I'm sorry, Carolina – but your hope may be false. For all I know, there really was no other video.'

A bird shot out from a tree, soaring across the sky. I watched its flight in despair. How could Luke's story end like this? I was supposed to be a detective, get every piece of the puzzle and make them all fall into place.

'Luke has been convicted by a jury,' he said, finally.

'You can't tell me that you believe their final judgement!' I cried.

'The point is, Carolina, nobody knows what happened. I know it's frustrating, but we can't know the truth, and sometimes growing up is about acceptance, letting go. What more can we do?'

For a week or so, I accepted his words. I hung out with Rob, I did my homework, I went back to birdspotting. But something inside kept telling me: *I can't accept it, I can't. I have to keep fighting.*

Mr Abdul thinks that this is a nice, cosy dinner that will help us move on, cheer up, get into 2017 and forget about Luke. Not as far as I'm concerned.

'These crisps are good,' Rob says, reaching for the bowl. 'I think they've got rosemary on them.'

I think of Luke in his cell, eating the dire prison food, rotting away inside.

I smile and tell him that I need the loo.

In the hallway, I bump into Apoorva bringing out more bowls of snacks. She tells me it's first on the right at the top of the stairs.

It's easy to spot Astra's bedroom. There are three rooms, doors closed, and hers has her name on it in black Gothic letters. I knock gently and when nobody answers I let myself in.

Her room is a bit of a mess. I scan the muddle of books and clothes, Nietzsche and Topshop. The walls are blank except for a noticeboard with a collage of photos pinned on it. At first I feel awkward about touching anything, but I remind myself that I have two, three minutes at most before someone wonders where I am. I rummage around. No sign of the videocam – I guess she took that with her. I look at the shelves and pull out a tattered copy of *Beyond Good and Evil* by Nietzsche. I flick it open and notice that there's a signed message scrawled it in, from Sebastian, wishing her a happy birthday. He's even added a quote: *To live is to suffer, to survive to find some meaning in the suffering.* I note a sheaf of paper in the book; I pull it out.

It looks handwritten, like a letter or a page from a diary, but most of it has been burned away. The writing looks familiar.

> That's the trouble with my situation – so many lies, all
> stacking up like a house of cards. I know that one day
> it will come toppling down on me ...

Eva. *Eva's diary.*

Siobhan said someone had stolen it from her locker. My dad insisted it was a fake and somehow managed to have it discredited as inadmissible evidence, although not everyone was convinced. Siobhan, Rob, Rivka – they all thought that the extracts printed in the newspapers were the real thing.

I fold it back in the book and hide it under my jumper.

Just as I'm on my way out, I stop to look at the photo collage on Astra's noticeboard. Every single picture is of Sebastian. Sebastian wearing tennis whites; Sebastian smoking a cigarette; Astra and Sebastian with their arms around each other. It looks more like the sort of thing you'd create for a boyfriend than a brother. There's something disturbing, even obsessive about it. They look similar enough to be twins. I shiver, hurry out and head downstairs. In the hallway, I grab my rucksack and quickly shove the book inside. I can hear the others chatting away in the living room. I go back in. Nobody asks me why I took so long. I sit down, grab some of the fancy crisps.

My mind is ticking too fast for small talk. I think about confiding in Mr Abdul, but I don't trust him not to make a mess of things; he's too ambivalent about Luke. The photos of Astra and Sebastian, the diary page. Did they steal her diary – was there something incriminating in there? Were they the ones who sent it to the press? And did they change it any way? What if Astra is not the fragile victim that she appears to be? What if she was the one who found Luke's knife in the woods that night? What if Sebastian was the one helping *her*?

I don't know how this ends and I don't know who it ends with.

Epilogue

Siobhan

I'm in my bedroom with all the lights off. A single candle flickers on my dressing-table, making shadows spirit across the walls. The candlelight illuminates the photograph, propped up against my mirror: Eva, sitting on a swing, laughing, her hair flying out behind her with the wind.

Eva, I address her, *how are you feeling? It's all over now.*

The candle pirouettes on its wick and I sense Eva is closer, listening in.

We can say goodbye, I whisper, *now that he's been caught. Luke will be locked away for years.* I swallow. *You can find peace.*

I feel tears raw in my throat. I don't want her to go; I want Eva to be with me always. That's selfish, though. She must be so tired, after all these months of waiting for justice to be done.

Oh Eva, why did Luke kill—

The candle trembles in a sudden cool draught that dislodges the photo. It falls right into the flame—

'Oh God!'

I jump up run to the door—

'MUM! FIRE!'

She comes bounding up the stairs, cries out in shock, runs into the bathroom, spinning the taps, filling a bowl—

I spot a bottle of water by my bed and fling it over the fire. Mum runs in and sloshes more water on top of the hissing embers.

Blackened rivulets drip from the dressing table onto the mauve carpet. I retrieve what's left of Eva's photo, her face all scorched and stained.

Mum opens the curtains and windows as wide as they'll go; bright morning sunshine streams into the room.

'Siobhan, how many times have I told you not to use candles up here!'

I open my mouth to apologise, but all that wells up are tears. I feel so embarrassed, but Mum is lovely. She sighs and pulls me into a big hug.

'I know it's a difficult week,' she says, stroking my hair.

Just as I said Luke's name, the photo burst into flames. It's a sign, a definite sign. She's at peace now and ready to say goodbye. I try to explain, only my voice is all hiccup-y and snotty. Mum makes soothing noises, then pulls away and passes me some tissues.

'Anyway,' she says. 'I've got something that will cheer up you. There's some post from your new publishers.'

'What!'

I follow her downstairs, still drying my eyes. There's a fat envelope sitting in the hallway. I open it up and pull out several contracts. My agent got me a book deal just before Christmas, when subscribers to my vlog hit the 3 million mark.

Right at the top of each contract is my name! And the title of my book, *Coming Through the Darkness*. And the publication date: June of this year.

'Hey,' Mum says, 'your dad and I should have a look over those too, just to make sure they're okay. Oh, my clever daughter!' She gives me another hug.

I carry my contracts into the kitchen and sit at the table with some juice. In the garden the trees are pale and anorexic but the sky is blue and brilliant with wintery sunshine. I open the last page of the contracts, and sign my name with a big flourish. My heart sings with joy, but then the guilt comes, pinching me once again.

The week after Eva died, I went into a bookshop and was overwhelmed with a deep hatred for all the piles of paperbacks. It was irrational and unfair, but that's how I felt. All these writers who got their books published while Eva never had her chance. Now here I am, with my own title coming out soon, all by a total fluke. I'm not even going to pen it myself, to be honest; my agent says I can bounce ideas off a ghost writer, and she'll do the tricky writing bit for me. I close my eyes and picture myself holding my very own book in my hands. There'll be a glam picture of me on the back cover, and one of those little pretentious author biogs inside and then – the dedication page.

For Eva, for ever and always.

I smile and I feel Eva smile with me.

Rob didn't throw his usual New Year party because his parents were around. He's having one tonight instead, now they're off skiing in France. I was in two minds about going, but Rob insists that we have to let the past go.

We nearly fell out during the trial. Rob was furious with me about the evidence I gave – right up until the day of Luke's final confession.

I'm glad I wasn't in court on those days. I still remember Rivka's call, her sobbing and repeating Luke's halfway confession. *I stabbed her.* All the lies I told actually fitted with Luke's tale – he *did* have the knife at the party. When I heard, I wept until I felt sick and wrung out, but afterwards there was an underlying peace, knowing that I'd done the right thing. This was the paradox: if I'd told the truth, it would have been a fiction. What I exaggerated was an intuition of what was really going on.

I used to love hanging out at Rob's place, but tonight, as I walk up the path to the ivy-covered porch carrying a bottle of Baileys, I'm conscious of an echo of that fatal night. It's impossible not to play the *what if* game: *What if we'd stayed in that night, what if I'd insisted Eva come home with me when I left early?* Inside, the house is packed with students laughing, chatting, drinking, but all I see are memories – Eva's last dance, Eva in the corner, kissing Luke. Then I overhear a guy joking: 'So Rob, who's going to get murdered this time!' A ripple of awkward laughter.

'I'm sorry, but that's sick,' I protest. That shuts them up.

My mood doesn't improve when Rob tells me that Luke is going to appeal. His tone is casual, but he is clearly delusional and still believes Luke is innocent. Apparently he has grown pally with Carolina again and they're working on the case together. They've got some kind of amazing new secret evidence. So they say. I'm seriously starting to wonder if we can stay friends.

'I hope Carolina comes tonight,' he says wistfully.

'Why?' I ask. 'She's a freaky geek and her dad's a peedy.'

'*Siobhan.*' Rob looks at me, half-admonitory, half-affectionate. 'Just try to relax and enjoy the night, okay? Let's do what Eva would have wanted – and party properly!'

I force a smile, feeling bad. This appeal nonsense will surely take forever and there's no way a jury is going to ever let him off, anyway.

So I make myself a cocktail, drink half of it down fast. I lean against the kitchen counter, wondering if I might even have a dance, when I spot Sebastian in the hallway, chatting with someone. Several people are looking over at him and pointing, but Sebastian keeps his cool. How unfair, I think, that his reputation has been tarnished for a crime he had no part in.

367

Then Rob spots him. His expression clenches like a fist.

'He's got a nerve, turning up here!'

And he makes as though he's going to tell Sebastian to leave, but I grab his arm and pull him back.

'Rob,' I protest, 'Luke's the one who was charged, and even if you do believe Luke didn't do it, Sebastian was cleared and deemed innocent, okay? It's not fair. Eva wouldn't like it – wouldn't have liked it – if you cause a scene . . . '

Rob exhales, then mutters: 'Very well. But if that bastard causes any trouble, he's out.'

'Sebastian never causes trouble,' I point out.

Sebastian, looking over and sensing conflict, gives us both a cautious smile. Rob replies with a terse nod. Then he spots some new guests and hurries off to schmooze them.

Sebastian comes wandering up.

'I didn't get to see you at New Year's,' he says, surprisingly warm and friendly.

'Well, you never asked me out,' I point out, sipping my cocktail through a straw.

'You didn't text,' he replies, as though I'm a temptress who deliberately set out to tease him. All of a sudden he puts his arm around my shoulders and we're all very cosy. I remind myself that Sebastian can be very charming one minute and not so charming the next, so I shouldn't get sucked in, but I can't help it. I can feel heat pulsing my cheeks as he leans in and whispers: 'Why don't we go outside?'

*

It's freezing out here, but who cares? Sebastian leads me down to the bottom of the huge garden. Rob's house is lit up in the distance. I don't have to sleep with him, I tell myself, we will go as far as I want to go. But God, he is so handsome; the moonlight caresses his face as though even the moon wants to bed him. Sebastian flicks some leaves away from a wooden bench and we sit down beneath the prickly shade of a holly bush. The garden fence is low and rickety and we're facing the woods – and they look like a dark, evil huddle to me tonight.

'Luke went down for your friend's murder,' Sebastian says.

'Uh, yeah.' I frown, because his tone is very casual, as though we're discussing a holiday Luke took.

'You think he did it?'

'Of course – the evidence was solid. I mean, you told the court yourself that you saw Luke guide her into the woods. You do think he did it, don't you?'

Sebastian shrugs. 'I feel it's all very convenient. I mean, there was one surreal week where they tried to pin the whole thing on me. Insane.'

'Yeah.' I frown, wondering whether or not to ask him about the piece of paper I found, the fact that his handwriting looked so similar to Eva's. I worry that it will spoil the mood, and my head is all swimmy from the cocktails and Sebastian keeps on tracing little strands of hair away from my face with his fingertips. He says something more about how it was fair enough that they brought him in – after all, he was there that night in the woods, by chance – but his words blur as his fingers stroke

369

my cheeks and circle my lips. Then his lips touch mine. I've forgotten what an amazing kisser he is. Joy sparks through me: *Oh Eva, I'm so glad I came to this party in the end.*

'I actually think it's really funny that Luke went down,' he murmurs into my ear, gently biting it. 'Because as it happens, I'm the one who killed Eva.'

'I'm sorry?' I sit up, my heart pounding in shock.

Sebastian stares into my eyes, unblinking, still smiling.

'I went into the woods. Luke had left her behind in that pit; she was lying there. It was too deep for her to get out and she was calling for help. Luke's knife was just lying there. I don't know if he just dropped it. So I picked it up, dropped into the pit and stabbed her. It was fine though, cos I had water with me, so I could wash off the blood after. I took her mobile away and destroyed it.'

'I—' My voice won't work.

'The trouble was that Astra, my half-sister, actually followed me and filmed a bit of the whole thing. She's studying film and she loves horror. She spliced a bit into a short film she made and loaded it to YouTube to get at me. She kept on putting it up, taking it down, playing games with me. In the end, I had to threaten to kill her too to shut her up. But it's fine – she owes me.'

'She owes you?' I ask in a shaky voice. A panicky voice in my head is screaming that I ought to get my mobile out, record his confession. But it's buried somewhere in the depths of my bag.

'We had a pretty awful childhood. Our dad worked in a

local bank and he was on the school advisory panel. Everyone used to say how charming he was, what a great guy he was. Boy, he had everyone fooled. By night, he was a different man. He used to lock me and Astra up in a room and torment us, play games. He'd ask which of us wanted to suffer punishment – the other had to watch. And I always volunteered. I always protected her.

'So,' he concludes, his eyes boring into me. 'She owes me.'

I stare at him, rigid with loathing and horror and fury and – and then he laughs.

'I'm sorry,' he says.

'You think it's funny?' I hiss. 'You think it's funny that she died?'

'No – I was just kidding. Of course I didn't kill her.'

'Oh – Jesus,' I say, very quickly. 'Oh my God.' I breathe out. My heart is still frantic. 'Wow.'

'I had you there for a minute, didn't I?' He nudges me. 'You see how easy it is convincing someone?'

'Yes – you sure did . . . ' I nudge him back weakly. I want to add that I don't think it's a very funny joke, but I'm all turned upside down, from the bliss of the kiss one minute and the cruelty of his confession the next. 'But – but – did you really have such a bad childhood?'

He hesitates, then he gives a small nod. I feel so sorry for him. No wonder Sebastian has been so mixed up and messed up and he's been so hard to date. He never told me much about his family and I should have asked. I had no idea.

371

All the same, his joke was out of order. I'm not sure there's any excuse for it, but before I can tell him what I think, Sebastian starts kissing me again. He holds me with a kind of need and desperation. Perhaps I can help to heal his tortured soul. He groans and pulls me in tight, his hand on the small of my back, and I want him so badly. We hear noises in the distance, voices approaching – someone is hanging empty beer cans on the trees for a laugh. Sebastian whispers: *Why don't we go into the woods, we'll have more privacy?*

He stands up, offering his hand, and there's an odd glint in his eyes, as though he knows I'm disturbed by the place, but he wants me to enjoy the thrill of it. I take his hand and we go through the back gate. *Whose woods these are I think I know*, he recites in a dry, flat voice, and I murmur how much Eva loved that poem. Then he falls silent and tugs at me to hurry on, drawing me quickly into the dark fog of the trees. In the distance, there's a sudden cry and I jump and laugh, because I think it's just an owl. But Sebastian doesn't respond at all and I realise I'm really not sure where we are and all of a sudden the tiniest fear sparks inside me and I'm wondering if this is a good idea after all ...

Acknowledgements

Many thanks to my excellent agent, Hellie Ogden, and all at Janklow and Nesbitt. To the brilliant team at Atom: my editor Sarah Castleton, Olivia Hutchings, Stephanie Melrose, and Madeleine Hall.

Thank you to David & Leesha for a comfortable northern base, where much of this book was written.